They Say She Tastes Like Honey

BY MICHELLE SAWYER

alyson books
los angeles

MANUFACTURED IN THE UNITED STATES OF AMERICA.

THIS TRADE PAPERBACK ORIGINAL IS PUBLISHED BY ALYSON PUBLICATIONS,
P.O. BOX 4371, LOS ANGELES, CALIFORNIA 90078-4371.
DISTRIBUTION IN THE UNITED KINGDOM BY TURNAROUND PUBLISHER SERVICES LTD.,
UNIT 3, OLYMPIA TRADING ESTATE, COBURG ROAD, WOOD GREEN,
LONDON N22 6TZ ENGLAND.

FIRST EDITION: OCTOBER 2003

03 04 05 06 07 **a** 10 9 8 7 6 5 4 3 2 1

ISBN 1-55583-811-1

LIBRARY OF CONGRESS CATALOGING-IN-PUBLICATION DATA
    SAWYER, MICHELLE.
        THEY SAY SHE TASTES LIKE HONEY / BY MICHELLE SAWYER.—1ST ED.
        ISBN 1-55583-811-1
            1. LESBIANS—FICTION. 2. CANCER IN WOMEN—FICTION. 3. CANCER—
    PATIENTS—FICTION. 4. GREENWICH VILLAGE (NEW YORK, N.Y.)—FICTION.
    I. TITLE.
    PS3619.A98T47 2003
    813'.6—DC21   2003052478

CREDITS
• COVER PHOTOGRAPHY FROM PHOTODISC.
• COVER DESIGN BY LOUIS MANDRAPILIAS.
• A PORTION OF THIS NOVEL ORIGINALLY APPEARED IN *A WOMAN'S TOUCH: NEW
  LESBIAN LOVE STORIES*, ALYSON PUBLICATIONS, JULY 2003.

For Pen

Chapter 1

Greenwich Village. Birthplace of the American Beat Society. Original home of the "come crash at my pad" crowd. Romantic. Eclectic. Funky. Unpredictable. Multicultural. Each corner you turn unveils something. And it all looks so harmless and fag-happy and pink, with dozens of places to find a good bottle of wine and black cats sleeping in the sunlight of flower shop windows.

The Village is also a place to get mugged. Everybody says it's the city, you know, downtown Manhattan, where all the shit is—and don't get me wrong, downtown Manhattan does have its shit. Pre-Rudy Times Square was no place to fuck with either. But the Village can be far more dangerous, I think, especially for those who don't live here. Deceptive. Streets twist and turn and spin you around like you're drunk. I once came across a tourist, happily intrigued, following a trail of red footprints. "Where does this lead?" asked the man, bearded, cardiganed, camera in hand. I couldn't say. And of course, I didn't dare tell him that the footprints were not in red paint, but blood, baked into a patch of light-colored sidewalk. I didn't dare tell him that the path he was following was more than likely someone's last. I didn't dare tell him that Jack Kerouac had died quite some time ago. For in New York, even death is art. And in the Village, it's best to keep secrets.

But with all of its odd curves and dark stairwells, Greenwich Village is the place to be if you're, well, a lesbian. And I hardly think that tiny Piqua, Ohio was ready for their prized Piqua Peach Queen of 1974 to come bopping out of the closet. I moved to the Village in my early 20s and stayed. Straight people live here too. Take my friend Trish, for instance, who came here to check up on me and met Hal, with whom she became totally infatuated. She married him, and they now have two girls with great teeth (Hal's an orthodontist). Trish has known me since long before I was the Peach Queen. As kids we skipped rocks across my aunt's pond and had tea parties. As teens we skipped school, listened to Led Zeppelin, and dared each other to inject ourselves with insulin shots we stole out of my grandmother's purse. Trish was the first person I came out to, as she sat stoned and giggling uncontrollably under the tampon machine in our high school bathroom, and when I started to cry she stomped out her joint and hugged me and told me it was OK. To be gay, that is.

Trish is dying now. Liver cancer. She found out six months ago.

That's when I started having the dreams again, dreams of being locked in a basement with no light. And that's also when my asthma came back. And that's also when I stopped jogging every day and instead started drinking every day, and it was this particular hobby that spawned a recent injury: After a tequila-soaked evening at Pete's Down the Street, I overcorrected after missing one of my front steps and toppled down to the sidewalk to land square on my ass—to my amusement (at the time). But the next morning my left ankle was the size of a baby's head. Sprained, but in a peculiar manner: Most twisted ankles turn inward; a "high sprain," however, is achieved by twisting the ankle outward, thus tearing a long list of ligaments, some of which might never heal entirely. Others would take weeks. A "high sprain." Sounds like an award.

Or a cocktail.

Crutches were a bit unnecessary; no, instead they gave me this velcro-belted, neon-blue nylon deal—a shoe, I guess, to wear over my cast—with hospital-white rubber tread. I immediately dubbed it "das boot." The thing made me claustrophobic, I couldn't walk for shit, and it was so damn ugly I thought I'd die. And the pain! Even with an enviable stash of Percocet at hand, the pain was unbearable. In a good-hearted effort to help, one of my employees loaned me a cane made out of a petrified and seriously stretched bull penis. Me, a bull dyke? It is to laugh.

"Steve got it for me on eBay. For our anniversary," said Allen, surprisingly stoic as he passed the enormous phallus to my waiting hands. I had rarely seen him sans smile since I'd met and hired him a few years before. This was, apparently, a somber occasion and, of course, a very special cane. I attempted to put forth an air of...reverence?

"Thank you, Allen." I fondled the cane at its handle, which seemed the safest place to touch, as it was wrapped in a braided cloth tape at the curve. The shaft itself resembled approximately 28 inches of beef jerky, dry and veiny and made of not-so-mysterious beef parts usually slung to the scrap heap at the slaughterhouse. "I suppose this sort of thing is very rare."

"Actually, no." Allen seemed embarrassed. "I used to think so myself until I stumbled upon this very item for sale in a Vivian Pring catalog."

Known throughout the east coast as the queen of cheap mail order, Vivian Pring was synonymous with monogrammed silver-plate Christmas ornaments and made-in-Korea vinyl moccasins. Vivian Pring sold the kind of shit that wasn't at all funky, just junky, and the very thought of his betrothed's love offering originating from such a tacky place obviously didn't set well with Allen.

"It was Larry Hagman's! I got it through a celebrity auction!" Steve scampered out from behind his desk, clipping a potted palm with his shoulder as he made his way over to us. "Two years ago, after he got the new liver, he sold some of his, you know...ephemera. And this!"

And, well, that made sense. With a new liver, one would never have room for a bull penis in one's life. I made a mental note to pass this bit of info on to Trish, should she ever be in the position.

"Together three years, and he presents me with this." Allen rolled his eyes. "One would have expected a set of crystal."

"It's a genuine bull penis," Steve said. "From the head bull at the Southfork Ranch. Perhaps he used it to keep Sue Ellen in line."

"Perhaps." I nodded, turning it over and over in my hands, looking for some mark of beauty or interest or...something.

"Anyway, it should help you get around until that ankle heals up. It's quite supportive. There's a metal rod that runs the length of it." Allen tugged nervously at the thin knot of his silk tie. A "pimp knot," he'd always called it, careful to craft a tiny dimple in its center with the tips of his soft, nimble fingers.

"Why, that's very sweet of you." A metal rod? I wondered if it could be removed to leave the bull penis hollow. I imagined somehow rigging a Super Soaker to the cane, a Super Soaker loaded with...warm cream? Let some tourist elbow me on the street and I'd give them a sticky blast! "It's lovely, really. A lovely thought. I'll be proud to use it."

So there I was, this tragic, crippled figure, hobbling out my front door with J.R. Ewing's petrified bull penis in one hand and my Prada bag in the other. Tiny Tim in a gray Armani suit—the one that makes me look like Sigourney Weaver in *Working Girl*, or so I've been told. All this cloaked warmly in my shin-length monstrosity of a coat, a man's coat tailored nicely to fit my lanky frame, its black cashmere impenetrable to harsh New York winter winds—a treasure I'd awarded myself on a visit to Barneys in those happier days when I actually gave a damn about how I looked.

The news of Trish's impending doom had changed me. I'd lost just enough weight to be under suspicion. (My secretary came right out and asked me one day if I had, as she called it, "the virus," to which I'd cheerfully informed her that no, I didn't, as I always made my vibrators use protection.) Gray hairs were popping up through the Auburn #5 more frequently, and I'd been leaving them. Gray suit, gray hair, gray world... And then she came.

Joseph, my regular driver, never minded blocking a lane of traffic to park and properly escort me to the cab. Joseph, however, was away on vacation, leaving me in the incapable hands of Giuseppe, a nervous dwarf who barely spoke English and insisted upon pulling his cab into actual parking spaces—no matter how big a tip I offered. And so, with enough prescription drugs in my body to eliminate any pain I might experience throughout the next millennium, I gimped my pitiful self down the front steps and was steeling for the agonizing hike to the car when, dear God, along she came.

Black hair, and I do mean *black*, like *Elvis* black. Big, soft brown eyes. Rollerblades. A bright blue backpack. Foreign maybe. *Romanian? Cambodian? Cher?*

Whatever her nationality, the girl was startlingly beautiful. And young. Probably didn't even own a heating pad. Definitely hadn't even entertained the thought of making that first, demoralizing purchase of Lancôme Wrinkle Recovery Cream. She snapped her gum loudly and proudly and just as I was envisioning her on the cover of the first lesbian Harlequin romance novel... SMACK! This guy trotted up behind her, slammed her headfirst into my wrought iron fence, and took off with her backpack. In an instant she wiped out on the sidewalk, landing in a crumpled, though not entirely unattractive, heap. I knelt down, nearly falling myself—no thanks to das boot—and gently touched her face with my fingertips. Her eyes fluttered open. I smiled in relief. She stared up at me with an innocence that turned to panic as she reached up to touch the blood that had run down the side of her cheek.

"It's all right," I said, surprised at myself for sounding so soothing and maternal. "You've just got a little cut. A bump and a cut."

I pulled her hand from her face and held it in mine. The morning had been cold enough already, but it was starting to rain now and would soon turn icy. I slipped off my coat and covered her with it. A few people gathered, probably tourists, but most everyone kept right on with their city pace. Assholes. Someone had called an ambulance.

Dismissing the diminutive Giuseppe, I decided to ride along with her in case the police needed a witness, as if it would make a difference. And though I sat, arms folded, freezing my ass off, I couldn't help but be taken aback by her beauty. Not in a lustful I-wonder-what-she-looks-like-naked sort of way. Not at all. Well, not entirely. It's just that she looked so...sweet. And soft. Like we all look when we're young and still believe in things.

"You wear Chanel No. 5," she said, grinning up at me. *Snap!* Again with the gum.

"Why, yes, I do," I said, flattered that such a pretty young thing would not only recognize but comment on my signature fragrance. I glanced at my reflection in the ambulance window. Not bad for my age. Late 30s or early 40s or whatever I was telling myself that day. A little hagged out, a bit rode hard and put up wet, as they say, but then so was Madonna.

"My mom wears Chanel No. 5," she remarked.

I laughed to myself. "Figures."

Chapter 2

"You're smoking again," Trish said. "You wheeze in your sleep."

I jerked awake, already feeling the kinks from my nap in a standard-issue hospital-room chair. Trish looked good, considering. Sometimes I wished she'd look worse so it wouldn't seem so unreal that she had cancer.

"Oh, you're awake," I said, shaking and shivering, my clothes still damp enough to cling.

"No shit," she said, straightening her bedclothes. Good old anal Trish. Chronic hand-washer. Organizer of my silverware drawer. Light of my life. "What happened to you? You're all wrinkled."

"Got caught in the rain," I said. "Some guy shoved a girl headfirst into my fence this morning and stole her backpack."

"No kiddin'!"

"Yeah, I, you know...I rode with her to the hospital." I lowered my gaze. "Filled out the police report and everything. Not like it'll do any good, but..."

"Mm-hmm." Trish smirked. "So did you ask her out?"

8

"Oh, no. No, no. She's just a kid. 23...24..."

"Pretty?"

"Ravishing," I admitted, then blushed.

"I love it! There's hope for you yet!" Trish pointed toward my cane. "What the hell is that?"

"Oh, this old thing? It's a petrified bull penis."

"Oh, yeah, well, now that I see it, how could I not have known?"

"It's also a cane," I said. "I sprained my ankle. Princess Grace strikes again."

"It isn't broken?"

I shook my head. "A high sprain."

"Sounds like such an achievement."

"It happens when you bend the ankle outward, and it hurts like nobody's business." I moaned and rubbed my calf, then I threw my hand to my forehead. "I'll never play the violin again!"

"Tripping over empty tequila bottles?"

I casually flipped her off.

"I would have brought you something," I said, ever-so-slyly changing the subject from my rampant alcohol consumption to my unlimited generosity. "I just didn't know what you needed."

"Well, hey..." She snapped her fingers. "I could use a new liver! Maybe a magazine..."

"Well, hey..." I snapped my fingers. "I saw one in the gift shop, but didn't know if it was your size."

I rested my head on the mattress beside Trish's hand and started to cry. This was nothing unusual. I tried to be strong about the whole situation, but sometimes the unfairness of it all was overwhelming. During each visit there came a point where I just cracked. She tousled my hair.

"Mace?"

I didn't answer. I had no answers for anything. Nothing made sense. She had a beautiful family. She had a life.

"Ma-cy?" she said softly and singsongy. "Macy's Thanksgiving Day Parade?"

I closed my eyes and took a deep breath.

"Little friend?" she whispered. "Are you home?"

"I'm fine."

"C'mon, girlie. Don't be so weepy. This whole 'My Best Friend Is Dying' thing is turning into a bad made-for-TV movie."

"Starring Tori Spelling," I said, blowing my nose.

"Yeah." Trish snorted. "As you." She reached over to check my forehead. "You're sick, missy."

"On the verge." I nodded. "Feel like I'm coming down with something."

"It's no wonder. You probably haven't eaten a decent meal since I've been in here." Trish reached for the phone. "Hal's got a meatloaf in the oven for tonight. I'll tell him to bring some over for you."

"No."

"What do you mean, no?"

"You don't have to worry about me."

"Well, tell me—if I don't, who will?"

"Hey." I grinned. "There's always my mother."

Trish frowned in disgust. My mother was a real harpy. When I finally had the guts to tell her I was gay, she told me I was "immoral and unnatural" and that I was no longer welcome in her home or her heart.

Period.

"Yeah, well, I gotta go." Standing, I tried my best to straighten out the wrinkles in my suit. "Last thing you need right now is to catch a cold from me. Don't worry, Trish. I'm a big girl."

"I know, but when you come in here looking like Liza, fresh from the club, I can't help it." She waved. "Go home and go to bed, for cryin' out loud."

"I will. I love you."

"You should."

"Wow." I slapped my forehead. "You are so Jewish."

"Don't smoke!" she called after me as I walked into the corridor. "You've got asthma, remember? And stop hitting the sauce so hard! You look like shit..." I could still hear Trish when I stepped onto the elevator. Six floors down, my dark-haired sorority princess had been stitched up and exited stage left. That was that. Case closed.

"Just missed her," the admissions clerk chirped.

"Story of my life," I said. "'Just missed her.' Maybe I'll have that tattooed on my ass."

I decided to stop by Pete's on the way home. No tough decision, no big surprise, as I'd been stopping at Pete's every day for the last six months, consuming enough tequila shots to encircle the Earth. It usually started at 5:45 P.M., right after work, but today, as I'd called in citing a "personal emergency," the process could start a little earlier.

It was 3, this time, when I took my first sip of Cuervo on ice from the big glass. The bartender knew it was a waste of time for both of us if she gave me a regulation-size shot. The tumbler she placed before me would last all evening, generally, and allow me to become gently smashed in my quiet little corner. But while I reveled in my privacy and, admittedly, self-absorption, I was hardly oblivious to the goings-on around me. The standard butches ogled and swaggered around the standard femmes. The selection of pretty youths trickled in from the club crowds, dancing loosely to the Alanis Morrissette tunes they'd selected on the jukebox. I sipped my Cuervo in my corner and wondered where I was supposed to fit in, how I had slipped out of my comfortable pocket in this odd, gay world.

In the '80s I had ruled Pete's with a wide-smiling self-confidence and a passion for playing pool. I'd listened to Blondie and I'd worn lots of black (which probably made me look like a member of *The Avengers*, but it must've somehow done the trick: I never went home alone). I'd worked at a travel agency, free to go anywhere in the world—cheaply. I'd sniffed cocaine whenever I wanted and felt virtually unafraid of almost anything. With the exception of commitment.

I sat and thought of all this in my corner. At 40-plus, I now wore designer clothes. I owned my own successful travel agency in the Village, and its success had enabled me to buy my apartment building on Christopher Street. I had been very lucky over the years and it showed, and I was at a time in my life when I should have been enjoying the vague air of sophistication I had achieved. Yacht clubs. Rolex watches. Polo ponies. Such things—appearances, frivolities—meant nothing, however. Well, almost nothing. The only person I had ever shared my secrets with was dying, and all the trips to Barneys in the world couldn't change that fact.

I lit a cigarette and examined my nails...*time to schedule a manicure*...and felt that sinking weight in my heart and my stomach again. Selfish or not, the feeling was very real. Without Trish, my life would be eternally fucked. How dare she have cancer? How dare she die?

"God, how long has it been?" a throaty voice asked from behind me. "Two years, maybe?"

I turned, and the voice was that of Naomi. Tall, but not as tall as I am. Short blond hair. She was a singer I had met a few years back in Manhattan. Yet another reminder of my bad judgment, for the whiplash of our "relationship" left me waking up to find all cash, credit cards, and personal checks missing from my handbag in a crummy hotel room. "Sorry" was all that was written on a piece of paper I found on the TV. At least she apologized.

"My, my...the ghost of Christmas past." I was aware of my slurred speech—but hey, who was I trying to impress?

"You're drunk," she stated, and looked at me with...pity? "You never used to drink before 6."

"Yeah, well, I use alcohol to cope with people *stealing* from me. You know, I swore if I *ever* saw your thieving ass again, I'd..."

"You'd what?" She smirked, gesturing toward the bull penis. "Chase me with your cane? Shit, Macy, what happened to you? You used to have a sense of humor." She sat down, facing me. "What do you say I buy you a drink? Huh? Let bygones be bygones. Come on, Macy. We had a lot of fun together."

"If you call hours of orgasms fun, well..." I shrugged. "Yes, I guess we did have fun together."

She smiled, reaching across the table to touch my hand.

"I'm sorry," she said.

"I know," I said. "I got the note."

What happened shortly thereafter I cannot explain, as I consider myself a fairly logical person and my actions were totally devoid of any logic. I was angry upon seeing Naomi, but the anger stirred other emotions within me.

Not in my heart exactly, but, well, in other places. It was just like I remembered: more of a game than sex. But it was a physically satisfying game, the details of which I'll not divulge (except for how she used her middle finger and a plastic spoon to make me come five or six times). Anyway, I wasn't proud of myself as I lay alone on the edge of the bed. My strange surrender had not been due to any true passion but to exhaustion. I had felt just as drained and spent before our desperate little tryst as I did after it.

It was 4 A.M. when I awoke, trembling like a junkie as I sat up and swung my legs over the side of the bed. I coughed, and my chest felt as if it would explode. Sick. Sick. Sick.

"Naomi, where's my coat?" I asked, my voice deep and hoarse.

Nothing.

I grabbed her shoulder and shook her. She moaned.

"Naomi, where the fuck is my coat?" Then I remembered... the girl... the gum-cracker. She had it. I peered out the hotel room window and saw a brick wall. Ha. "City view," we called it in our travel brochures. Rain slid down the bricks. I was freezing and had no coat. Fabulous. My suit lay in a crumpled pile on the floor. I reached down and picked it up...still damp. My head pounded. For a moment I stood shivering in my underwear.

"What are you doing?" Naomi asked, eyes closed, barely stirring.

I studied her. Probably just in town for the weekend. She had no idea where I lived, and I liked it that way. Yeah, I could sleep with her, but I didn't want her knowing my personal information. Sex has always made me illogical.

"Breakfast," I told her. "I don't know why, but I'm starving. Howard Johnson's, here I come."

"OK."

And it was that easy. My exit, I mean. Once dressed, I slipped on her black leather deal with the Warner Bros. logo embroidered on the back and slipped out the door. That was that. No muss, no fuss. No awkward exchange of phone numbers. Two minutes later I was ducking into a cab, begging the driver to please turn up the heat. So long, sucker. And off we went into the New York morning, zipping down Fifth Avenue at some ridiculous rate of speed. And I was thinking about...jeans.

Her jeans.

How they were stonewashed or acid-washed. Something not yet classic—not ever destined to be classic— and definitely not current. Not even close to stylish, honey. Not in the least.

I laughed. I laughed until it hurt. No loss, you know. No great catch ever cracked her gum and wore stonewashed jeans.

It was only about two hours later when I woke up in my own bed, hacking so hard I saw flashes of light—Christ, I hadn't even closed the front door—groaning involuntarily from the shocks of pain that racked my body when I tried to get up. In fact, as I lay there silently analyzing the situation, it was rather like a full-body migraine. Oh, goody. The flu. My apartment had a somewhat slanted, murky look. This wasn't right. A dream perhaps? The front door clicked shut. *Gently.* Afraid, I kept my eyes closed—and heard careful footsteps.

Suddenly, I'd had enough. So what if this *was* a psycho killer? So fucking what?

"I don't know who you are," I croaked, "but I'll give

you $50 if you bring me a glass of water before you kill me." One last request, you know. It was only fair.

My head throbbed from the sound of my own voice. Frustrated, disoriented, and just plain scared, I started to cry. Just as I did so, a hand lifted my head and a glass was held to my lips. I drank, cool water soothing my throat.

"Mom?" I don't know why I said it.

Someone laughed and said, "No."

I opened my eyes.

Unbelievable.

It was her: the girl who'd been mugged in front of my apartment. Pretty. Sweet. Girl-next-door-ish. I squinted in disbelief. Yeah, it was her, all right. I closed my eyes and allowed my head to fall back against the pillow. It had to be a dream, I rationalized. Some twisted hallucination. Pretty soon she'd have two heads and would start shoving hot dogs into donut holes. No one this attractive could just wander in.

"I'm sorry, the door was open," I heard her say, heard her feet shuffle uneasily. "I just wanted to return your coat. And to thank you. I didn't mean to bother you. It's just that..."

She paused. I opened my stinging eyes and saw that she'd moved closer to my bed, looking at me—into me— with those soft brown eyes. For a moment it seemed she might cry, but she held back her tears and just looked at me like I was Christ himself.

"It's just that most people just turn their backs or walk away, and you didn't." She smiled. "You helped me. I had to let you know how grateful I am."

Nice person, I thought. *Manners. Dropping by to return my coat and to thank me personally. Dropping by and looking, well, fantastic.*

"I've been here," she continued, "in the city, for two years now. Alone. And sometimes it's cool...it's an adventure. But sometimes it just sucks."

And with this I was feeling a bit weepy myself. Not like it took much for that feeling to surface, as I'd been on a self-pity sabbatical from reality all morning. All year, essentially.

She leaned over me, touching my face with caution, touching me with her cool, soft fingertips. I gazed upward to see the smooth, girlish face hovering over me shift into an expression of concern.

"It's my fault." Her gaze moved down with guilty resignation, as if she was set to confess a homicide.

"What?" I had to know what all this tearful melodrama was for.

"You were soaked in the rain when you waited with me the other day. You gave me your long, beautiful coat." She spoke slowly. "It's my fault you're sick."

"Well, now, it's not like I have the plague," I began, not entirely sure of the truth of that statement, but before I could continue, I realized the girl had vanished.

Great, I thought, shaking my head. *A little flu and suddenly I'm Camille, lusting after my young lover on my deathbed. Pathetic. Even my hallucinations let me down.* Embarrassed, I fell into a restless slumber, until several minutes later when I felt her wrap around me from behind. Cool, silky skin seemed to absorb my fever as her round, naked breasts pressed against my back. Her right arm draped over me as she reached around to caress my ribs. We said nothing to each other, but she knew precisely where to touch me with her delicate hands, pulling the aches out of my body. My skin felt electric. I had never been so awake, so relaxed, so alive. It was sublime.

For hours, we lay without words or complications. Drifting. Safe. The incident with Naomi seemed distant now, almost like I'd been someone else just hours before. There was no need for games or dances, no roles to play this time. It was a rainy fall Saturday and I lay awake, naked and feverish and held by a beautiful stranger in my own bed. It was the single most perfect moment of my life.

Chapter 3

Light spilled in through the slivered blinds of my floor-to-ceiling bedroom windows, signaling morning to my puffy eyes. Outside, the slang of garbage men filtered through the traffic noise. Inside, the cordless blared through my eardrum, and I snatched it off its base in one ring. Trish.

"So, who is she?"

"She...?" I said. "She who?"

"What? Is there more than one *she* there with you? Are you hosting some swingin' lesbian slumber party, or what?"

"And if that were so"—I slipped my hand under the mattress and pulled out my secret lipstick—"would I answer the phone?"

"I suspect not." Trish sighed. "So who was she?"

"Who?"

"The girl who answered your phone, ass."

The girl who answered my phone?

"Oh, yeah," I said, the little nightlight coming on in my head. "The girl who was mugged the other day. You know—the one who cut her head on the fence." I blotted

19

my lips on the bedsheet—brazen burgundy—and groaned at the collage of pill bottles that littered my bedside table.

"And...?"

"And what?"

"And now she's your personal assistant or love slave or whatever, answering your calls and shit, telling me you're sick, that she's sorry but you're still sleeping, she'll take a message, blah blah blah?"

"She answered the phone? What time?"

"Around nine. So, did she spend the night?"

"Not exactly." (Technically speaking, she had only spent the morning.)

"Hey, hey, so you slept together?"

"Yeah, I think...well, no...I mean, I think..."

"Don't tell me you were too drunk to remember, for God's sake."

"Trish, I've been sick. Can't you hear it in my voice? I feel like shit."

"You sound like Demi Moore, goddess of implants."

"Exactly. Thank you," I snapped. "No, I was not too drunk to remember. If I seem a bit foggy, it's because I've been ravaged by the flu from hell. Jesus..."

"So..." she sighed. "Feeling any better?"

"Yeah, my...uh..." I felt my forehead for verification. "My fever's gone. I still feel like my chest is full of broken glass when I cough, but it's much better. You know...not so tight."

"How's the asthma?"

"What asthma?" I laughed. "Asthma, shmasthma. Hell's bells, who cares about asthma?"

"How did this girl, this...what's her name?"

"I don't know."

20

"OK, how did this *unknown girl* end up staying the night?"

"She just showed up."

"And you said 'Hi, I have no idea who you are, but you're young and probably good at answering the phone. Come on in and let's have sex and you can sleep over.' Was it something like that?"

"No," I stated. "We didn't have sex, I don't think."

"You don't *think*?"

"We slept together in the nude, but I don't think we did anything."

Trish laughed a long time over that one.

"Help me out here, babe. I don't get it."

"I was already in bed when she got here," I explained. "She told me how grateful she was for being nice when she was mugged the other day and all that and that she felt bad because I'd caught the flu and the next thing I knew, we were in bed together."

"Slut!"

"No, I was just sick with this fever, you know, and this girl, this...this beautiful creature just crawled into bed and curled up with me."

"Like spoons."

"Huh?"

"You've never heard it called that? It's when one person curls around the other from behind. Like spoons in a drawer," she explained. "It's called 'spooning.'"

"Yes. Right. Like spoons."

"Naked," Trish probed. "She simply coiled around you and slept and you were both...naked."

"Yes, Judge, a mere case of spooning in the nude. That's pretty much it."

21

"Pretty much? Hmm...where did she keep her hands?"

"What?"

"Did she grab your breasts?"

"I don't think it was as much of a grab as it was a graze."

"Like she was reaching around?" she asked. "Not actually going for them, not actually copping a feel, but kind of brushing them accidentally?"

"You know, you're getting awfully interested in the details here. Is there something I should know about you, princess?"

"Hey, hey, look here, missy, I'm only examining the facts. Somebody has to be objective about this little fairy tale. I don't like the idea of someone taking advantage of you when you're in a Nyquil coma."

"She wasn't taking advantage of me. She was massaging my bronchial tubes," I said. "My chest."

"She was *what?*"

"I woke up covered in Vicks and the bed was empty." I shrugged. "And that's the facts, ma'am. All pretty innocent, really, except for the naked part."

"Oh, ha ha. So, where is this little dreamboat?"

"From the sound of it, she's taking a shower." I sat up and grimaced at my reflection in my dressing mirror. "Jesus, I've gotta go. I look like Queen Elizabeth. Listen, I'll call you later, Trish. Bye."

I heard the water shut off. My eyes fixed on the bathroom door. She would be out any minute. She. She with the island-black hair and calm eyes. No name. Hell...no need.

The door opened with the usual creak and she stood in the doorway, towel-drying her hair and wearing one of the flannel shirts I sometimes slept in. Long legs. Shirt open just enough to expose her cleavage, which was not enormous—no Silicon Valley here, thank you—but very nice.

"Sorry I left the television on." She continued drying her hair.

I hadn't noticed, but yes, the TV was on. *What Ever Happened to Baby Jane?* was playing with the volume down, no doubt on some Ted Turner station.

"So, you like old movies?" I asked, which was a lame attempt at conversation, I know, but it was an attempt, nonetheless. Bar talk with a stranger was different than, well, post-shower talk.

"Not especially," she responded.

Great. So she wasn't big into conversation. Not a big talker. Shit, what did that matter? We could get past it.

"So, you have a thing for crippled older women?"

She smiled, exposing this funny little bit of an overbite. Not bucky beaver teeth, mind you. Not overdone, not Rosanna Arquette. Just right. "Very funny." Then she began brushing her hair in long, slow, even strokes I hoped would never end. I envied that brush. "Oh, yeah, I forgot to ask. What happened to your foot?"

"Tragic war injury—no, it's just a bad sprain."

(What was I supposed to tell her? That I fell down drunk?)

"How long will you have to wear that cast?"

"Eight weeks, if I don't cut it off myself before then."

"Sounds like you're feeling better."

"Much," I said, breathless at the sight, the motion of her brushing that black, shimmering hair that spilled over her shoulder. Dear God.

And then it hit me.

"What's wrong?" She stopped brushing, just stopped

and stood there, looking at me like she wanted to know what the hell I was thinking about, what the hell that flash was that just went over my face.

I couldn't help it; I had to know. Too many so-called relationships had left me scrambling for the Valium bottle. This would probably be a good time to break out my eighth-grade debate team extemporaneous speaking skills. You know, start off by saying something about our world being...oh...full of conflicting desires. Something like that.

"Should I sit down for this?" she joked.

It wasn't a big deal, and yet it really was. The whole bisexual thing may have worked just swell for others, but not for me. No sirree, Bob. I'd never liked sharing as a kid, and I wasn't ready to start then.

"OK, tell me..." I took a deep breath, which actually wasn't very deep, as the old neurotic asthma was starting to kick in—but at least I was on my way. "If you were, say, a toy, a doll, or something..."

"Yes?"

"You're a toy, a doll—and your mate takes you out of your box to play with you." God, this was lame. "What would your instructions say?"

"I don't know—contains small parts?" She giggled and threw up her hands in surrender.

"What else?"

"God, what are we on the *Newlywed Game*?"

I cleared my throat. "What I'm asking is, would your instructions have a diagram that said anything like, oh, 'Insert penis into slot B'?"

She tilted her head like a dog when it's listening, like the RCA dog—what was its name?

"You're asking me if I'm bisexual?"

Nipper! The RCA dog's name was Nipper. I always did the stupid trivia self-distraction thing when things got intense. She'd figured it out, all right. She was smart. Smart enough to be profoundly insulted by my stupid-ass little guessing game. She'd be gone soon. My one chance at having the intuitive lover I'd always wanted and I was blowing it. "Yes," I said. "Yes, I'm asking you if you're"—I didn't even like to say it, much less hear it— "bisexual."

Blech. *Bisexual.* A word so ugly I felt like clearing my palette after saying it. Bicentennial, biodegradable, bionic...bisexual. Ah, yes. The tease for both genders, the ultimate flirting-with-disaster, just-in-for-the-weekend type of relationship. Not even respectable enough to be a relationship really. Just a fuck. A fuck with repercussions, like drunken husbands who stumble home unexpectedly and want to kill you or watch both of you, or—worse yet—join in. Heartbreakers. Cheaters. These were the bisexuals, in my eyes. Bitter? You betcha. But I had plenty of case studies upon which to base my bitterness.

The name Kimmie comes to mind.

Kimmie was the first, and by that I mean the first one I really had a thing for. Rain brought us together.

Rain and fresh-cut flowers.

I was brand-spanking new to the city when we met, clicking my heels down the sidewalk one average Saturday morning, having my cigarette and still a bit in the tourist mode—you know, wearing my crumpled David Bowie T-shirt and a pair of blue jeans with a big rip right under the left cheek of my skinny white ass; sunglasses on at 6 A.M. and still thinking I was cool. Still taking it all in: the sounds and smells, the sense that I was in some ancient place, so eager to be swallowed up by the history and fame and sheer size of New York. Feeling very invisible and still mildly jiffed from the record-breaking amount of coke served to me during the prior evening's antics.

Needless to say, I wasn't paying attention to the sky, so the rain took me by surprise. Such a downpour was not unwelcome in the early morning's summer heat, but it was inconvenient. My makeup ran, my clothes were soaked, and instead of clicking my heels I was forced to slog through the mess as I slicked the hair back out of my face. A green awning sheltered two carts of flowers in front of a convenience store, and I ducked underneath it for shelter. Cursing, I flicked the remainder of my waterlogged cigarette out into the gutter—and began to laugh to laugh at myself. Kimmie emerged just as I was hit with the heavy fragrance of fresh lilacs. She propped open the convenience store's front door with a brick.

"Got caught in the rain?" Her slight Southern drawl added to the charm of her loose print dress, ankle bracelet, green eyes, and kitten smile. I didn't stand a chance.

"Rain? What rain?" I squeezed a stream of water from my T-shirt. "Just an excessive perspiration problem is all. That damned Secret just isn't doing the trick."

She threw her head back and howled with laughter, uncharacteristic of the Lands End catalog model type I'd pegged her to be. "I have an umbrella," she said, her green eyes sparkling like chips of jade behind long, curly bangs. "And I live just over there. You can pop over for a spell and dry off if you like."

Well, I'll be. Not since Ellie Mae Clampett had I been so disarmed by a hillbilly. So pop over I did. Kimmie suggested I borrow her robe while she put my clothes in the dryer. What was the harm in that? So we drank coffee and played cards and talked a while at the kitchen table, just small talk mostly. She was from Prestonsburg, Kentucky, and had moved to New York to study interior design.

I observed her as she spoke of wallpaper and floor coverings, watched in fascination as her full lips formed the words "levelor blinds" and as her delicate hands brushed the hair from her face. She was young. Pretty. And so was I, so I ignored the signals I've since learned to detect and react to accordingly. For all I knew, she was just a good-hearted Southern belle who looked, as they say, "hotter'n Georgia asphalt."

An hour or so passed. As I shed her robe to slip back into my own clothes, off went her bedroom light and on came Tammy Wynette's "Stand by Your Man" from a stereo I couldn't see. I spun around in the darkness, fumbling for the light switch, and then she jumped me. *Wham!* Arms and legs latched around me. Momentum knocked us back against what I assume was her vanity table, as I could hear perfume and cosmetic bottles flying everywhere. Kimmie grabbed a handful of my hair and jerked my head down hard—*shit!*—locking her lips against mine and steering us to fall onto the bed. We missed, tumbling to the floor in a heap. The record skipped, I heard a rip, and off came my red bikini underwear. So set the stage for our brief liaison, relationship, or whatever you want to call it.

As you might expect, from that point on I couldn't get enough of her, but not for the reason you might presume. It was not for the sex. With Kimmie, sex was almost mechanical; she didn't seem to care who I was, only that I was there for the wild ride. Fast and bumpy, like a dirt bike. There was no cuddling or sweetness. Afterward, I often felt used—and, well, empty. Like a whore. An exhausted whore.

But aside from the strenuous yet dissatisfying sex, things could not have been better. Kimmie was cute and fun and bright, with a bent sense of humor that led her to coax me into eating what I later discovered was horse testicle soup at an ethnic festival (not bad with crackers, by the way). We attended concerts and plays, ate out, and caught movies together. Real dates, you know, with hair spray and kissing under the porch light and everything. We hung out together two, maybe three nights a week, and sometimes more. Things were just swell.

Then one Saturday night this big slob of a guy came strolling in on us. Kimmie was in mid-lick, completely detached, as usual, from everything in reality including me, so she didn't hear a thing. I, on the other hand, had a perfect between-the-knees view of his stubbled, doughy face peeking up from the end of her bed. He was slightly disheveled—OK, sloppy, if you ask me—but not from work. I looked at him, at his hands and his form. He was soft. Perhaps a bit privileged in his upbringing. A mama's boy, maybe. Here was a boy who'd spent more time practicing the violin than fixing cars or playing baseball. And now, the sheltered boy had grown up.

Still spoiled by someone, I thought. *Probably the pet tortured artist of some easily charmed benefactor. A poet without a cause.*

"Hi, guys," he said, like it was nothing to find his wife or girlfriend or whatever in the sheets with another chick.

What to do? What to do? No entry in the *Homo Handbook* for this situation. So I flashed my best smile and waved hello. What else could I have done? We were nailed, busted, caught right in the act. Scared shitless, I readied myself for that big, raucous confrontational moment, the moment when the materialized. But what happened? The guy reached up and tapped Kimmie on the shoulder. She looked around and grinned.

"Hey, you made it!" she said, all happy and huggy and—oh, Christ—acting like she'd invited him; because, of course, the slob was her husband, a musician who spent most of his time touring the tri-state area with his band, Sin-ergy. Bob was his name, and Bob did not mind coming home to double his pleasure. No, Bob liked the idea. A lot.

"Don't let me interrupt." He sat down on a wicker bench.

Wicker. What a stupid thing to make furniture out of.

Anyway, ol' Bob liked the idea so much he couldn't resist whipping his wiener out of his pants.

"Please go on," he said, so polite, proceeding to masturbate right there...IN FRONT OF ME!

Kimmie returned to the task at hand, but having never liked the idea of love as a spectator sport, I had a hard time concentrating. And sure, it had been love: a fun, frivolous kind of love with no real glitches other than the sex thing— and, of course, the Bob thing. I mean, maybe I wasn't cool enough or liberated enough or sophisticated enough. Whatever it was, I couldn't handle it. For Christ's sake, the guy actually sat fondling himself while his wife gave me head. And not very good head, at that. So for the first and last time ever, I faked it. Moaned, quivered,

rolled my eyes...even topped it all off with a kittenish little squeak. And yeah, it was wrong. You should never fake
it. But I had to get out of there. It was beginning to turn
my stomach.

"Kimmie." He was hard. And it was a big one—
especially for such a pudgy little freak. All puffed up and
no place to go. "I'm ready to slip it in your ass. Are you
ready?"

Kimmie shrugged. "Sure."

Right then I decided it was best to relinquish my front-row
seat to this debacle. Gracefully, I excused myself to "fresh-
en up," retrieving my clothes from the floor as I left the
room. Didn't even bother to put on my shoes and socks.
Through dirty puddles and sidewalk litter, I padded all the
way home as fast as my big, bare feet would take me. Fred
Flintstone would have been proud.

She whose warm curves I'd convalesced in was now
looking at me with a child's eyes.

"I'm not bisexual."

Whew!

"I'm sorry, I wasn't trying to be rude." Words came
easier now, but I still wanted to smoke. Scanning the bedside table, I saw keys, Tums, but no cigarettes.

"What are you looking for?"

"My cigarettes."

That's it. She'd probably thrown them out, or hidden
them. Trying to "do what's best." Control me. Splendid.

"Eves?" she asked. As if she had to ask.

"Yes," I snapped, knowing she was about to give me
some sanctimonious speech about how she was "saving my
life" by throwing them in the trash, blah, blah, blah, some

kind of healthy, idealistic, youthful bullshit like that. And, oh, was I ready. You bet I was. But before I could let loose with my "this is my life" diatribe...

"They're right here." She picked them up from the kitchen counter and tossed them to me. "I think you've only got a couple left." She began to brush her hair again, curling the brush from underneath this time. "I almost bought you a new pack when I went out earlier, but I wasn't sure if these were yours or not."

"What's this? Just toss them to me like a pack of chewing gum? No lecture?" I pulled the lighter out of the package and lit one, puffing it lightly, shaking my head in amused disbelief.

She frowned. "What?"

"Well, it's just that everyone gives me hell about smoking," I said. "And"—like it was a news flash, like she hadn't noticed I breathed like a fucking freight train in my sleep—"I've got asthma."

"I know. I saw your inhaler," she said. "But why should I get on your case for something you can't control? Nicotine is a very powerful drug." She pulled her hair back and fixed it with a rubber band. "You can't help yourself."

"Oh!" Miss Perfect. "And I suppose you've never smoked?"

"I didn't say that."

"Aha! So you have!"

"Nope." She folded her arms and smiled. "Never."

"What, are you Amish?"

"So, not smoking makes me Amish," she said, pointing to my CD collection. "I guess listening to Tina Turner makes you Buddhist."

"No," I said. "I'm not Buddhist."

"Oh. Well, then..."

"I'm black."

She laughed. I smiled my wide smile.

"Anyway," she said, "back to what you were saying earlier..."

"About bisexuality?"

"Yeah."

"I don't like it," I said. "It's like saying you're a vegetarian, then sneaking off to Burger King. It's a lack of self-discipline that's unfair to everyone involved." I folded my arms, ashamed at how imperious and judgmental that must've sounded, but it was true. To me, anyway. So there.

"A lack of self-discipline?"

"Precisely." I meant to blow out some smoke to make a point, but the grace and drama was lost when I wheezed like an accordion.

"You say this as you sit there smoking a cigarette."

"But didn't you just tell me that smoking was beyond my control?"

"You think people have control over their bisexuality?"

"Perhaps," I said, wheezing my way into the beginning of an attack. Wonderful. I always lost my wind before I could win an argument.

She ducked into the bathroom and returned with my inhaler. My hero.

"I'll trade you this for your cigarette."

One puff and the wheezing began to dissipate.

"Sorry," I fibbed. "This hardly ever happens."

"The flu probably doesn't help." She sat next to me on the bed, rubbing my back in a circular motion. "I'm sorry. You don't need debates. You need rest."

"I'm fine," I said. "How smooth your skin is."

She drew me close and rested her head on my shoulder.

"So," I said, "I guess I should ask your name."

"It's Faith."

Faith. Of course. More of a cliché than a name. Wasn't Faith that sweet little gal the gunslinger always came home to?

"And now," she murmured, "I guess I should ask for yours..."

Our heads were nuzzled together, and I was warm and drunk with a fresh pleasure.

"What's your favorite place to shop?" I said. "It's big. Quintessential New York."

"Your name's Salvation Army?"

"Cute," I said. "It's Macy."

She linked her fingers in mine and we held hands like eighth graders.

"So, tell me, Macy. If you were a doll, what would your instructions say?" Faith leaned over and gave me a small but generous kiss on the lips. The first real kiss I'd had in...God, who knows? Not counting, well, Naomi.

"Fragile," I said. "Some assembly required."

She kissed me again. Cherry Chapstick. Yum.

"Faith?"

"Yes?"

"Congratulations. You're probably going to catch my flu."

She kissed my neck.

"Just think of it as my first gift to you."

She kissed my collarbone.

"Nothing like a viral infection to show someone you care..."

She opened my robe. Her hot breath tickled my right

breast as she slid down and kissed my nipple, licking the tip with quick, sharp little licks.

"Oh, my..."

"Macy?"

"Huh?"

She stopped and looked up into my eyes. Sweet Mary, Mother of Jesus! My whole body was numb.

"Huh?" I couldn't form any real words at that point. Shit, I was lucky to get out a grunt.

"Would it be all right if I made love to you?"

Chapter 4

Gee, that was a tough decision.

"I'm kind of new at this," she said, leaving a trail of soft wet kisses as she made her way down, at last reaching my...

"Oh!" Jackpot.

"I'm sorry." She paused. "I told you I was new at this."

"Th-that's OK, sugarplum." Sugarplum? How the hell did that come out of my mouth? "You're doing just fine." I reached down to run my hands through that thick, black hair of hers. "Just fine." Sugarplum. Christ. Sex for me was like holding a baby—it made me say the dumbest things.

I'd planned to take a shower, but didn't. Night came sooner than I expected. I'm sure there were stars out and all that. I'm sure someone sensitive like Elton John would have composed some tender love ballad after such an outstanding sexual experience, but that was pretty much impossible, since the only chords I had ever learned on the guitar were to "Gypsies, Tramps, and Thieves" as a silky-haired, Cher-emulating teen. And yeah, it may have made a mint for

Sonny and Cher, but it was hardly the right song to play to your new, nurturing, gifted young lover who had just succeeded in ringing every bell in your body.

So I slept, without the aid of alcohol for the first time in months. Faith slept as well, lying on top of me with her smiling face nestled peacefully between my breasts. No place like home. She stirred only once, rising to bring a glass of water in an effort to drown my dry flu cough, and when I thanked her she said:

"Will you come away with me?"

And, now, well, you have to understand. I hadn't known this girl but for maybe a day and a half, tops. I knew only her first name. No idea where she came from, how old she was, what she did for a living, so naturally I said yes.

"Great!" she said. "Just for a couple of days."

"Where?" I asked, not that it mattered.

"Michigan," she said. "I have a house there. On a lake. It's very private." She climbed back into bed. "You'll like it there."

"On a lake, huh?" I raised my eyebrow. "So, does this mean I'll be pissing in a hole outdoors? Bathing in a stream? Beating my clothes on rocks?"

"You can if you like."

Fucking lake cottages. Shit. Musty. Cold. Spiders the size of terriers.

"Sounds great."

"It's a house, not a shanty," she said. "It has everything—bathroom, kitchen, fireplace. Everything you need." She slid her arm around my waist. "Just for a couple of days. It'll be good for you. You can bring a book and nap by the fire."

"This isn't going to be one of those trips where we have

to kill our own food, is it?" I crossed my eyes. "Because I kilt a barr when I was but four."

"There's a market down the road. And everything's already dead, for the most part."

"Including us, if they find out we're lesbians."

"Oh, brother."

"I'm just being realistic," I said. "I don't think ol' Gomer's gonna take too kindly to us shacking up next door. We might blight the crops or sour the milk or something. I know how it is. I'm from Ohio. Sisters there are of the knife-carrying, flannel-clad variety. They're tough because they have to be."

"It's not like that, Macy." She stroked my hair. "It's a very liberal community."

I turned and kissed her and looked into her eyes, wondering what she saw in mine. Inadequacy? Fear? I remembered being 10 years old and Mrs. Lawson our neighbor gave me $15 for mowing her tiny lawn—*fifteen dollars!*—and how I'd looked at her as she placed it in my hand and thought, *I don't deserve this, but I think I'll keep it because I need it.*

As I looked at Faith now, I thought the same thing.

Trish answered her phone on the third ring.

"It's me," I said. "How is everything?"

"Everything's pretty cool," Trish said. "Hal just called. I guess Ashley's going out for cheerleading. Can you believe it? I have created a cheerleader. But it's good for her to keep busy, you know. Katherine works so many hours at that fucking McDonald's I'm threatening to report it to the child labor board. So, what's up with you? You sound a little better than yesterday."

"Yeah," I said. "I just wanted to let you know...I'm going away for a couple of days. Monday and Tuesday."

"Really? Where? Someplace suitably exotic?"

"Well...yes. As a matter of fact, it is rather exotic," I said, opening a drawer to select the proper watch. "I'm going to Michigan."

"Michigan? What the hell's in Michigan?"

"Lakes, fudge, multicolored leaves," I said. "And my friend. You know, the girl who answered the phone. She has this place in the sticks, and..."

"Oh, no, Macy. Tell me you're not going off with some stranger to the middle of nowhere."

"She's not a stranger anymore. Her name is Faith."

"Faith?" She laughed. "Don't tell me. Hope and Charity are her sisters, right? You shouldn't be out traipsing around anyway, Macy. You're sick."

"Will you listen?" I screamed. "I am not sick!" And this powerful statement was immediately followed by a dry, spasmodic hack that lasted a good full minute.

I sipped some water and got a grip.

"Trish, I appreciate your concern as a friend. And I know my track record for self-abuse has been extensive as of late, but I'm feeling much better, really, and Faith is very nice, *and* I haven't had a drink in two or three days."

"Macy, I still don't think this is a good idea."

"I am not asking for your approval," I said. "I'm just, you know, just letting you know. I'm going to be gone for a couple of days."

"Macy..."

"OK? So if you need to reach me, you have my cell phone number. Otherwise, I'll call you when I get back to town. Love you. Bye."

I took another hit off my inhaler and fell back against the pillows.

Faith's place in Michigan was nothing like I had expected. A big, sprawling lakefront house. Ten rooms. Sparsely but comfortably furnished. Old, with huge windows trimmed in green that opened outward to face the lake. Not only was it located in the sticks, but it was nearly half a mile off the road, obscured from view by a wall of enormous pine trees. Secluded was an understatement. If Howard Hughes could come back as a house, this would be it. The lake itself was so blue it looked artificial, bright bright bright like the Brady Bunch's back yard, and flanked by marshes that served as nesting grounds for the biggest fucking birds I had ever seen: big, gray, prehistoric-looking bastards stepping slowly through the weeds, knees bending precariously in the tall swamp grass, stepping like tall, gawky men. Jeff Goldblum gangly. And, as I spied from the milky windowpane this flock of Jeff Goldblums lurking so close to our domicile, Faith peered over my shoulder. I flinched when she touched me.

"Sandhill cranes," she said. "Cool, eh?"

"They make me nervous," I said. "They look hungry. They don't have teeth or anything, do they?"

"I don't think so," she laughed. "I'll take our bags upstairs. Just kick back on the sofa, and I'll be down in a sec to build us a fire." She started up the stairs. "I'll put flannel sheets on the bed and crank up the furnace."

"Good idea. It's like an icebox in here."

"It's the wind off the lake. I'm afraid the insulation leaves something to be desired," she called, and I could hear her flipping sheets and blankets upstairs. "I'll bring down the electric blanket."

A man's purple dress shirt over a bright yellow tee. Faded paisley-patterned jeans. This was her ensemble of the day. In her presence, fashion had not seemed so important. But now, alone, I rolled my eyes. Winos dressed better. Marginally retarded winos. Color-blind, marginally retarded winos.

The sofa was Naugahyde and had been patched in several areas with silver Duct tape. It looked slick and cold and entirely uninviting, but was actually quite comfortable. Not bad for a dorm reject.

We hadn't talked much on the plane, what with being wedged between the standard criminally overweight, sweaty passenger on one side and the inattentive mother with a squalling snotty-nosed child on the other. Once again, I kicked myself for not planning ahead, forced into the city-bus-at-best comfort of flying coach. It was prudent, as always, to tune out—you know, hit the drink cart and try not to focus on the whole concept of traveling in a thin metal tube, thousands of feet in the air.

Anyway, the plane ride hadn't exactly been a plethora of conversation, and as I sat on the sofa awaiting Faith's return I felt a bit overwhelmed, isolated—maybe even homesick. After all, I had no idea where I was, and it was so damn cold. And quiet. And *still*. Every so often, I could hear the wind whistle and the house creak and pop, like we were on some creepy old barge that was listing to the side, ready to capsize. But this was no remake of *The Poseidon Adventure*. There was no Shelley Winters on board to save me. Just Macy, all alone, feeling small and helpless in the middle of nowhere. I didn't even know where the toilet was.

I thought of calling Trish. My cell phone was in my bag, but certainly there was a phone in this empty hulk of a place. As Faith had told me, she wasn't Amish or anything. I sat up to go look for it, but stopped. What could Trish do? Worry. Shit. And worrying would be the last thing she of the compromised immune system would need. Sigh. I missed Trish, though. There was no TV, never mind cable, and, let's face it, this Faith chick hadn't presented herself as a stunning conversationalist. What if we had a fight? The girl could ditch me here and no one would know about it, or worse yet, she could hold me captive like that bitch did to the guy in *Misery*.

Oh, God. Maybe Trish was right. Maybe I had been thinking with my twat, and my twat had never been a good decision-maker. In my long career as a lesbian, my twat had made numerous poor choices. Erica. Nadine. Debbie. Guadalupe. Martha. Ingrid. Naomi (ugh). Not even the stock girl at Valu-Mart was safe from my clutches. Yes, I had seriously tramped-out over the years, collecting piles of relationships that had all ended in one form of disaster or another. The list of freaks and bitches was longer than any kid's Christmas list. I had been bad bad bad bad bad bad bad and it was time for retribution. My comeuppance, so to speak. My karma.

Promiscuity led to HIV for some. I, on the other hand, would face a lonely, frozen death in the Michigan woods as punishment for my wicked, wicked ways, trapped with a woman whose wardrobe indicated, at the very least, some form of mental instability.

Of course I could not call Trish.

My chest tightened. It was happening already, and this time it probably wasn't even an asthma attack. More like a heart attack. And it was all my fault. I had to flip out when Trish told me she was dying. I had to stop jogging and start smoking and drinking and running around like Dean Martin or something.

"Macy?" Faith's footsteps pounded across the hardwood

floor. "Oh, my God, I couldn't find it!" She produced my inhaler. "It was in your bag. Here."

And thus, my dramatic death sequence was almost immediately extinguished by sucking Proventil into my lungs. Relief! Faith clutched me in her arms, and I immediately felt silly for doubting her. Faith, with her olive skin reflecting radiantly against her bright-yellow T-shirt. Wow.

"Man, I had to dump out that whole bag of yours before I found it." She stroked my cheek. "Might be a good idea to keep an extra one of these around, eh?"

"OK."

Christ. The girl could've asked me to remove my spleen with a shoehorn and I would've said "OK." I burrowed down into the mothball-scented folds of the baby-blue electric blanket she'd brought down with her. Not much of a blanket—lumpy, moth-eaten, worn thin—but my teeth were beginning to chatter, and as long as we didn't plug it in...

Faith blew onto the Bakelite plug attached to the blanket's cloth cord. "Let's fire this thing up."

"You're trying to k-k-ill me, aren't you?"

"Huh?" She finished plugging in and reached for a log to toss on the fire.

"This thing has got be a f-f-ire hazard."

"It's seen better days," she shrugged. "But it's clean and still seems to work OK. Think of it as an antique."

"Vintage?"

"Vintage," she smiled.

Was it my imagination or had the wires within this tattered wreck of a home appliance stiffened with life at the initial jolt of electricity? I tried my best to resume settling snugly into the electric blanket of the living dead. Anyway, Faith wouldn't endanger me, right? This whole trip would be an excellent opportunity for us to build trust in the formative stages of our relationship. Besides, the thing didn't work. How could an electric blanket, no matter how sinister in appearance, be even the least bit treacherous if it didn't even heat up?

Uh-oh. Time for one of those "awkward silences." No problemo. This was normal. I could handle it.

OK, maybe not.

"Do you think I should get a haircut?"

"What?"

"I asked if you thought I should a haircut," I said.

"And where did this question come from?"

"Just making conversation. Just eliminating the silence." I ran my fingers through my hair. "So, what do you think? I wouldn't even debate it, but the last time I had it trimmed she kind of went wild and I ended up looking like Sandy Duncan—you know, the one who used to do those Triscuit commercials."

"The woman with the glass eye." She crumpled newspaper and shoved it between the logs. "And it was Wheat Thins, not Triscuits."

"Oh, right," I said.

"I like your hair. I think it's great the way it is." Faith's back was still turned to me as she struck a match and set the yellowed newspaper ablaze in three places, blowing to feed the flames. "I wouldn't change a thing about it."

"You don't think it's too long on top?"

"Not at all." She looked over her shoulder at me and grinned. "Actually, the way you have it right now, with your eyes, mouth...your whole face, I guess. And your height. You look a lot like that woman in *Copycat*."

"Sigourney Weaver."

"Yes." She cocked her head. "But I'm sure you've heard that before."

Had I ever.

The staple of my travel agency was my particular talent for arranging gay and lesbian pleasure cruises. Six days at sea, one long party. Bands, comedians, attractive individuals of every sexual orientation imaginable. And I was their ringleader. The queen of queens, so to speak. Well-dressed and well-coiffed. Up all night and loving it. Champagne and rented jewelry. And all the girls girls girls telling me how glamorous I was, how I looked just like Sigourney at the Oscars, and how would I like to join them for a drink back in their rooms? Cha-cha-cha.

Faith finished building the fire, and it changed everything about the house. No longer frigid, isolated, dreary, asylum-like. It was cozy now. Peaceful. Home.

But just as I was about to drift off, my blanket sparked into a sudden spasm of competency. Not wanting to sizzle like the better half of a BLT, I pushed it down to cover only my legs. "So you've got a thing for Sigourney Weaver?" I asked as the blanket's heat built to the point of nearly singing my day's growth of leg hair. I tossed the blanket far off to one side on the sofa, shrinking away from its white-hot heat. "Got a few posters of Lieutenant Ripley on your bedroom wall, eh? Maybe that's what makes me attractive to you, my vague resemblance to…"

"It's not a vague resemblance, it's quite strong." She crouched beside the sofa. "But it's not her I have a thing for, Macy." She pulled my hand to her lips and kissed it. "It's you."

I couldn't help but blush—yes, blush—at how corny and sweet and delightful the moment was.

Chapter 5

Suddenly I felt angry with myself for not chasing down—or for not being able to chase down—the dirty little prick who'd mugged her in the rain. I could just see myself, just *see* myself: five years younger, black mascara and red lipstick, the tails of my black leather trench coat flying as I hauled ass in the 60-yard dash down Columbus. Right behind the dirty little prick, right on his heels.

But this cinematic vision had not been possible. Even without das boot, I still would've run out of steam after a few hundred inches—well, maybe centimeters—at best. As it was, my damsel in distress had remained in distress, with me hovering over her. Yes, I had just merely stood there, weak and horny and afraid of being sued because she'd been injured on *my* property. Useless.

"What's wrong?" Faith playfully traced my lips with the tip of her index finger.

I said nothing, only shook my head, as I didn't want to cry and feel even more like a sniveling wuss than I already was.

"I'm going to the store." She bent over and kissed me

on the cheek. "Just down the road. Are you hungry for anything in particular?"

Here was my chance to do the standard innuendo response, to wink and say something cheesy like "Just you, my little tenderloin." And with anyone else, I would've cut loose with such a comment, however disgusting it may have seemed. But no, not this time. This was Faith, who had cradled my flu-withered frame to hers without any empty promises.

I gave her a meek little smile. "Not really."

"Still not feeling very well, are you?" She touched my face and sighed as she zipped her coat. "I'll be right back, OK? Just make yourself at home."

And with the roar of a rented Jeep Cherokee, Faith left.

Alone with myself, I poked at the fuzzy folds of the demon electric blanket. It was cooler now, thank God, at least a touchable temperature, at least somewhat less threatening, but I kept my eyes on it as I stood from the sofa and backed away, step by awkward step. The room had warmed enough to warrant an exploration of this sprawling barge of a house. No sense in being shy about it. Nothing wrong with looking around, getting acquainted with the layout of things. Not like I would snoop around in her stuff or anything—no, no—just, you know, get a feel for the place.

I opened the first door I came to and found—tah-dah!—a closet. It was bare, except for some wire hangers and a full-length mirror on the back of the door. I checked my reflection. Yikes. In six months of letting myself go, I had become some kind of Nancy Reagan freak of a woman, with my big fucking head teetering upon my long, scrawny bod like a bobbly-headed carnival doll. Gaunt. Dark circles.

Heroin chic. Keith Richards in drag. I had to do something quick. I looked hard into the mirror. My tits. That was it. My tits looked pretty good. The weight loss hadn't affected them; in fact, they appeared larger now. And they hadn't sagged to my waist. Still hanging high and dry, from the look of things. Still relatively nice, bouncy-looking tits. I unbuttoned my blouse one more button. Yeah. Not bad. I sucked in my breath and stuck out my chest, examining my profile. Not bad at all.

I was still posing, coughing that loud, lingering cough, when I heard a door creak open in another part of the house.

"Faith?" It was a man's voice. "Is that you croupin' around in there?"

Heavy-heeled boots pounded through the house, and before I knew it the Marlboro man was standing before me. Carhart coat. Cowboy hat. A deeply lined face, a stiff blond mustache, and ridiculously blue eyes that—dare I say it?—twinkled. Twinkled! He stepped closer.

"My God." He removed his hat to expose wavy, reddish-blond hair. "I am so sorry, ma'am."

"Oh, no. That's quite all right," I said. "You just startled me." Though I'm not sure "startled" is the proper word for what he had done to me just then.

"I'm truly sorry. I had no right to just barge in like that."

He extended his hand and I took it. Hell, you *bet* I took it—shocked at how warm and rough and just plain big it was. He smelled of Aqua Velva.

"Hey, no problemo," I gushed.

My God. Was I flirting? It sure felt like it. Shit. Since my years in the Village, I'd all but forgotten about the whole rugged thing.

"I'm Marcus." Marcus smiled a smile that cut right through that thick mustache.

"Macy." I nodded, then smiled right back at him, showing all the teeth I could possibly show, praying there was nothing stuck between them.

Marcus's pheromones were like chemical warfare. "Like I said, I really am sorry. I heard someone coughing up a storm..."

I patted my chest. "Well, that was just poor old sickly me. I'm, uh, just trying to shake this flu." How strong he probably was, like a little bull. Short and square. In his 40s, maybe, but still a very nice build, and if I had ever been inclined to be with a man, Marcus would've been my type. Yes, yes. Marcus would probably fuck you blind, go bust his ass on the tractor all day, then come on in and fuck you some more. Ya-hoo. Ride 'em, cowboy.

"Sounds like a pretty bad bug," he said, and I involuntarily giggled. *Christ, get a grip on yourself, Gidget.*

"Well, you know how it is. You get old, it's tough to shake these things." Oh, God. There it was. My signal for him to compliment me, to tell me how I didn't look so old, blah, blah, blah. Holy shit, I was baiting him. Flirting. WITH A GUY.

"You better not say that." He cocked his head. "You don't look like you're even close to being as old as me."

Ah, yes. And the dance had begun. I had fished for a compliment. He was fishing for information about my age.

"40." I said, playing along. Miss Nonchalant.

"42," he said. "I guess we're not that far apart, are we?"

"Nope."

We both laughed. The nervousness between us was escalating. And I stood and stared at him and puzzled to myself: *What would a real penis feel like?* I'd never felt a cock inside me that didn't come with a warranty. Why bother? But I was in the minority. Maybe I was missing out. Nine out of ten women couldn't be wrong, could they?

"What happened to your foot there?" He pointed to das boot. "What'd you do, kick your husband too hard?"

"I'm not married."

"Oh."

Silence. A pause, then...

"You?"

"No." He lowered his gaze for a moment, perhaps recounting some hideously failed relationship, then looked up at me again. "So, you're a friend of Faith's?"

Faith. That's right. I *was* here with Faith. Faith. My beautiful young lover—badly dressed as she was. So who was this man anyway, this Marcus character? A relative? A friend? And why the hell did he have a key to her house?"

"Yes, I am." I folded my arms. "And you?"

"Just a friend of the family," he said. "I check on the place when she's gone."

A door creaked open and slammed shut.

"Hey, Marcus." Faith entered, carrying two bags of groceries. "I see you two have met."

"Yeah, I...uh..." Now it was his turn to blush. "I thought I saw a car here earlier, so I stopped by to let you know I fixed that pipe under the sink." He looked back at me. "Guess I'll be going now. You girls call me if you need anything."

"It was a pleasure meeting you," I said.

"You take care now." Marcus winked, tipped his hat, and left.

"Thanks, Marcus," Faith called after him, setting the grocery bags down on the table.

"Nice fellow," I said all cool-like, returning to the sofa, covering up with the blue electric blanket (now set on "low," it produced just a docile whisper of warmth) and praying to God she wouldn't make eye contact—not until the whole Marcus thing was out of my head. I was not so lucky.

"You liked him!" Faith stepped in front of me, grinning, hands on hips.

"Yeah," I said. "He seemed like a nice enough guy."

"Nice enough to unbutton your blouse to your navel, I see."

"It's not unbuttoned to my navel, my little exaggerator." I buttoned my blouse back up completely. "I was just, you know, letting the girls get some air. You gave them quite a workout last night. They're not used to such abuse."

"You're going to sit there and tell me that when I walked in here, you guys weren't checking each other out?"

"Sexually?"

"Yeah, sexually."

"That's absurd." I closed my eyes, hoping to disappear into the lukewarm folds of the blanket. Not possible.

"So you didn't find him attractive at all?"

"OK, so he was handsome," I admitted, raising my hands in surrender. "Just trying to get in touch with my straight side."

"Very funny." She crawled onto the sofa, lying on top of me. "Just don't get any big ideas, Miss 'Bisexuality is like saying you're a vegetarian, then sneaking off to Burger King.'"

I hugged her tightly. "Faith, I promise you, I will never *ever* sneak off to Burger King."

And I kissed her, partly to make a point, partly because

I just felt like it. Kissing Faith was easy. There was nothing awkward or rebellious about it, no sensation of "proving myself as a lesbian" or any crap like that. It was sweet and simple and unrehearsed.

"Here, don't lie flat on your back." She slid over and sat on the edge of the sofa next to me, pushing a pillow under my shoulder blades.

"What? Why?"

"If you elevate your shoulders, it's easier for you to breathe."

"Like the old woman in the Craftmatic Adjustable Bed commercials."

"Pretty much, wheezer."

"Oh, you're so funny. Ha ha. Just make fun of the poor, decrepit asthmatic woman who waited with your sorry ass out in the rain"—Faith slid her hands up and began to slowly unbutton my blouse—"sacrificing her health for an ungrateful brat like you."

"Now if I'm so ungrateful, why would I bring you here to take care of you?" She started at my neck and began kissing her way down, carefully reaching my breasts. "What, no bra today?"

"Didn't you know? Today is International Bra-less Day," I said. "It's on the calendar. Hallmark even has cards."

"It is a day to rejoice," she said. Then she took my left nipple into her mouth.

I let out one of those uncontrollable sex noises, something like a whimper. She stopped.

"Too hard?"

"No, but I think I'm lactating."

She laughed. I coughed. Faith stood and walked to the

kitchen, returning with a red bottle and a spoon. She climbed up to straddle me on the sofa.

"That reminds me," she said. "Open up."

"A present? For me? How sweet. You shouldn't have."

"Hey, remember." She poured a spoonful. "You wouldn't be walking around barking like a trained seal if you hadn't helped me that fateful day."

"And I also wouldn't have my nipples so erect I could cut diamonds with them if it wasn't for that fateful day."

"Shut up and swallow this."

"Gee, I guess we know who's the 'man' in this relationship, now don't we?"

"Now, just a minute..."

"You're the one who's going around telling me to shut up and swallow."

"Well, you're the tall one..."

"So? Look who's on top!"

"So?"

"So...that *is* the traditional sexual position for the male of the species."

"So I'm nontraditional," she said. "You swear like a man."

"You sweat like a man."

"You drink like a man."

You dress like an indigent drifter, I wanted to say, but instead I said, "You fart like a man."

She gasped. "I do NOT!"

"Do too," I said. "Like a big chili-eatin' trucker man, my sweet."

"Well, then, my sweet—just what do you call *that*?" Faith pointed to my cane, which was leaning in a corner under the hat rack, just next to an umbrella. "You're the one with the penis!"

At this point I realized how ridiculous it was to have assumed Faith was a poor conversationalist.

"And you're older," she added smugly.

"That I am." She had me there. "How old are you, anyway? 13?"

"24."

"Well." I slapped her thigh. "Nice to know I won't be going to jail for this little adventure."

"OK, open up before I spill this crap all over you."

"Yes, sir." I saluted. It was cherry cough syrup, strong and disgusting, but I swallowed it anyway. "Thanks so much."

"Sorry." She put the bottle and spoon down onto the floor. "I know it's gross, but it should help."

Once again she began to nuzzle my breasts, gracing them with a flurry of soft, warm kisses, and it all felt so good, so right, so natural. God himself could have told me it was wrong, and I wouldn't have believed him. This was the most moral, correct, decent thing I had ever done.

Our lovemaking was long and leisurely, and once we'd finished, I felt warm and complete. I wanted to tell the world about it, or at least tell Trish, but I couldn't. I had finally entered into something that Trish could not be a part of. I had—drum roll, please—a relationship. The real thing, built on something other than cruise ships or booze or boredom or all of the above. But Trish would not appreciate or understand this. She couldn't. She had found Hal and lived happily ever after. How could she know what it was like to live off microwave entrees and schedule your nightlife around *Melrose Place*? How could she know what it was like to be alone? Not to mention that she seemed to hate Faith for no apparent reason, which should have created a major problem for me but somehow did not. As a matter of fact, I kind of liked it, which is pretty sick, sure, but I can't lie about it. Everybody has feelings they're not particularly proud of, right?

Chapter 6

I was damn proud of myself for making dinner that night. I hadn't actually prepared a meal in months, so it was fun—you know, an event. I'd brought two bottles of serious French Merlot along with me, and I proceeded to pour myself a glass, sipping it as I cooked shredded cabbage and kielbasa. I clicked on the crappy little AM radio next to the toaster and sang along to "Hotel California," swaying and stirring and buzzed just enough to not give a shit whether I was in tune.

At one playful moment, Faith embraced me from behind, peering over my left shoulder. "You're using apple in the sauerkraut?"

"Well, of course." I kept dicing. "The trick to making orgasmic sauerkraut versus mediocre sauerkraut is in the little extras, *ma cherie*. A few rings of hot pepper, mushrooms, and—most importantly—diced apple. Takes away the bitterness without making it sweet." I lifted the lid from the stainless steel cooker. "See? See that? It's perfect. Almost too perfect. Should be in a museum. I look at this and you know what I see?"

Faith rolled her eyes. "I'm afraid to ask."

"I see a well-mixed tequila sunrise, little beads of moisture glistening and rolling down the sides of a tall glass." I pulled the spoon from the pot and held it like a microphone. "I see a red rose in the stage just before it blooms. I see Elizabeth Taylor in that white slip she wore in *Butterfield 8*..."

"I hope this is the wine talking."

"Oh, no, this is the Zen of cooking talking, my friend. This is art. This is about becoming one with the kielbasa."

"Sounds painful," said Faith. "Oh, look, I forgot to unpack a bag of groceries." Sipping my wine, I watched her pull out a package of bacon, some eggs, olive bread, pasta shells, Celestial Seasonings red zinger tea, and...a tiny, white box. Lozenges. Luden's. Wild cherry flavored. And the sight of them broke my heart all over again.

Vi.

Vi always had a box of Luden's wild cherry throat drops in her purse, Vi being my father's second wife and my stepmother. I know this because she spoiled the living shit out of me and let me do pretty much as I pleased, which included plundering her purse to try out various lipsticks. It was 1965 when they married, a whirlwind courtship after meeting at an appliance convention in Las Vegas, and I'll never forget seeing her step off the train with my father that gusty October Saturday afternoon.

Slow motion. Sloowwwww motion, here...

From a monotonous sea of navy, beige, brown, and gray clothing emerged a shiny red dress made of Tokyo silk. When Vi Rogers stepped down off that train, everyone—men, women, children, small dogs, *everyone*—turned to see who it was. Funny, I was only 5, but I remember the details clearly. That red, shimmering silk dress, cloaked in part by her long, black, leopard-trimmed coat. (A "swing coat," I think they called it.) Black leather gauntlet gloves. She paused on the platform to pull a Lucky from its gold case and lit it, herself, with a matching gold lighter, surveying the crowd over the rims of her black sunglasses. She walked with the strong, straight posture of a woman unstooped and unstopped by life, and she was the only one in the whole train station, the whole state of Ohio, with a tan.

Outgoing but not obnoxious, Vi easily became the top salesperson at my father's appliance store, the first to have the sense and ambition to seek out large contracts with apartment complexes and institutions in the tri-county area. Confined to a TB sanitarium as a child, she said winter "wore her down," so when the entire town attended football games or went skating or caroling, Vi stayed home. Being the puny asthmatic kid I was, I generally stayed with her and soon came to look forward to our time alone. She had grand stories of New York and L.A., of her three marriages, of her daughter who had drowned when she was only 5, and I quickly learned that the longer she sipped her Southern Comfort in front of the fireplace, the more revealing and tumultuous her stories became. One evening, after letting me drive her Cadillac down one of Piqua's dirt roads (I was 10—told you she let me do anything), she shared something with me that she said she had never shared with anyone else.

Following the death of her only child in 1954, Vi announced to her first husband that she wanted a divorce. Figuring that such a request was the result of a nervous episode, Vi's husband conferred with her mother and had her committed. Two weeks into her stay at the hospital, she tired of pissing her pants during "experimental shock therapy" and of fighting off the guards after lights out, so she escaped. Running the train tracks for miles, penniless and shoeless, at last she found and secretly boarded a slow moving train and rode for hours. Treated to a view of what she called "America's backside," the cluttered backyards and chicken coops scattering the countryside, Vi indulged in her first real sleep in months.

According to her account, everything was pretty peaceful until the train stopped midway to Chicago. It was then that a bum joined her in the boxcar. Ed was his name, he told her, and he seemed harmless enough, sleeping off a drunk at the other end of the car. Some time in the night, however, Ed got some ideas. She awoke to find him on top of her, her mouth covered by a filthy hand as she attempted to scream, his foul breath turning her stomach.

Vi was not a large woman. 5-foot-2, maybe 110 pounds at the most. But she managed to wrestle free from the vomit-stinking old bastard and scramble for a weapon, anything that could be used to battle for her dignity in the boxcar that night. What she found was a piece of a 2-by-4, and as Ed the bum lurched toward her, she swung it like a baseball bat. The sound was hollow, she said, like a coconut, as the board connected with his skull. Ed crumpled to the floor, and it was then, watching the blood seep out of his wound and staring into his blank pupils, that Vi knew she had killed him. Of course, she'd done it without really meaning to—albeit without much remorse. His death produced no great loss to society, no vacancy in anyone's life. She knew that. And it *had* been self-defense. But it was 1954. As a woman who had escaped from an asylum, what rights did she have?

Vi pulled a wallet from his back pocket. It contained,

surprisingly enough, $26. The enclosed ID belonged to another man, a victim of Ed's light fingers, no doubt. And while crossing a swamp somewhere near Gary, Indiana, she rolled his body out of the boxcar and into the night, saying a prayer under her breath that was more for her own soul than for his.

Such a tale might have frightened some kids my age, but not me.

Vi taught me how to enjoy becoming a woman without losing myself. A real woman, she explained, knew how to bake a chocolate cake without having it come out lopsided. True. But a real woman also knew how to, say, throw a football and fire a rifle. Vi taught me to buy small bottles of expensive perfume rather than big bottles of the cheap stuff, as well as how to change the oil in a car. Vi Rogers had been the first person to show me that being female was not always a liability, so why should I care if she killed some bum who was trying to rape her 15 years ago? She made me feel good about myself, and you know, I think she would have been extremely cool about my homosexuality, but I never got the chance to spill my guts to her. By the time I realized that I was what I was, Vi had died of a heart attack at an office Christmas party. I was 18, and manning the spiked punch bowl, when I watched her sink to the floor after doing the Locomotion with half the sales staff. She was only 49.

"Hey, you." Faith touched my arm and I flinched. "You're crying."

Jesus. So I was. Nice. One minute, I was happily quipping the light fantastic over a pot of fabulous sauerkraut. The next, I was in the middle of a teary-eyed flashback. Way to go, Sybil.

"Nothing moves me to tears like Polish sausage," I said. "So tell me. How'd you score such a righteous pad?"

"I did it the old-fashioned way."

"Prostitution?"

"No." She laughed. "I inherited it."

That made sense, but I was still curious. And besides, the more she shared, the less I would have to.

"Inherited it from who?"

"My grandmother. She knew I'd never have a husband to support me, so..."

"You told her?"

"I didn't have to." Faith pulled some plates from the cupboard and began to rinse off the dust. "She was smart about things like that."

"Intuition?"

"You could call it that. She was Native American."

"Native American?"

"Right." She giggled. "By the way, are you Polish?"

"What?"

"Well, with such a strong appreciation for kielbasa, I just thought..."

"No." I tasted the cabbage. It wasn't quite ready. "I'm actually part French—on my father's side."

"Really?" she said.

And so continued our lovely drone of small talk. We spoke of prom dates and favorite paintings, of ex-lovers, and first pets, and all those other things new lovers speak of.

The one thing I loved about Faith's kitchen was the dining table: Sturdy planks brush-painted blue. There we sat, feeding sloppy spoonfuls to each other, giggling and licking each other's fingers. It was one of those moments

I'd always heard of and thought were ridiculous.

Cooking had tired me, and after phoning in to check up on the office, I relaxed on the Naugahyde sofa, reading *Valley of the Dolls* and dozing off and on. Faith sat at the other end of the sofa, reading a magazine with my feet in her lap. The crappy little AM radio still played in the kitchen. For nearly an hour, I rested better than I had in months, full of kielbasa and wine and a whole variety of pleasantries I wasn't accustomed to. Peaceful visions replaced my usual nightmares. How wonderful wearing your favorite pair of socks is when your feet are in the right lap.

I had stirred momentarily and had been headed shamelessly back into doze mode when she looked up from her copy of *Rolling Stone.*

"I don't have any family," she said.

I opened my eyes. How strange that she would say such a stark little statement just out of the blue like that.

"No?"

"No." She shook her head. "My grandmother died. I told you about that. And my parents..." She had tears in her eyes, but was holding them back, something she was obviously accustomed to doing, something I had never been very good at. "They're like, these...migrating grifters. I don't even know where they are."

"You don't have any idea?"

"No." The tears receded some. "What about you?"

I snorted. "We don't keep in touch."

"So you're the black sheep, huh?" She smiled and began rubbing my foot.

"Black sheep, they could handle. Gay sheep, they could not." I patted my cleavage. "Sweetheart, have you seen my glasses?"

"They're on the floor with your book. I took them off while you were sleeping." She lifted my foot, inspecting. "Nice socks." She grinned. "I mean...sock."

"Wool and cashmere blend," I said. "Great for keeping dry and cozy." I frowned at my cast. "I can't wait to get that damn thing off. It itches like crazy."

"I'll bet it does. So anyway, where do you go for the holidays?"

"Hmm?"

"You're not in contact with your family, so...?"

"A friend's house. Trish. I think you spoke with her on the phone."

"Yeah, I remember Trish. She sounded very..." Faith raised her eyebrows. "...territorial."

"Maybe a little." I laughed. "She and I have been friends since, basically, birth. She's just looking out for me. It's sort of a big sister thing."

"Are you sure that's all?"

The insinuation pissed me off a tad. Trish was an attractive, funny woman whom I adored, respected, loved. But I had never, *would never* think of her in that way. How could this even cross her mind?

"Just what are you trying to say, Faith? You don't even know her. We grew up together, OK? She's married and..."

"Macy, I'm sorry. I..."

"...she's dying." And it occurred to me, just then, that for a few hours I had let myself forget. How could I? I began to cry—a real cry, you know, the whole cathartic package, complete with heaving sobs and wailing and snot pouring and hands yanking at my hair. I cried so goddamn hard I thought I was going to hyperventilate and throw up. Faith clutched me to her chest and rocked me, pleading with me to stop, telling me over and over that she was sorry. Pretty soon, she was screaming her apology, whether from confusion, frustration, or just trying to be heard over the din. But tears, like everything else, eventually run out, thank God, and as our emotions slowly wound down we were left holding each other in silence. When I caught my breath at last, I bowed my head.

"She...um..." My voice was shaking, my hands were shaking, but it was time to talk about it. I had already gone this far, already exploded with no warning. "She has cancer." And as I said the "c" word, I felt that awful, gnawing feeling in my stomach, like the cancer was eating away at me too.

Faith looked at me with her big, beautiful eyes. They were brown, like mine, but not like mine at all. I looked back down at my hands, afraid that she would see the emptiness, the regret. She deserved someone better, someone stronger, someone fun and young and unselfish. Someone more like her.

"Macy." Faith placed her right hand directly over my heart. I felt it beat against her palm. I said nothing, as there was nothing to say. She couldn't begin to understand.

I continued to stare down at my hands. Old hands, long fingers. And here it came. The waves hit me with an unwelcome familiarity. I was the bad one. I was the promiscuous one. I was the one with no family, no purpose. Why hadn't I been the one to get cancer? I'd asked myself that question repeatedly for months, but it was never any easier to face. It never went away, really.

"Macy."

My heart pounded against her palm. An angry heart. I looked at her, expecting a smile of pity or embarrassment. Instead, I found something else.

"Macy." She looked into my eyes with an almost stern concentration. "It's not your fault."

Not to get religious or gushy, but there are times when we crave certain words. Sometimes those words are "I love you" or "I'm proud of you" or, well, "Nice ass." The point is, we seldom ever hear those words from the ones we want to hear them from—or from anyone, for that matter. And no matter how many times you might say them to yourself, there is still that need, waiting to be recognized. The last time anyone told me what I wanted—or rather, needed—to hear, was back in Piqua, in my high school's rest room, when Trish told a stoned 18-year-old me that it was OK with her if I was gay.

"Macy?"

Now I really wanted to hear Faith say it again, to hear it come from someone who wasn't paid to say it, who wasn't some fucking shrink on the East Side.

"Macy, it's not your fault she has cancer."

The lump in my throat vanished, and I smiled at the sensation of her hand on my heart. She wore Lucky Brand jeans, which I duly noted upon spying the little LUCKY YOU shamrocks inside her fly, and I shucked those jeans off her with a speed and agility that surprised even me. Not bad for a beginner. See, I had always thought it better, more—I don't know—more ladylike, to receive than to give. I'd never had the urge, never felt compelled to—how shall I say it?—return the oral advances of a partner. Call me a selfish bitch. Call me Ishmael. No one had ever seemed to mind much. But for some reason, Faith's essence didn't drive me away. No, no, it pulled me in. And in I went with a vengeance, searching like I'd lost my keys in there or something. Firm, golden thighs pressed against my ears till the only sound I could hear was the thunder of my own breathing and my own heart pounding faster, faster. I slid my hands down the small of her back and down around the cheeks of her firm, perfect ass. Her body hitched as I pulled at her. I felt her hands slide into my hair. She guided me up a bit. I obliged. And in the warm, muffled darkness, I felt like a star suspended in the night sky. Orion, the hunter. Macy, the lover. And the joy, the power of pleasing Faith, was overwhelming.

Chapter 7

"Have you ever been with a man before?"

"Huh?"

It had startled me since, quite honestly, I hadn't really been paying much attention, having succumbed to the temptation of taking a long soak in the claw-foot tub upstairs. With das boot propped on the tub's edge at one end and my head hanging back at the other, it must have looked like an awkward, uncomfortable pose. *Au contraire.* A glass half-full of that exquisite French Merlot remained in my hand as my arm dangled over the side. Relaxed and content, I'd caught myself snoring several times.

"I said..." Faith stood in the doorway, only mildly perturbed at having to repeat herself. "Have you ever been with a man before?"

"In bed?"

"No, to Disneyland. Yes, in bed, silly."

"Nope," I said it cheerfully, a bit drunk, draping a warm, wet cotton cloth across my eyes. I said it like I was proud of it or something, and I guess I was.

Though the desire to change my sexuality had plagued me at certain times throughout my life, I had never had any doubts. While cleaning our garage at only 10 years of age, I'd stumbled over a few *Playboy* back issues and had secretly coveted the nude photos of Marilyn Monroe. Treasure! My tiny hands deftly stashed the naked goddess behind an old road sign my brother had stolen. Henceforth, all confusion and prepubescent sexual anxiety could be instantly eradicated by sneaking a peek at Norma Jean's plushy posterior behind that sign in our garage.

"Never? Really?"

"Really."

"Haven't you ever wondered what it was like?"

"Yeah, maybe," I said. "But I've also wondered what it would be like to have my tongue pierced. Doesn't mean I'm going to rush right out and do it though."

"Oh, I can just picture that. Miss Conservative with a stud in her tongue." She laughed. "Well? Aren't you going to ask me?"

"What? If you've got a stud in your tongue?"

"Very funny."

"OK. Fine. I'll bite. Tell me, Faith, have you ever been with a man?"

"Why do you say it like that?"

I lifted the washcloth from my eyes.

"Like what?"

"Like in that smart-ass way of yours. Like it's a joke."

"Come on," I said. "Looking like you do? Why, I'll bet half the football team whacked off to your yearbook photo."

"Even if they did, that doesn't mean I slept with them." She frowned. "I don't make assumptions with you, Macy. You shouldn't with me."

"Geez. OK. All right. Goddamn." I rested the base of my wine glass on the tile floor. "I'm sorry, OK? Shit. You don't have to give me that look."

"What look?"

"That look that says, 'Macy, you're a jerk.'"

"Jerk?" She cracked a smile. "*Jerk* was not what I was thinking."

"Inconsiderate boor, whatever," I said. "I'm sorry, OK? So, come on, out with it. Have you or haven't you?"

"What?"

"Oh, for Chrissakes...*slept with a man!*"

"Yes."

Yes? I hadn't been prepared for her to say yes. It shocked me, just a touch, just enough to shut me up for a minute. But everyone wasn't like me, didn't have to be like me. You know, gay from day one, untouched by man, all that. Besides, it was probably a long time ago, but just in case...

"How old were you?"

Oh, God. Please don't let her say it was last week.

"Sixteen," she said.

Sixteen. I thought of the scenario with the guy of guys alive in his 501s and ready with a rubber in his wallet: He pushes himself on top of her. The scent of MD 20/20 and Clearasil hangs heavily in the air of his Chevy truck interior. Bob Seger wafts out of the tape deck. Or Journey. Oh, my baby, my darling Faith, deflowered unceremoniously—wedged between Bubba Somebody and an unknown piece of hunting equipment. Disgusting.

"Sixteen." I said it this time. "So?"

"So I worked for the Naselrods..."

"The Naselrods?"

Yikes. What sounded like a probing instrument at an ear,

nose, and throat specialist's examination room was obviously someone's name. This was bound to be interesting.

"Yes, their name was Naselrod. Jo Naselrod and her husband, Steve. She called herself Jo, Jr., after her dad." Faith squished up her brow, remembering. "You know, I think her husband's last name was Bennett, but everyone called them 'the Naselrods' because that was the name of their business: Naselrod Jewelers. Her folks had owned it and wound up leaving it to her."

"Her, meaning Jo Naselrod, Jr.?"

"Right," Faith continued. "Anyway, I started going out with their son, Rex. Student council president, captain of the football team. You know..."

"Setting things up nicely," I said, as I too had selected the "perfect boyfriend" in high school. Mine was Andy Babcock. Track star. Great teeth. Everyone used to say he looked like Bruce Jenner. And eventually all the guys in school started calling him "Andy Sadcock" as tales of my frigidity began to spread. "Nice guy, affluent family..."

"Affluent for my little town."

"Right. So you were dating Rex..."

"We'd been seeing each other, for, oh, I don't know, what seems like a long time when you're a teenager?"

"Six months?"

"Not quite that long, but close." She shook her head. "And we decided it was time." Her voice dropped off. "So...we did it."

"Where? Sorry, but I'm intrigued."

"In his house, his parents' house." She looked down with shame. "In his bed," she said. "In his room."

"Oh." I hoped she'd leave it there. Leave it at that. But no.

"I knew it wasn't right." She still didn't look up. "Right then, I knew it wasn't, but I had to. I mean, what could I do?" Faith looked into my eyes. "What was I supposed to do?"

I could see, then, that she was reliving the whole mess. It was brewing in her eyes. Frustration, confusion, disbelief. All the crap, you know, all the shit that hits you when you finally realize there's nothing you can do to change.

"Sure," I said, wanting to touch her, but I was in the tub after all. I simply couldn't reach.

"He fell asleep, like, immediately." She laughed a little, relaxed a little. "So I went downstairs."

From the change in her tone, I could tell something good, something juicy was coming. I sat up a bit, leaned forward, antennae fully extended. "And?"

"They had these big, wing-back leather chairs in front of the fireplace..."

"Brick or stone?"

"What?"

"The fireplace. I'm sorry, but this is an important story and I'm just trying to get the whole picture."

"Brick."

Such details must have seemed inconsequential to her, but not to me.

"Anyway, I sat down and I was crying and I felt a hand on my shoulder. And it was Jo, Jr. His mother."

"And?"

"Well, it freaked me out, at first. I mean, she was supposed to be away for the weekend and there I was in my nightshirt, sitting in her living room. Busted."

"What did she look like?"

"She was probably 5-foot-6 or 7. An OK body, not fat or anything, but kind of weird."

"Sporty? Built rather boyish? Strong enough for a man but made for a woman."

"Yeah," she agreed. "She had a unique face. Blue eyes. Very cold, blue eyes. A nice mouth. It's hard to describe. I mean, she was really attractive..."

"More so than me?" God, it just slipped out.

"No!" She said it with such surprise that I believed her. "No, nothing like you." She perched on the edge of the bathtub. "Hmm, how can I define this? It's like you have movie-quality good looks. People look at you and say, 'Wow! Who is that?' Sophisticated. Classic. Breathtaking. Elegant. But Jo"—Faith shook her head—"Jo was attractive in more of a scary kind of way. Kind of striking, like— oh, what's her name? The one with the Eurythmics?"

"Annie Lennox?"

"Yes!" She snapped her fingers. "Kind of, um..."

"Androgynous?"

"Yes!" Faith pointed at me in acknowledgment. "Very animalistic looking."

"So, she put her hand on your shoulder, and..."

"And she sort of crouched down, got on her knees in front of me. She put her hands on my shoulders." Faith stood and bent to place her hands on my shoulders. "And I'm thinking, 'God, she knows. What if I lose my job at the jewelry store?'"

A pause. I clutched the smooth, rounded sides of the tub and looked at Faith. I knew what was coming, pretty much. I'd been around when it came to things like this. My expertise, however, made it no more comfortable to hear the facts unfold. She'd been 16 at the time of this little incident. Just a baby.

I cleared my throat. "What did she say?"

"She looked at me all funny, like she was really assessing me, like a snake. And she said, 'It's not so bad, sometimes, Faith. But it's not for everybody.'" Faith released my shoulders and eased back onto the edge of the tub. "I was hypnotized," she continued. "My entire body was hot...shaking. I'd never felt that way before." Faith's eyes closed and her nose crinkled with a secretive smile. "And then she went down on me. Right there in the chair, with her son—my boyfriend—upstairs asleep."

I slid my hand under the tub, behind one of the claw feet, and retrieved my cigarettes. No sense in hiding them—or anything else, for that matter—at this point. I fiddled with the pack and thought of sweet baby Rex, dick shriveled from sex, all snug in his twin bed under his flannel football logo sheets. Pennants from State decorating the walls. Souvenir sombrero from a family trip to Mexico hanging over the headboard. And mama downstairs giving all her best to his best girl.

Around 10 o'clock, we retired to bed like an old married couple. Faith slept beside me, her arm draped over my thighs as I sat working out a first draft of the next cruise itinerary on my laptop. The room was a touch on the drafty side, and Faith had insisted that I sleep in my sweats so I wouldn't be chilled after soaking in a hot bath for so long. Two days together and she was already bossing me around. How precious. I'd been typing and thumb-scrolling diligently for more than two hours when she flinched, realizing I was still awake, and groaned.

"Good night, Macy."

"Good night, John Boy."

I kept right on typing. I'd hire a new DJ this time, and

spice up the menus, maybe throw in a casino night with slot machines, yeah, and blackjack...

"Macy." She sounded bitchy.

"Yes, my little miracle that walks on earth? How may I serve thee?"

"Turn out the light and go to sleep."

"Oh, come on, Mom. It's not a school night."

"Macy..."

"Is the light bothering you?" I was trying not to lose my temper, here, or my train of thought—but you know how it is when you're right in the middle of something and someone commits *workus interruptus*. "Because I can turn the light off if it's keeping you up."

No response.

"Faith?"

Obviously, she'd drifted back to sleep. Good.

I picked up my cell phone to check my voice-mailbox. There were two messages. The first was Trish, wanting to know if Faith had killed me and sold all my useable organs to a Japanese underground transplant ring. Would I please call if I had a chance tomorrow morning? Check in. Spill the details. This was a relief. I hadn't been disowned. Message number two was from my advertising rep at the *Voice*, quoting me costs for the spring and asking me to call and reserve space for the first quarter as soon as possible, blah, blah, blah.

As the dullness of the real world crept in, I studied my sweetheart as she lay beside me: her long lashes, her button nose, her expression warm and forgiving—even in sleep. I closed my laptop and clicked off the light. Her upper arm poked out from under the covers. I kissed it.

"Good night, Snow White," I whispered.

Chapter 8

Two hours later I woke up with the cough from hell. With an extra blanket thrown over my shoulder and a pillow tucked under my arm, I headed dutifully downstairs to the sofa. There was no sense in both of us losing sleep. Embers from the fire still gave off a toasty glow, and I chucked another log into the fireplace to give it a boost. My glasses and book still lay on the floor, so I continued where I'd left off, not minding the solitude in the least. I thought of Faith, upstairs sleeping peacefully. And I thought I might like to make her eggs in the morning, after I got a little rest myself. Wind rattled the front door, and I sluggishly rose to secure the latch, stopped in my tracks by the moon, full and lavender and hanging over the lake. My eyes gravitated to the long dock that cut through what was left of the weeds still standing in the snow, and I was reminded of the summer I spent with Dad and Vi in a rented cottage when I was probably around 16. As with many cottages, there had been a lake, a private one, and next to our dock was a dilapidated shed listing precariously to the right. One morning while farting around and swimming with some kids from up the road, I conned one nimble boy into climbing atop the shed and tying a rope around one of the overhanging tree branches. What followed was a day of each of us yelling "Geronimo!" and swinging out from the roof of the shed to crash into the open water below. It wasn't that far up, maybe only 20 feet or so, but it seemed like forever before you hit the water. Sometimes after that, when I knew everyone was asleep, I would sneak out to the dock and slip out of my night-gown, scaling naked to the shed's roof and standing there in the moonlight. It was the point right after letting go of the rope that was the absolute best, when my body sailed through the air, young and newly curvaceous, eyes closed and back curved like a dancer in the Russian ballet, greeting the moon in a brief moment of flight before slicing into the cool, slow waves below. The intoxicating secrecy of my late-night excursions was lost, however, when Vi entered my bedroom one evening, flashlight in hand, grinning. "Hey, Moon Goddess," she whispered. "Next time you feel possessed to take one of your midnight dives, warn me first so I might keep your father from catching you. I don't think he'd approve."

"There you are."

I turned with a jerk. Faith stood before me, yawning.

"Hey!" I said, then I lowered my voice. "Hi there, little girl."

"I rolled over and you were gone." She leaned groggily against me and hugged me. "Couldn't sleep, huh?"

God, even her hair smelled nice. It was the middle of the night and she still smelled so fresh and so good. I couldn't help but bury my face in the sleepy sweetness of her neck and hair.

"No, I couldn't sleep," I murmured. "I'm sorry you woke up alone."

"Oh, I'm not alone." She slid her hand around and

gave the right cheek of my ass a healthy squeeze.

"Hey, hey..." I squirmed and jumped and let out a deep laugh that echoed through the house. Faith laughed with me and we made our way from the window over to the sofa and collapsed onto it, shifting around and pulling the blanket up until we were relatively comfortable.

"God, you've got your pillow and everything down here with you." She winked. "Planning to ditch me for the night, huh?"

"Not true," I said. "It was out of courtesy that I left."

"Courtesy?"

"I was a little on the restless side, that's all."

"That's all?"

Was she suspicious? Insecure? Just playing around? I wasn't quite sure. "No, actually, it was your body odor that drove me away. I think it's time we took one of those long walks on the beach and had a talk about things You know, underarm deodorant, feminine hygiene spray..."

"Thanks." She nodded wryly. "I'll get some tea and you can fill me in on the tampon thing too."

"I'll get it." I said it, but I didn't mean it. Sometimes we all just say things because we should, when in actuality we have no intention of getting up to do anything.

"Nope." She stretched and headed for the kitchen. "Stay put."

So I did, soothed by the sounds of her house slippers scuffling across the linoleum. She was humming too. "Norwegian Wood." "Mandarin orange OK?" she called out, filling the kettle with water from the tap. "It's the only one with no caffeine."

"Sure," I called back. "That song is about an affair he had with Marianne Faithful, you know."

"Huh?"

"The song you're humming," I said. "If I'm not mistaken, John Lennon wrote that about an affair he had with Marianne Faithful."

"Really? How cool!" The gas flame on the stove's burner came alive with a low thump. "Who's Marianne Faithful?"

I laughed. At least she hadn't asked, "Who's John Lennon?"

The tea was warming and pleasant, and combined with the lazy heat from the fire, I felt a bit heady. Not such a bad thing though—not with Faith nestled against me on the sofa. She adjusted herself and the blanket and shoved another pillow under my shoulders before taking her usual position: Head between my breasts, arms wrapped around me in an embrace that was not constricting but still firm enough to stay in place throughout the rest of the night. Faith's skin reminded me of a Dove soap commercial, the kind where the husband writes in to the company extolling the radiance of his wife's epidermis. *Dear Dove, My lesbian lover has the most incredible skin. She's used Dove for years, and...* I lay there for a long time, caressing her face and hair. Admiring her.

"Macy?"

Uh-oh. I was keeping her awake. She was, undoubtedly, pissed at my constantly playing with her hair and ear and...

"I love being with you," she said, tightening her embrace.

I wrapped my arms up around her shoulders, careful not to pull her hair. "I'm afraid I haven't been very entertaining lately."

"Macy, I don't want to be entertained," she sighed.

I stared up at the ivory ceiling, following a crack in the plaster from one edge to the other.

"This is the first time I ever wanted to wake up with someone," I said.

"Yeah." She raised her head and looked at me with a smile. "Me too."

"Even though I'm an asshole sometimes?"

"You're not an asshole, Macy."

"Even though I'm 400 years older than you are?"

"Even though you steal all the covers and your breathing is louder than the dishwasher in my apartment." She laughed.

"I see," I said, pretending to look hurt.

"So, what do you want for breakfast?"

"That's right. Go on," I said. "Say something cruel, then try to bribe me with promises of bacon and eggs."

"I was thinking more along the lines of blueberry pancakes."

"You've got to be kidding."

"Serious as a heart attack."

"Throw in a couple of sausage links and I'll forget all about what you said about me and the dishwasher."

"Done."

We shook hands and giggled and curled back into each other's arms.

"Macy?"

"Yes?" I was beginning to drift off.

"Let's not leave."

"Huh?" My eyes fluttered open.

"Each other." She yawned. "Let's not leave each other when we get back to New York."

"All right," I said, giving her shoulder a squeeze,

watching the crack in the ceiling fade as I fell sound asleep.

Old houses with all their creaks and whistles can launch one odd thought after another, or so I discovered that morning. As I lay with Faith, my eyes half open in that surreal state of just-interrupted sleep, odd thoughts piled up in my head. There were a lot of bad people out there in the world. A lot. And it absolutely disgusted me to think of Faith at the hands of another mugger or thief or...God...a rapist. The thought of some degenerate grabbing at her with his dirty hands made me ill. It also made me think of the gun I'd taken from my brother Elliott's bedroom when I left for New York. I still had it, the dreaded .38 Special that had inspired him to stand before his dressing mirror and do his best DeNiro "You talkin' to *me?*" spiel. I'd caught him doing that one morning as he stood bare-chested in his brown corduroys, aiming the shiny, nickel-plated pistol at his own reflection. Sworn to silence about the gun, I learned that he kept it in his sock drawer—way in the back.

Elliott was in prison when I moved to New York. I boarded the Greyhound with the Smith and Wesson tucked into my cosmetics case and said nothing about it to anyone. He owed it to me for being such a worthless dong over the years. Besides, better in my hands than his.

I still had it. Kept it hidden conveniently between my mattress and box spring, along with the small assortment of vibrators I'd collected over the years. Occasionally, when I fumbled around in the dark, desperate for one gadget or another with which to pleasure myself, my hand would touch its grooved, wooden grips and I would instantly pull away. Being reminded of its presence could blow my mood.

Sometimes it may have enhanced it. But the fact remained that I still had the gun. Not that I had ever been particularly afraid of intruders. No, I don't know why I'd hung on to it for so long. But now, now that I had someone to protect against New York's finest array of deviants, I was glad I'd kept it. If men had guns to demonstrate their power, then women had guns to blast their little marauding balls off.

I opened my eyes wider. Maybe I should get a better alarm system? Maybe a rottweiler? Take a class in martial arts? I stifled a laugh. Shit, what next? String barbed wire around my apartment and lock Faith in some giant pink case like she was my own little life-size Barbie? The laugh turned into a cough. And as I sat up a bit, Faith raised her head and pointed her finger as menacingly as someone as sweet as she was could point.

"You," she said, her eyes unopened, "are going to the doctor first thing when we get home."

It was after 8 when I awoke, and Faith was already in the kitchen. I gimped upstairs to the bedroom, found my phone, and dialed. "Hello, little friend," I said, my voice husky and deep.

"Who's this?" Trish asked. "Is this my long-lost friend who was last seen with her underage lover in the heart of the Michigan woods?"

"Baby," I whispered. "Don't you know who this is? It's me, Joey Heatherton."

"Well, well, well." She snickered. "Just how are you and Lolita faring way out there in *Deliverance* country?"

"Good. Great." I missed her. "It's beautiful here. You'd love it. Biggest birds I've ever seen. Cold though."

"So, how's tricks?"

"Tricks are pretty damned good, considering," I said.

"Considering what?" asked Trish.

"Considering she's fine. Terrific." I was beaming. "Unbelievable."

Silence. Then... "Well, good...I *guess*."

"You know, just be happy for me. Just once."

"I am happy for you."

"I mean, Jesus, Trish, just give her a chance. You're gonna like this one, I swear. She's in there making me blueberry pancakes as we speak."

"Macy, I'm happy for you, but..."

"For crying out loud, do you know when was the last time I had real blueberry pancakes?"

"Hey, that's great, Macy. But tell me, how long have you belonged to the Pussy of the Month Club? Hmm? Tell me."

"Jesus Christ!" I yanked at my hair with my free hand and sat down on the bed. "Come on! That's just...just vulgar. That is not fair at all."

"I'm serious. At least once a month you're telling me..."

"It's not once a month. OK? Blatant exaggeration, here. Blatant exaggeration."

"Once a month *at least* you're telling me, 'Oh, I met the most wonderful woman! Oh, we met on the cruise or on the plane or wherever and just hit it off.'" Her voice became flat. "The next thing I know, Little Miss Wonderful is hitting you up for cash or has a giant cop for a husband or deals drugs or..."

"Trish!" She was right. She was always right. And I got so angry, so frustrated, so fast that...fuck! I started to cry.

"Macy." Her voice had softened.

"Why do you always have to make me cry and feel like

an idiot? Why do you always have to piss all over my parade?"

"Macy?"

"This is different." I kept my sobs as quiet and controlled as possible. I didn't want Faith to hear this. I didn't want her to hear me pleading our case for courtship. A bigger person would've told Trish to back off. And with anyone else, I would've. But, shit, what can you do? Shut up, I guess. Shut up and buckle like a belt.

"How is this one different?"

"She's just..." I couldn't think of any poetic way to say it. "Nice."

"Nice, huh?"

"Yeah. N-n-nice," I always shook when I cried, and sometimes—obviously—I stuttered. Not like Mel Tillis or anything, but enough. Crying always makes me feel like such a pitiful weakling. But the whole shaky, stuttering mental patient thing is just the pits. I was a grown-up, a success, almost 6 feet tall, but I felt like a reluctant third grader forced to stand up in class and recite answers to the homework I hadn't completed. God, what a mess.

I took a deep breath and blew it out noisily. The asthma was starting up. Peachy. I closed my eyes. *Think! Think of something! Serene cows in a pasture! Clouds! Anything! The new Versace spring collection...*

"Macy?"

"Just a minute, I'm..." Oh, God, the more I thought of that spring collection, the slower my pulse and breathing became. "I'm just..." I almost laughed, but instead concentrated on taking slow, deliberate breaths. *The spring collection...*

"Macy, relax."

"Oh, sure," I said. "How considerate of you to tell me

to relax when you're the one who got me all riled up to begin with. Well, I don't need you to tell me to relax, I can tell myself to relax."

"OK..."

"See? I'm fine now." And by then I was, and I was also rather proud of myself for escaping an asthma attack, as if I'd become a poster child for self-control or something. Ha.

"I didn't mean to upset you. I only..."

"I know." I nodded. "And you're right." A nervous laugh slipped out. "She'll probably fuck me over like everybody else, but what can I say? I'm a sucker for a pretty face."

It was true. Trish was right. Only a matter of time before the wheels came off the wagon. What was I thinking? What could she possibly want with me? Money, maybe. Or maybe some sick "Mommy" complex. No, it was probably money.

Money, I thought. *It always comes down to that.*

"You're never going to believe what my oldest child found in the dictionary." Trish had mounted a swift change of subject.

"What?"

"The term *going down*!"

"No! In the dictionary? At last, my lifestyle is being given the recognition it deserves."

"Yes!" said Trish. "I heard her blabbing on the phone to one of her little warped friends about it, so I checked it out and, sure enough, there it was."

"No, that's incredible. What did it say?"

"Something like, 'to perform oral sex on another.'"

"As opposed to on yourself?"

Trish broke into a laugh, and I followed. We needed to

laugh, even if it was over something weak. I pulled the phone away and coughed a big, weird, heavy cough even I didn't like the sound of.

"Yikes," I heard her saying as I lifted the phone back to my ear. "That's nasty."

"Same ugly cold I had the last time I saw you," I said. "Only uglier. But don't worry, I'm going to see Germaine when we get back to the city."

"Jermaine?" she asked. "Jermaine Jackson?"

Smart-ass. I guess Germaine was a funny name, but I never liked calling her "doctor," so one day I just started calling her by her first name: Germaine.

"Yeah, Jermaine Jackson," I responded. "We're pretty close. He promised to show me a few new dance moves."

"Super." She sounded tired. "Macy?"

"Yes?"

"Go enjoy your pancakes."

"OK."

I pressed the "end" button and put the phone back in my bag.

Chapter 9

"What's this?"

It was my silver charm bracelet, and she was wearing it. Over the years I'd grown particularly fond of silver. It felt cool and clean against my skin, and I liked the way it looked on me when I had a good tan. Nothing against gold really, although it has a way of multiplying into gaudy, Liberace-esque messes around the necks of the middle-aged. With silver, however, you can never go wrong. In various fits of various emotions, I'd accumulated an enviable, if a bit plain, collection of silver jewelry from Tiffany's. There was the cruciform pendant, a simple bauble that resembled the symbol for the Red Cross, only it wasn't red. From their Atlas collection, I'd selected a silver ring with roman numerals encircling its wide band. Silver, bean-shaped earrings. And, of course, the charm bracelet. Delicate and simple in its design, the Tiffany's charm bracelet was so light you hardly felt it on your wrist. Only the soft jingling of its tiny totems served as a reminder of its presence. It was my favorite piece. And now, for some unknown reason, she was wearing it.

"Oh!"

I'd startled her as she stood working at the stove, the smell of sausage filling the room. "I found it on the floor this morning. It must've fallen off your wrist last night while you were sleeping. I put it on so I wouldn't forget to give it to you." She held up her hand, smiling at it in approval. "Cute."

"It's from Tiffany's, little girl." I sat down at the table and lit a cigarette. "So don't get too attached."

Ha. And I ain't just talking about the bracelet, sweetheart.

"Uh-oh." She set a cup of coffee before me and mussed my hair. "Looks like someone woke up on the wrong side of the couch, grouch." Faith removed the bracelet and dangled it in front of me. "Here you go, Jackie O."

"How clever. A poet." I snatched it from her hand. Faith bent down and kissed my forehead.

"Whoa," she said, pulling away. "Warm." She returned to the stove, forking a few sausage links out of a frying pan and onto a platter. "Your cough sounds a little better this morning, though."

"It should. I practiced all night."

"I know." She set the platter on the table. "I was there, remember?"

"Oh. Right," I said. "So sorry to have disturbed your sleep."

Faith placed her hands on her hips and stood before me. "Look, Macy. I don't know what the problem is."

"Oh, Christ." I took another sip of coffee, frowning. "Don't get your panties all in a wad."

Faith said nothing. No nasty retort. She just stood there. Tears came to her eyes but didn't fall, and oh, hell, my heart just sank right to my stomach. What a flaming bitch I was.

"God, Faith, I'm sorry." I stumbled to my feet and moved toward her.

Faith's voice quavered. "You know...it's OK if you're in a bad mood sometimes. Just fill me in. That's all I'm asking." She turned away and went back to the stove. "I'm not a friggin' mind reader."

"I know you're not." I slid my arms around her from behind, my head resting on her shoulder. "It's just that I don't feel well, and..."

"I know you don't feel well, baby." She turned around and held my face in her hands. "That's why we're going to the doctor as soon as we get home. So hang in there and have some breakfast, OK?" She pulled me close, kissing me on the neck and rubbing my back, whispering, "Poor baby, poor baby."

I did nothing to resist, as I rather liked being Faith's poor baby. I liked being coddled in the middle of the kitchen with a huge breakfast waiting on the table. I liked closing my eyes and running my hands over her. I even liked the crappy little AM radio playing Carole King on the counter. "Well, it's too late, baby, now, it's too late. Though we really did try to make it..."

Soon after breakfast, we packed our things and headed for the airport. Eating our weight in pancakes affected each of us with dramatic difference: Faith wandered around, droopy eyelids, mellow and content in her Mrs. Butterworth stupor. I, on the other end of the spectrum, had more spastic energy than a 4-year-old jiffing on a Twinkie buzz. Needless to say, I was dying to drive, and after going into a nonstop *Rainman* mantra regarding such—"I'm an excellent driver. Excellent driver. Definitely Kmart. Three minutes till Wapner. Excellent driver"—Faith screamed and threw me the keys. On the way we encountered a car that had struck a deer. The car itself had incurred minimal damage, but the deer—a doe—lay on her side in the center of the road, legs splayed, head raised up for her last look around. As our Cherokee crawled by, the fallen doe followed my gaze until we had passed. Imagine that. Me, Marcella Antoinette Delongchamp. The last living creature she might make eye contact with. Ever. It hurt me, then haunted me throughout the rest of our drive and flight. I tried to convince myself that she'd only been stunned, you know, that she was probably able to walk back into the woods, shaken but unharmed. But no. No, there had blood on the pavement—I had seen it spilling out from under her—and her legs were a mess. No. So I made a decision that maybe later when I was alone someplace I might want to pray about it. Not a formal prayer. Not "Our Father, who art in heaven..." No, nothing that would make the Pope proud. Just take a minute to ask God to tell the doe I was sorry and that I hoped she hadn't suffered much. That's all. It would be the first time I'd been inspired to pray since Trish got sick six months before, the first time I'd even considered prayer as something other than an exercise in futility.

I wondered if she would stay. "She" being Faith. I mean, she probably had pets and all that; plants to water; laundry to do. Part of me expected our interlude to end at the airport. You know, the usual kiss-kiss-buh-bye-two-ships-passing-in-the-night type of thing. But when she opened the taxi door, I scooted over—an inviting, if not desperate, maneuver. Faith got in without hesitation, and as we passed through the tunnel and into the city, I was glad to be back. I saw a Roy

Rogers Chicken and wanted to cry. Almost home! Soon our cab had reached the Washington Square Arch.

"That park used to be a cemetery in the 1700s," I said, doing the dull tour guide thing, which served merely as yet another distraction tactic to avoid having a small-scale nervous breakdown and begging her to stay the night. "Yellow fever. Killed hundreds of people."

"That's what killed Mozart, isn't it?" she asked, but it wasn't really like a question. Faith seemed nervous too, and for the last remaining minutes of the cab ride, we didn't look at each other. Not directly, anyway. I paid the driver and we all moved around to the trunk to get the bags. I looked at the sidewalk. And then I looked at the fence, which would need to be painted in the spring. And then I looked at Faith.

"Well," I said, trying to work up the nerve to say it, say it, say it! But before I could say it—whatever "it" was—she was headed up the steps with our luggage. I unlocked the front door. Inside, in the elevator, there was still no talking, no eye contact. My apartment was on the fifth floor, the top, and it took fucking forever to get there.

"Thanks." I threw my coat on a chair. "You can just set those anywhere."

"OK."

I stood, wringing my hands. "I, um, I've got to take a shower."

"Yeah, me too." She stood looking at the floor.

"OK." I clapped my hands together. I couldn't ask her to stay. It would be too needy. But, God, it had all seemed so weirdly close, so powerfully intimate. But like the cliché went, things were not always what they seemed. She'd probably said all those things then just gotten bored with me or something. I knew how things went. Hell, I'd been there myself.

"So, what's keeping you?" She finally locked eyes with me, smiling. Cocky about it. Fine. Let her eat cake. If she wanted to be that way, then fuck her. She could let herself out. I'd just go right on in and take my shower and she could just go directly to hell.

I threw up my hand and waved before turning to enter the bathroom. It felt good to get out of my clothes. I turned on the shower, un-velcroed and removed my geriatric walking boot, and wrapped my cast in a plastic garbage bag before stepping under the jet. The stream was cold at first, hard, and I let it run down my face. Fuck her. But wait—I wasn't being fair. I mean, if the girl had to go home and tend to her responsibilities, that was normal. That was OK. Everyone has responsibilities. She couldn't be expected to just hang around and nurse me all the time. Right? I lathered my hair with shampoo. Right. I could just write the rest of the evening off as Elvis time; you know, lie around watching television, dreaming of fried 'nanner sandwiches and girls wrestling in white cotton panties. Buy mama a Cadillac. That King, boy, he sure did know how to live. I smiled, rinsing my hair, my lower back cramping from the strange way I had to balance my cast on the stall's edge to keep it dry. Yeah, I had it wrapped, but I didn't trust the whole garbage bag concept.

"Hey, you started without me."

What the hell?

I jumped and let out a short burst of a scream. Faith pressed against me from behind. Naked! Naked! Naked!

"Did I scare you?"

"Oh, no," I shook my head. "No, no, the stroke I just

suffered was from prolonged exposure to Christmas lights. Yeah. It had nothing to do with the paralyzing shock wave of fear I just experienced." I sighed. "Hi."

"Hi." She giggled. "Just lean back."

"What?"

"Lean back against me." She pulled me back against her, one arm holding me at the waist, the other braced firmly as she clutched the railing at the top of the shower stall. "I've got you. Go ahead and do your thing. I won't let you fall."

Awkward as that was, she had the right idea because my back stopped cramping. I lathered my body, directing the hot water to hit right below my collarbone, the place that felt so raw and stingy when I coughed. Wonderful. And as an added bonus, just when I thought I was finished, Faith opted to reach around and slide her fingers inside of me, rocking back and forth until I slumped against her and twitched, our pose resembling a lesbian reenactment of the Pietà. Catholics around the world questioned their heterosexuality at that moment, I'm sure.

"Are you hungry?"

Was I hungry? Was I ever.

If you're out to count calories, it's best to stay away from Virgil's, my favorite spot in Manhattan. Big and clean with plenty of Patsy Cline blaring throughout, Virgil's was home to enormous burgers, homemade onion rings, and mustard coleslaw, all the foods a body craves during that postcoital feeding frenzy when a garden salad just won't do. I'd found Virgil's one night as I wandered in such a haze, ditching Tess, my flavor of the evening, after an argument at yet another mindless fashion bash in the nearby Royalton

Hotel. It was then that I found the true meaning of "comfort food," shoveling pulled pork and potatoes into my eager mouth, washing it all down with great tumblers of margaritas on the rocks.

That night with Faith, I happily indulged in country fried steak and several honey brown lagers, regaling her with tales of my early years as a reluctant teen pageant beauty. Someday, I promised, I'd greet her at the door wearing my tiara and nothing else. I also promised I'd call Germaine from work the next morning to schedule an appointment. Waiting for a cab, I took just one drag from an after-dinner Eve and doubled over, hacking. This was starting to become a nuisance. Enough, already. Germaine and I were old friends, so I knew she'd squeeze me in. It would only require a few minutes out of my day, anyway, just long enough to let her slap an icy stethoscope to my chest, proclaim it a virus, get a slip for some pills, and be on my way.

Chapter 10

Reality is a hideous thing. I'd always fashioned myself as one who would retire young and live that sort of lush, lavish life. Barbara Hutton–ish, you know. Jacqueline Suzanne, baby. High tea at the Drake. Lunch at 21. Falling-down-drunk in the ankle-deep red carpet at the Plaza Hotel. Waking up at the crack of noon. Lover after lover after lover. But there is such a thing as paying the bills. You know, work. And when you own your own business, there's no one to blame but yourself when things come crashing down. Even with the tight little crew I was lucky enough to have, there was still a great deal to do. And I had been slacking off. What with the whole borderline alcoholism meets sudden romanticism of my life, things had suffered a bit. Advertising had let up and, consequently, so had business. Not enough to turn us into street people, but it had definitely taken a dip. We had our standard holiday bookings, of course, but things could have been better.

It was around 4 A.M. when I made it to the office to get cracking on the new ad plan. Generally I used major sources sparingly. Electronic media only occasionally. Print was a great source for couponing, so I ran a lot of ads in the *Voice*. Suggestive but tasteful (?) advertisements aimed at our target audience of predominantly single and upwardly mobile gays, with slogans like "Come Cruise With Us" and photos of same-sex, scantily bikini'd couples captioned with the line "Hot Enough for Ya?" got a lot of attention. Very effective. We gave away trips for raffles benefiting the AIDS Foundation and enjoyed tons of free publicity for our generosity. We threw wicked parties and sponsored local events. We devised a point system where anyone spending money with us earned significant discounts on tanning packages, meals at favorite local eateries, jewelry... Anything we could tie in, we did.

So I was back in the saddle, so to speak, for the first day since my siesta in Michigan. I entered to find a pack of Nicorette on my desk. How subtle. My staff was small but persistent, and their mission to help me quit smoking for good was a valiant if sometimes annoying one. Lavinia, our receptionist, often left stacks of American Lung Association pamphlets in my IN basket.

She was an odd one, that Lavinia. An ex-stripper who'd lost her washboard abs and her job when she became pregnant, she had all but begged me for a full-time 9 to 5 two years ago, and I'd caved. As it turned out, she became quite an asset. Men liked her for her curvy, buxom shape and tiny voice, not to mention because she came off like an airhead. She wasn't, though. Women liked her because she was a working mom. I liked her because she typed like she was on crack. Lavinia, the minority in our office, was terminally straight, but we didn't hold it against her. She liked me and seemed to respect me, so I made a conscious effort not to stare at her tits.

"Welcome back." She stepped into my office at around 8 A.M. "The gum's from me."

"Fantastic. Thank you." I grinned and held up the package of gum, posing emphatically. "I'll think of you when I'm chewing it."

"You do that." She laughed. "I'm going to Dean & DeLuca. Do you want anything?" She paused. "No, let me guess." She frowned and folded her arms in a very austere impression of me. "'Black coffee. Not espresso. Not cappuccino. No stupid cinnamon sticks or whipped cream. Nothing foo-fooey. Coffee is not meant to be cute.'"

"Actually..." I thought for a moment. "I believe I'd like some toast. No, a bagel. With strawberry cream cheese."

"A bagel?" She stepped back in surprise. "With strawberry cream cheese?"

"And an orange juice. A large orange juice. And a large hot tea." I reached into the pocket of my Lagerfeld slacks and pulled out a fifty. "Here. Live it up. Breakfast is on me. See if Allen and Dave want anything. They say breakfast is the most important meal of the day, you know. And if you have a minute, could you please stop and pick up a box of Kleenex? I'm all out, and there's something truly unsettling about using toilet paper."

"Sure." Lavinia looked confused—maybe even frightened.

"What?" I took off my glasses and looked squarely at her. "What's the problem?"

"Who are you?"

"What?"

"You're not one of those pod people, are you? Or a clone?" She squinted, puzzled. "A victim of an alien abduction maybe? Or is this a drug thing?"

"Lavinia," I said it crisply, enunciating every syllable, like I always did. I liked the name, liked saying it: La-vinn-ee-ah... There was such a rhythmic quality to it. "La-vinn-ee-ah, what are you talking about?"

"Gee, I don't know. I mean, you come bouncing into work in casual clothes. You're...you know...*eating*." She smirked. "You're all smiley and everything and you obviously took a bath in cologne this morning. Not that I'm complaining, but what gives?"

"The question is not *what* gives, but *who*." Dave came trotting in behind her with his usual toothy smile. Both in their 20s and boyishly charming, Dave and his lover, Allen, were my customer service team. Working together, they could sell even the most embittered old queen a trip to Tahiti or wherever else was paying them the most commission. Soulless, unstoppable little bastards. I loved them.

"I don't know what you're talking about." I put my glasses back on and glanced down at some receipts on my desk, trying to curb a smile.

"Macy, give it up." He tapped my desk to get my attention. "Who's behind curtain number three?"

"Well, if you both have nothing better to do—like, for instance, *work*," I said, still examining the receipts. "I suppose you can meet her this afternoon."

Dave applauded. "Late lunch?"

"Doctor's appointment," I said. "I'll be leaving at 3 today."

"Stopping by to accompany you to a doctor's appointment. So considerate! And so soon. Tsk-tsk-tsk!" he laughed. "You know the old joke..."

"First comes love, second comes marriage..." Lavinia piped in, not one to be left out.

"You know what lesbians do on their second date?" he asked.

I looked up, trapped, as Dave loomed over my desk. "What?"

"Rent a U-Haul."

"Not true, not true," I said. "Now go on. Out. Get breakfast. Make us some money. Do something to make me feel like you're worth what I'm paying you. Out! Out! Out!"

Good God. I had only a few months until the next cruise. I had to start hooking them now or face the plight of empty cabins, a no-no in my book. People love a sense of urgency, that "hurry up, it's selling out fast" feel. I needed to start pushing this cruise.

Now. Special offer! Book now for best rates! Blah, blah, blah. Sixty-eight phone calls later and the frenzy had begun. I had no voice left, but I had a kick-ass ad campaign.

Cruise ships held approximately 1,800 to 2,000 people. At at least $1,500 each, our cruises had the potential to gross over 3 million dollars. After expenses, we usually took in about half that, but it was still a nice chunk. Three cruises a year and I was set. Anything on top of that was just gravy on the potatoes. Charity banquets, mailing lists, radio, television, print... Every queer within a 200-mile radius was going to hear about this, and it was up to me to be their pied piper.

Three o'clock came before I knew it, and I was utterly annihilated: hair pointing in all directions, lipstick nonexistent, voice all but completely useless. A scary old broad, indeed. Faith showed up looking like some lovely, ethereal waif-goddess, of course, all glowing skin and dark eyes. Perfection personified. And it was all mine. My appointment was at 3:30 P.M. so, thankfully, we had to rush. I did manage, however, to make the obligatory introductions in my hoarse falsetto, which did not go unjibed. (Dave kept making the most asinine references to Butterfly McQueen—"Miss Scarlett! Miss Scarlett!"). And to make the moment even more embarrassingly sappy than it already was, Faith had brought me a gift. Awwww. And it was an appropriate gift, at that. A scarf. It was long and chenille. (Quality chenille, not the cheap stuff.) Slightly fringed at the ends. Black. Thick. Cozy. And as she reached up to wrap it around my throat, I was filled with pride for my darling little trophy, scooping my arms around her and leaning in for a kiss. It was my first public display of affection in years, thank you very much. The first one ever at the office.

Dave tapped me on the shoulder and whispered "Jesus, even *I've* got a boner!" in my ear, which, considering he was the gayest man in the free world, was truly an event. Lavinia just stood there, not sure how to react. Not because of the whole lesbian PDA thing (as this very straight mother of two had seen it all and then some even before coming to work for me), but because she was shocked to consider that her boss could be so...well, tender, I guess. I could practically see the wheels turning in her mind as she tried to find the connection between my showing a normal amount of human affection and my consumption of strawberry cream cheese. Still, all in all, the air, the whole vibe, was unexpectedly gracious and for a moment it felt very much like a family kind of thing, like I'd brought her in to meet the folks.

The elevator was out of order, which was standard. And Germaine's office was on the fourth floor, wouldn't you know. Impaired as I was, what with das boot and everything, I still managed to pass by the majority of her clientele on the stairs like they were standing still. Many of them, in fact, *were* standing still. Old people, methadone cases, assorted fruits and nuts, all smoking or ranting or two-handedly clutching the staircase railing, or all of the above. Germaine's partner in practice had discovered the outrageous profits available to doctors who welcomed government assistance cases; thus, her waiting room had come to resemble a panel of guests on *Jerry Springer*.

Germaine herself was a tubby dyke with a good complexion and glasses. She was in her early 40s, but because of her chubbiness and upbeat disposition, she appeared much younger. Not that I found her irresistibly attractive, no. But she did look remarkably young for her age. She was clean, yuppie-ish, like somebody's hip, happening mom on a sitcom. A Jew from the Bronx, Germaine reminded me—largely because of her communication style—of Trish, only more restrained. They even looked a tad alike. Just a tad. Not like they were sisters or anything. Not like they were the dreidel twins. But they both had thick blond hair and seemed to delight in giving me shit about not taking care of myself. Both were dry and candid and just nosy enough to really get on my nerves. And both knew they could get away with it.

"Macy!" She waltzed into the examination room, eyes never lifting from the notes in my file. "You know, my friend Kristy...you've met Kristy, haven't you?"

Why, I thought, scanning the room—*Is Kristy in here with us? Is she going to be part of my examination?*—before I realized that Germaine was, well, just being weird.

"I don't believe I've had the pleasure." Oh, God, one day back in the city and I was already on auto-lie. Yes, I did know Kristy. Indeed. Biblically, in fact. So did everyone else on the last cruise I'd booked. What a giant slut, and a gold-digging one at that. Don't tell me Germaine had taken the bait.

"Well, Kristy and I rented... Oh, what was it?" She looked up at the ceiling for inspiration. "*Death and the Maiden*. Yes. Just last week, and I said, 'Wow, Kristy, do I ever have a patient who's a real ringer for her.'" She continued perusing my file. "So, aside from the fact that you broke your leg without telling me, what's up?"

"I didn't break it. It's a high sprain. It's when the ankle..."

"I know what a high sprain is, Macy. I'm a doctor, remember? I'm your personal physician, actually—though you wouldn't know it from the number of checkups you've been in for. Anyway, next time you have to pay a visit to the ER, how about giving me a call?"

"I, um, I'm sorry. I will."

"Let's hope so. Anyway, as I was saying, What's up?"

"Not much, really." I shrugged. "A cold, I guess."

"You guess?"

"I guess." I smiled, raising an eyebrow. "I did not come here of my own free will."

"Oh, really?" She smiled back.

"I now have someone concerned with my health."

"Someone special? You? The eternal bachelorette?"

"See for yourself." I gestured toward the door. "She's right out there in the waiting room. In a chair next to that hideous rubber tree plant you refuse to get rid of."

"One moment, please."

Germaine ducked out for a minute or two, then came rushing back in.

"The pretty one?" she whispered. "Right next to the plant? Black hair? Tan? Big eyes?"

"Yes, ma'am!" I was so proud.

"Good for you!" She felt my throat—my glands, I suppose—then opened a package that contained a tongue depressor. "OK, open up." I did. "Sing! Aaaaah."

I complied. "Aaaaagh."

"Hmmm. We'll need a throat culture." She scribbled something in my file. "Been running a fever at all?"

God, woman, I thought. *Just shut up and give me my pills and let me the hell out of here, OK?* I hated doctor's offices. Even knowing Germaine, amiable sort that she was, it was still a doctor's office and it still gave me the creeps. Who knew what disgusting ailment the last person to sit on that table had? Crabs, perhaps? Scabies? I was starting to itch just thinking about it.

"No." I shifted uneasily, tearing the paper that had been used to cover the padded table beneath me. Great. It probably tore directly under my ass. I was now probably sitting right on the spot where some welfare case had plopped her clap-ridden booty. Terrific.

Germaine made more notes.

"How long has this been going on?"

"Oh, I'd say maybe a day or so. Not long."

"Cough?"

"No, not really."

Germaine looked at me. She frowned.

"It's a virus, Marcus Welby. Enough with the 20 questions. I don't want any tests. Just write me a prescription and I'm out of here. Let me get off this table before I contract herpes or something worse. I know what can happen at doctor's offices. I've seen *20/20.*"

Germaine frowned again, then reached for the door.

"I'll be right back. In the meantime, I need you to remove your blouse."

"That's what they all say." I winked, unbuttoning my cuffs.

A few minutes passed before Germaine returned with Faith in tow. I immediately folded my arms in front of me. Shy? Another first. Funny. You can strip bare in front of your doctor or your lover and not think a thing of it, but both of them at the same time? No way.

"Ten minutes alone with another woman and you just whip your blouse off, first thing," Faith whispered into my ear.

"I hope you don't mind, Macy, but since you have a history of fibbing, I sought a second opinion."

"Shit. You two are ganging up on me. It isn't fair. And I am probably sitting on the same table as some anal warts patient. LET ME OUT!"

"Now, just wait a minute, here..." The tone of Germaine's voice put the kibosh on my tirade. "Faith says you cough all night and can't get any rest. She says that when you do fall asleep, you wake up after a few hours, often with an asthma attack. She says you've had a fever, off and on, for about three days. And..." She tilted her head. "You still smoke. Anything else?"

Nothing like a smug, smart-ass doctor to make your day. Not to mention a girlfriend with loose lips. Whatever happened to confidentiality?

I threw up my hands. "Do what you gotta do," I said.

Germaine chuckled and placed her stethoscope to my chest, listening. "OK, kiddo. Deep breath. Through your mouth."

I followed her instructions, inhaling with marked difficulty and exhaling with a high-pitched whine of a wheeze, providing repeat performances of these sickening sounds whenever she moved the stethoscope from one area to another on my chest and back.

"Any pain?"

"What are you asking me for?" I pointed to Faith, who was seated on a high stool in the corner wearing a very sheepish expression. "She's got all the answers."

"Macy..." Germaine shot me a look.

"It burns, stings," I said through clenched teeth. "Right here. Right below my collar bone."

"Nothing in the rib area?" She prodded my side.

"No," I said. And I wasn't lying.

First, there were chest X-Rays. Then blood tests. Sputum cultures. The spirometer. Temperature. Blood pressure. Breathing treatment. Injections: one in the arm, another in the ass. And then one more blow into the spirometer to measure my lung functions *after* the medication in the breathing treatment had been given time to take full effect. We were there nearly four and a half hours and I was angry and beat when it was finally over. The diagnosis was asthmatic bronchitis, about which Germaine issued a stern warning regarding the complications that could occur if I didn't take proper care of myself. Contagious? Doubtful, but that would be verified by the tests. Also, she suspected I was anemic.

All this information breezed by me. She'd lost me, lost all credibility, when she'd brought up her relationship with Kristy. How could I trust her judgment when I personally knew that Kristy, the newfound fire of her loins, was easier to make than microwave popcorn? Yeah, sure, the girl had a nice set of breasts. Positively buoyant, from what I could remember, complete with one of those trailer park tattoos of—what else?—a bleeding rose, no less, conveniently located next to her left nipple. What class! And, well, yes, I can honestly confess that I did enjoy whiling away a few hours on the big boat with old lusty Kristy, as I'm quite sure she enjoyed scoring numerous free drinks at my expense. But Germaine? Come on. Germaine was a doctor, for crying out loud. She was supposed to have some common sense.

I pouted most of the way home. It was my right, I figured, after the shit I'd been bullied into.

Things looked different at my apartment. Cleaner, brighter. Fresh flowers stood in a vase on the dining table. A stack of various publications had been strategically placed next to the piece of furniture I called my "fainting couch"—*Cosmo, The Wall Street Journal, The Advocate, The Post*. It was mildly exciting in a childish way, to see them there waiting for me to read them. Like getting mail. As a kid, I had always looked forward to the nights when my stepmother, Vi, would emerge from her black Eldorado with a paper sack. The sack was not filled with boring crap like groceries, I knew that. We had a housekeeper who bought food, cleaning supplies—all those drab, necessary household items. No, the bags Vi brought home were filled with those cool little luxuries so many women love: magazines, liquor, cigarettes, and makeup. Friday night generally found her smoking leisurely in her chair beside the fireplace with a copy of *Modern Screen*, devouring every detail of Jackie Onassis's various jetset vacations in exotic locales. That Jackie was on the cover of nearly every *Modern Screen* magazine eventually came to confuse me: She hadn't been in any movies, had she? When I asked Vi about this, she explained, "You needn't be a movie star to be a celebrity," which I didn't quite understand. She said that people like the Gabor sisters and Kitty Carlisle qualified as celebrities without accomplishing much. But Jackie deserved her fame, her rank among Hollywood's "bigwigs," she said. Jackie was "the real deal."

Generally, I perched on a cushion on the floor, feeling privileged and appreciative in knowing that not only did Vi allow me to read comic books (something my mother detested), she condoned it. I mean, I could count on getting two or three per week: *Archie, Lois Lane*...even *Mad* magazine, which she thought was particularly beneficial because of its political satire and offbeat social commentary. She advised me that reading would increase my vocabulary and encouraged me to read anything I could get my hands on. Coming from Vi, I believed this. She was the smartest, most sophisticated person in the world, though she'd dropped out of high school in the tenth grade. And so I read, obedient and silent like a dog in front of the fireplace, lingering sometimes more on the advertisements than the comics themselves. Itching powder. Ventriloquist dummies. Sea monkeys. One hundred plastic Revolutionary War soldiers in their own cardboard replica footlocker. My personal favorite and the object of my obsession for some time was an ad featuring a photo of a tiny monkey sitting in a teacup. "Darling Pet Monkey" it read, "$10.95." A bit pricey for the time, but, hey, it *was* a real, live monkey.

Chapter 11

At night, I would stare at my bedroom ceiling, envisioning the adventures my darling pet monkey and I would share together. I decided that I would name him Ringo, after Ringo Starr, and train him to terrorize my asshole brother as he lay sleeping two rooms down the hall. Every school day, I would go to the library during lunch and read about monkeys, fantasizing that Ringo would come along in my lunch box, much to the amazement and envy of my many third-grade friends. He would be impish and endearing, and I would outfit him in tiny soldier and sailor outfits I planned to swipe from my brother's G.I. Joe collection. About that time, I started to work on Vi. Being worldly and generous, Vi was the obvious choice to fund my monkey lust. But, alas, convincing her of the merits of owning my very own darling pet monkey was not as easy as I'd expected.

"I'm sorry, sweetheart," she said, not even cracking her usual kind smile. "But no. I'm not sending away for any monkey."

"It's because I'm 8, isn't it?" I was on a mission, so I

threw in some drama. "You think I'm not old enough to take care of it. Well, I will. I promise." I grabbed her hand, begging. I had no shame when it came to the future of my darling pet monkey. "Please."

"It's not that I think you're too young. You're a very bright, responsible girl. But forcing a wild animal into our environment is just wrong," she explained. "It upsets the balance of nature. These people"—she frowned, but didn't raise her voice—"they steal these poor little monkeys from their own, natural environment and sell them for profit, with no regard for their health or happiness." At last, she smiled. "Monkeys live in the jungle, not in the suburbs."

I wanted to argue, but I couldn't. This was Vi. Vi, whom I idolized, who took me to museums and who brought me ice cream when I had my tonsils out. Shit. There had to be a way to win her over on this.

"Hey, Vi, get this," I piped cheerfully, sitting down at the breakfast table. "Tallulah Bankhead had a pet monkey."

I'd done my homework, scanning through her old magazines and books until I'd found the prized bit of information that was sure to end the monkey war. I knew for a fact that Vi had seen *Lifeboat* (starring, yes, Tallulah Bankhead) *six* times. And if Tallulah Bankhead had a pet monkey, well...

"Yes, she did have a pet monkey. In the '30s, I think." She folded down the newspaper she was reading, never looking up. "Trained it to sit on people's shoulders and shit down their backs, from what I've heard."

"Vi, for God's sake!" my dad gasped. Yeah, right, like he'd never said "shit" in his life. I got the feeling he was only acting appalled for my benefit, that he really liked a woman who could say "shit" at the breakfast table without flinching. His coffee cup did not hide his smile.

"Sorry, Bill, but it's true." She reached over and clapped me on the shoulder. "Nice try."

Little did I know it then, but victory would be mine, and soon, but not without a price. One day after a minor and typical sibling squabble, my brother Elliott shoved me into the chalkboard hanging inside our garage. The sharp corner of the metal chalk ledge caught me in the side of the neck. It was a deep cut, dangerously close to an artery, and—my God—did it ever gush. I cupped my hand over the wound and went inside. Blood seeped through my fingers as I stood staring at Vi in our living room, my mouth agape. It was then that Vi turned a strange color, a color I would later see come over an old man's face as he slid off his stool, dead right then and there from a stroke at the Dairy Delish where I waited tables one summer. Ashen. And it was then, witnessing her terror, that I knew I was in big, big trouble.

"BILL!" she screamed, so loud and hard it didn't sound human. Dad had been in his favorite room, the crapper, working diligently on the *TV Guide* crossword puzzle when her roar had reached him. Shirt half tucked into his unzipped pants, he hastily made his way into the kitchen where Vi had dragged me pressing a stack of dish towels against my gash, which still spurted like Old Faithful. Dad was tall and thin like me, gangly, and we had the same gift of coordination, so it was no shock when he fell down the front porch steps on the way to start the car, splitting his chin wide open. By the time we reached the emergency room, all three of us were covered in blood: me in my own from the geyser on my neck, Vi with mine (from holding me), and Dad from the slit directly in the center of his chin. The scar from said slit would eventually look more like a natural crease, prompting Vi to chide him with nicknames like "Spartacus" and "Montgomery Cleft."

Hospitals have a way of making you feel small and powerless, even as an adult. Being an 8-year-old strapped down to a cold table didn't exactly make for a warm and fuzzy memory. I screamed and shrieked for the better part of an hour as the big people in white worked over me, my fear gradually subsiding as whatever not-yet-tested-for-children 1960s tranquilizer sneaked into my veins. Soon everything seemed blurry and warm, and before I knew it I was in an actual bed and fairly comfortable, rubbing my eyes to see my mom and dad embracing at the foot of that bed. My mother was crying, which didn't bother me. She cried all the time. But seeing them together just then, like that, I forgot they were divorced. Maybe they forgot too.

Dad saw that I was awake and smiled, a huge wad of gauze taped to his chin. Mom was still crying, with her face buried in his chest.

"Hiya, babydoll." He squeezed my foot through the blanket. Mom looked up with bloodshot eyes, smiling meekly—ever the weak, blubbering female—and hey, there they were again. Bill and Phyllis. The Great American Couple. All smiles and hugs. Enough smarm to make Norman Rockwell reach for his paintbrush. All we needed was a faithful black Lab to pose at their feet. But what should've made me happy didn't. Seeing them all cozy like that made me nervous, made me wonder when the other shoe was going to drop. I didn't trust it, didn't trust either of them. Even at 8, I'd witnessed enough fights and suicide threats to be legitimately leery of their union. Right in the thick of things, they had sent me to a shrink, anticipating any anxieties I might have about the split-up. I had none. I was the only kid in America who was glad her parents were getting divorced. Sure, it was a minor pain in the ass at first. There were some adjustments. But things had worked out nicely for everyone, and I liked everything just the way it had come to be. Elliott generally stayed with Mom. I generally stayed with Dad and Vi. Cool beans. Why fix it if it ain't broke? And, hey, where was Vi? She'd make everything normal again, if anyone could.

I closed my eyes, feigning sleep so I wouldn't have to deal with my parents, and wound up falling asleep for real. They were gone when I woke up. Vi was there. For the first time, I noticed the wrinkles at the corners of her eyes.

"Well, look who decided to wake up," Vi said, and when she smiled the wrinkles became even more pronounced. Don't get me wrong: It didn't make her ugly. It made her human.

"I'm glad you came." Man, was I glad. With Vi there, I was no longer a defenseless kid. I had representation.

"I've been here all along, right out in the hall," she said, sweeping the hair out of my eyes. "Why don't you go back to sleep? Pretty soon your dad'll be back and we'll get to go home."

Dad had left, escorting Mom home, since she'd been too distraught to drive herself. Christ. A hangnail could make my mother distraught. And of course he had to leave, you know. Big Bad Bill to the rescue.

"OK." I started to close my eyes, then jerked. "Vi, don't leave." I lowered my voice to a whisper. "I don't like it here."

She didn't leave. She stayed, sitting in a hard, yellow chair. Leaning over, her head resting on my bed. Asleep. A nurse came in to check the bandage on my neck.

"Is that your mommy?" she asked.

"Yes," I answered. I didn't want them to make her leave. I didn't want to be alone in the hospital or, worse yet, in the company of my parents as they proceeded to hang all over each other.

The squishy soles of her white shoes squeaked with each step as the nurse left the room and closed the door behind her.

"Hey." Vi squinted up at me, head still resting on the edge of my bed. "When we go home..." She took my hand. "We'll order the monkey."

And sure enough, she kept her word. The next day I clipped the order blank carefully from the back cover of *Archie* and Vi slipped it along with a check into a business-size envelope. "GUARANTEED LIVE DELIVERY IN ELEVEN DAYS OR LESS!" the ad said.

No more than a week later, the box arrived. Vi signed for it and stood on the porch. I watched her open it and set it on the steps. She came back inside, solemnly holding an ice bag on her swollen jaw, the miserable aftereffect of a wisdom tooth extraction the day before, and I knew. I knew right then that Ringo the darling pet monkey was DOA. Vi told me to stay inside, but I couldn't. While she went to the garage for a shovel, I crept out to the porch. An odd, sweet smell arose from the holes punched in the lid of the box. I opened it and there he lay, curled up, eyes closed. Tiny fingers and hands—just like a little man.

"Oh, Macy, I told you to stay inside." She returned with the shovel, eyes downcast and wet with tears. "Just go on inside for me, will you?"

I felt responsible, not only for Ringo, but also for making Vi upset. I don't know which was worse. In all the times she spoke of losing her little girl, she never cried. And here she was with her jaw all black and blue, digging a monkey's grave. A monkey she'd sent for against her better judgment. Just to please me.

I took the shovel from her.

"I'll take care of it," I said, and I buried Ringo in his box, placing a rock with his name written in Magic Marker on the small mound of fresh dirt beneath one of my dad's prized apple trees.

Vi was upstairs when I came back inside. I could hear Mrs. Vasquez, our housekeeper, talking to someone on the phone: "It's Saturday morning and still he is not home." Mrs. V. continued to tell whoever was on the other end that she had seen my father's car at my mother's house that morning when she went to Patch's pharmacy to pick up a prescription for Vi. He'd left the night before to fix a pipe and had not returned. This happened all the time, Mrs. Vasquez explained. My mother would call on a Friday or Saturday night all worked up over some minor household crisis and off Dad would run, not to return until late the next day. Vi had told me he'd been working late. Shit. He'd been working, all right. "Poor Mrs. Delongchamp," lamented Mrs. Vasquez. "Here she is with her jaw puffed up like a baseball, all alone with the little girl. She needs a man who'll come home to her, not one who goes to his ex-wife."

I couldn't believe it. I mean, every male in the county had the hots for Vi. Christ, even Lila Mayhew, the check-out girl at Patch's, couldn't help but give her a second look. But all that and a bag of chips was not enough to keep old Wild Bill Delongchamp satisfied. No, he wanted the one who overdosed on Valium and cut out the crotches in all of his pants and chucked Pepsi bottles at his head. He wanted Mom.

I leaned against the wall for a minute, thinking. What would happen if they got back together? Elliott was in and out of juvenile hall (or, as he called it: "the juvi") so much it wouldn't really make a big difference for him. But for me? Shit. I still had the telephone numbers to the sheriff and police departments indelibly etched in my brain from the ruckus that ensued during their first bout of unholy matrimony. And hey, I had learned CPR in Brownies, which would come in handy on any of the countless occasions they would attempt to murder each other.

When I found Vi upstairs, she was in the bathroom, spitting blood into the toilet. I led her back to her bed, refilled the ice bag, and then brought her fresh gauze to pack into her cheek. I then administered two of the pills Mrs. V. had picked up. I took good care of her, I guess, for an 8-year-old. I even lay down beside her, sort of curling around her arm the way I thought her little girl might have done if she were alive. Clinging and letting her stroke my hair as her quiet sobs fell into an uneven snore. She was going to leave. I just knew it.

I envisioned her packing her monogrammed luggage and heading off to some foreign land, sipping a frozen cocktail in her bathing suit and sunglasses, a shirtless Spaniard gleefully applying cocoa butter to her shoulders beside an azure sea. There'd be swank nightclubs and tan lads in white tuxedos. Mystery. Romance. A world where she belonged. A world so much bigger than Piqua, Ohio could ever be.

So it didn't surprise me when I found the envelope she'd slid under my door that evening. It contained $30 and a note: "Gone to California to get some sun. Be back in two weeks." The note also said she could be reached at a cabana at the Beverly Hills Hotel and gave the phone number there, instructing me to please call anytime. She'd left Dad a note too, bulging in a sealed envelope atop his desk. He flipped when he found it. I mean, really flipped. Slammed his fists over and over on the desktop.

Then, for the next few weeks, he wouldn't eat and he slept in a fetal position on the living room sofa. Quite a stink over someone he'd been screwing around on for two months or more. Meanwhile, Vi called every day and offered terrific tales of her visit to the coast. She'd sat next to Chuck Connors on the plane, was spending her evenings dining at Chasen's and cruising Sunset Boulevard in a rented red convertible. "It never rains here," she told me. "This is weather to recharge your spirit." Then she added something about biorhythms. And while grabbing a bite at Musso and Frank's, some lady started snapping pictures and asked for Vi's autograph. She didn't know who Vi was exactly, but anyone who looked like she did had to be somebody.

So hey, who could blame her for soaking up all the attention and flattery and fame by association? Who could blame her for ditching her bland routine in the suburban Midwest to rub elbows with the stars? Not me. I was a kid, but even I longed for escape. Even then I felt out of place in our innocent little burg, burdened with secrets I might have to hide forever if I chose to stay in Piqua, though I was way too young to know what those secrets would turn out to be. And if someone like Vi could get out, well, by God, good for her.

That's why it was such a shock the day she came back.

Unbelievable.

I was over at my mother's house when I heard the honk of a familiar horn from the driveway. Vi entered without knocking, tan and rejuvenated, blue eyes flickering behind her sunglasses, sporting flashy new duds from Rodeo Drive. Elliott was out on a day pass from the juvi for his birthday, and he and Dad had gone out into the woods to bond and kill something. My mother had made a cake for the occasion, frosting it with her famous cream cheese frosting and displaying it prominently on the dining room table.

"Phyllis." Vi ran her thin, tapered finger along the edge of the cake, sucking the frosting from her fingertip. "I've come for my husband."

Holy shit. The sheriff was back in town, and I was glad. This was better than TV.

"He's not here."

I hid in the bathroom, looking on with anticipation.

"His car is in your driveway." Vi laughed a tight little laugh.

"He and Elliott are hunting in the woods out back." Mom wiped her hands on her apron and glared at Vi. "They said they'd be back by noon."

"Well, it's nearly 11:30 now." Vi glanced down at her watch and pulled out a chair. "I'll just sit here and wait with you if that's all right."

"Sure." Mom opened the cupboard and took out a cup. "Coffee?"

"Please."

Both maintained a chilling politeness until around noon when Dad and Elliott came stomping in. I kept a safe but observant distance from the situation, pretending to draw on a notepad in the hallway, listening for any mention of divorce or remarriage or anything revolutionary. Nothing. Dad threw his arms around Vi and swept her off the floor. They giggled and kissed, pawing at each other and frenching away, right there in my mom's kitchen. Hooray! And so brought the end of my father's Mr. Fix It expeditions to my mother's house.

Elliott went back to the juvi. And me, well, I remained content and properly spoiled at Dad's house as we all lived under the reign of Vi.

Chapter 12

Let's face it: Helplessness is not a trait most people look for in a partner. It's just not something that grabs you while perusing the personal ads. Sure, once in a while it might feel good to play the hero to a damsel in distress. Save the day. But it gets old, and frankly it worried me to have started a new relationship when I was so sick and whiny. Growing up tall, people had always taken me to be older than I was. Thus, I learned to revel in the responsibility and respect that was given to me automatically due to my stature alone. Throughout my life as a long, cool woman, I never slumped. Instead I learned how to dress to accentuate it. I wasn't some awkward Amazon. I was statuesque. When I walked into a room, a business meeting, a situation, I could generally take charge with little or no resistance. People trusted me. Abe Lincoln was tall, after all. And people looked up to him. They had no choice! And sometimes, they seemed more than a little intimidated by this Armani-clad, well-groomed, monolithic figure before them. I had power, an edge, and I liked it. Even when I had no clue what was going on, I exuded competence.

But Faith didn't know this side of me, the side that I most liked, the side that had bought a failing business and made it thrive. Since day one, she had seen only my vulnerability and neuroses. More than anything, I wanted to change her image of me from susceptible to unfaltering. She deserved the best of me. But regardless of my determination to define my capabilities, I was still not at all well. For hours, I lay bundled in blankets in my red leather recliner, conspiring to prove my worth to Faith. Some kid had fallen into the river again, according to the Channel 4 Action News Team. Silently I wished I had been there to plunge into the icy, polluted depths alongside him, emerging victorious, the still-living child held triumphantly in my arms. Quintessential photo-op. Yes, me, standing strong and tall in the middle of the river. Joan of Arc, Jr. A saint for modern times. And I would've done it too, or at least attempted it, had I not been so whacked-out on bronchitis and pain medication, so beached without purpose in front of the TV.

"Macy?" Faith called out to me from the kitchen, where she was furiously cooking something. She must've gone to the grocery store while I was at work, as I'd left my refrigerator bare, with the exception of half a bottle of wine and a jar of foul imported mustard I'd bought—on a whim—that had defied eating even before its expiration date had come to pass six years ago. The fridge itself was one of my first major purchases, a Sub-Zero with an elegant frosted-glass door and chrome fixtures, but it had never been of much use. Food came easy for me upon my arrival in the city. For the first two years, I lived solely on hors d'oeuvres. Fresh fruit, pates, canapés, cocktail sausages, cannoli...you name it; if it arrived before me speared with a frilly tooth-pick, I ate it. Such miniature delicacies were available to me in great abundance in the darker half of my double life. See, by day I led a relatively low-profile existence working full-time at Brickley Travel. I kept my nose clean and towed the line, as my boss was not one for change, but each day I saw opportunities that we, as a business, were missing. One par-ticular gaping hole in the market was, most certainly, the gay trade. I mean, hell, we were in Greenwich Village, for God's sake. Larger agencies were able to steal the bulk of our "average couple" customer base with huge discounts and promotional offers. We couldn't dream of competing for the mainstream crowd. But in time I would change our focus and our profits, snatching up the business for a fraction of what we would reap in profits in our first year alone. Long live Brickley Travel!

I took my time, however, never one to rush into any-thing hasty regarding money. Vi's life insurance policy had provided me with a considerable chunk, and I was com-pelled to invest it conservatively. Eager to learn things first-hand, I cheerfully earned my paltry wage during the day. A good girl, you know? Passionate about my job. Efficiency apartment. Discount at the dry cleaners. But at night, oh-ho! The night found me tending bar in my black brassiere, serving and smiling to the pricey dykes that gravitated *en masse* to a series of exclusive private parties held in a secret speakeasy above a video rental store and tanning salon. There I learned my true, predatory nature, flopping into bed each night, the pockets of my Gloria Vanderbilts bulging with phone numbers and tips. Gig after gig, I passed out more business cards than an Amway rep and built my customer base. Thus began my career. Macy

Delongchamp, lesbian entrepreneur extraordinaire. Snappy dresser with a vague knowledge of fine wines. One swingin' hipster of a travel agent. Not available for children's parties.

The older ones were the easiest. The married ones played a close second. Before long I had networked my way into the address books of New York's "*autre* café society." My name became synonymous with travel—and a fine lay to boot. Paying my price began to pay off. I had no regrets.

"Macy?"

"Yes?"

Something was working on my head, all right. Something trippy and tactile and slow. I stared at the frame on the wall. Not the picture in it, mind you. The frame. And remembered, just then, every detail of the 3-D picture of Jesus my mother had hanging on the wall of her living room. Trish and I would stop by to drop off her alimony check from Dad, stoned beyond reggae, and there I would sit on the couch, swaying back and forth, mesmerized by the 3-D Jesus picture that gave the illusion he was knocking on some door. What was he thinking? Whose door was he knocking on?

Knock, knock. Who's there? Jesus. Jesus who? Jesus, it's cold out here! Let me in!

"Macy, how much of that cough syrup have you had today?"

"Good question. I don't know. I just take a swig now and then."

"Um, Macy?" She'd discovered the bottle. "Half of this is gone already."

"So?"

"So it says here: one tablespoon every two to four hours."

"Really? That explains the herd of miniature German

Shepherds that keeps running through here." *Oh, man. Try some. Give it a shot! This stuff is better than ecstasy...*

"Great." Faith shook her head.

"Say, what is that delightful aroma I smell emanating from the kitchen?"

"Soup." She clanged a lid onto a pot. "And homemade bread."

I craned my neck for a peek.

"You look luscious in there, toiling over a hot stove," I shouted. "Like the Land O'Lakes maiden right here in my own home."

She held up a spoon and posed. "Our people call it maize."

I laughed. "Tell me," I said. "What's your favorite album?"

"Huh?"

"I mean CD." I slapped my head. "Sorry."

"I know what an album is, silly. I just don't think telling you would be a good idea," she said, tasting the soup.

"Why not?"

"Because it's setting me up to look like some shallow, adolescent twerp. I mean, it's discussions like this that beg for posing, you know?"

"Posing?" I frowned. "I'm afraid I don't follow."

"Posing. Posturing." She opened the oven door. "Acting. Like it's a test question and neither of us want to fail, so we'll make up some lie that will make us sound original and intelligent, and we'll end up finding out absolutely nothing about each other. It's a lose-lose situation."

"How's the bread coming?"

"Fine." She closed the oven door.

"OK, so I'll promise not to judge you. And I promise

not to lie to impress you either." I jerked my thumb over my shoulder in a "you're out" motion. "I'll even throw out opera and classical. Strictly contemporary music."

"And no foreign stuff." She eyed me suspiciously, oven-mitted hands resting firmly on her hips. "No sneaking in Edith Piaf or chants in Latin. Not even Selena."

"Done." I folded my arms and leaned back in my chair. "God, you're awfully defensive about this. You're not going to say, like, Debbie Gibson, are you?"

"No."

"Tiffany? David Hasselhoff? Nobody really bad like that, right?"

"No!"

"OK then, relax already and come out with it!"

"Fine." Faith folded her arms, stuck out her delicate jaw, and squared her shoulders. "Prince. *Purple Rain* soundtrack."

"That's the one with 'Darling Nikki' on it, isn't it? That song about the freaky girl who masturbated."

"With a magazine, yes."

Sordid! Kinky! Yes!

"OK. Any others worth mentioning? Any close seconds or thirds?"

"I really like that song by Roberta Flack."

"Which song? 'Killing Me Softly'?"

"No, it's...wait a minute. I'll get it." She closed her eyes and hummed for a moment, then snapped her fingers. "'Will You Still Love Me Tomorrow?'" She lowered her head. "I used to cry when I heard that song."

"Great song. You know who wrote that?"

"Who?"

"Carole King. I've got the CD. In fact, that's probably

my favorite album. Carole King's *Tapestry*." I sat up. "You should check it out some time. It's amazing. Classic."

"So..." She was at ease now, I guess. "Any close seconds or thirds?"

"Yeah." I closed my eyes, thinking. "*Best of Blondie*, Annie Lennox's *Diva*, and"—I smirked—"*Ella Fitzgerald Sings the Cole Porter Songbook*."

"Oh, she's smirking." Faith laughed. "OK, I'll bite. Why that one?"

"When I was very small, my stepmother would play that record on her hi-fi and she and my father would make love."

"What?!"

"It's not like they were perverts or anything. They kept the door closed. They were far down the hall."

I blushed just thinking about it, thinking about Ella's smooth, elegant tone. "Birds do it, bees do it..." And my father's whispering cry: "Oh, Violet! Violet!"

Which he never called her otherwise.

"I didn't know that's what they were doing then. I was only 6 or 7 maybe. All I knew was, the morning after she played that Ella Fitzgerald record, my dad was tripping all over himself to make her eggs, light her cigarette, do whatever she wanted. And my father wasn't like that." I burst into a short laugh. "Eventually, I figured it out. You see, one day I decided to play that record myself. And upon hearing it, I realized that the squeaking spring noise was not on the recording."

"The bedsprings?" Faith asked.

"Yes!" My maniacal laugh eventually subsided. "Guess you had to be there."

"Here." She came in and handed me a glass of orange juice.

"In the evening?"

"For calcium. And vitamin C. It won't hurt you."

"I don't care about calcium." And I didn't. After half a bottle of prescription cough syrup, you don't care about much.

"You'll care when you're 60 and your bones snap like twigs."

My, what a positive vision of my future.

"I won't need calcium when I'm 60," I said. "I figure I'll just loll around like an amoeba or boneless chicken or something. Soiling my Depends. Screaming at the neighbor kids to stay the hell out of my yard."

"A boneless chicken?" She laughed, and I realized that making Faith laugh was not only easy but incredibly rewarding. Carefully manicured fingers had ever so swiftly brought many a gal pal to orgasm in 60 seconds or less, but I would've worked for an hour just to hear Faith laugh.

She held one hand behind her back.

"What? What are you hiding back there?"

"A gift."

"A gift?"

She produced a round shape wrapped in brown, paper bag-like material.

"How sweet of you."

"I got it from a street vendor." She dropped her head. "It's no big deal, but..."

It was an orange. But not really. It was actually a maraca made to look exactly like an orange. And it did. I rattled it with glee. What a weird but terrific gift!

"For some reason, I thought you'd get a kick out of it."

"OK, you're asking for it. Ready?" I began shaking it rhythmically. *Shicka-shicka, shicka-shicka.* "Oooh, kind of a bossa nova groove. Yeah!"

"Oh, God." Faith knew she was in trouble now. Step aside, Streisand, I was preparing to really belt one out.

"How old are you again?" I asked, still holding a loose but consistent rhythm.

"23."

"Ready? OK..." *Shicka-shick*. "Well, she was just...twenty-three-eee. If you know...what I mean."

"Oh, God."

"And the way she cooked...was way extraordinaire."

"Macy..."

"What, not a Beatles fan?"

"So you like it?"

"Need you ask?" I thrust the orange maraca high into the air. "I love it. I love maracas. And the fact that it looks exactly like an orange, well, that only makes it all the more wonderful."

"I had a professor in college, in creative writing." She gazed at the orange thoughtfully. "One of the assignments she gave us was to imagine ourselves inside an orange and write our way out."

"Like, to tell how you got yourself out of the orange?"

"Right. I guess it was actually a metaphor for being born. She told us that at the end of class."

I guzzled the orange juice Faith had brought me and she took the empty glass. "One guy who read his assignment aloud said that someone was in there with him. Turns out he was a twin."

"How peculiar." I studied the orange. "So the orange represented a uterus?"

"Correct."

I took her hand, eyes still on the orange.

"If you were an orange," I heard myself say, "I would

125

never leave you. I would stay inside and lose myself in the folds and the seeds and the sweet, orangey smell."

"You would hide." With the cool touch of her fingers at my jaw line, Faith turned my face to hers. She looked into my eyes with that way of hers. Effortless forgiveness is what she offered—as if I was no mystery or puzzle that required days, weeks, years to be solved, as if she'd be perfectly happy if she never figured me out completely. Maybe I didn't want to be understood. Maybe acceptance was a worthy substitute for understanding.

"I *would* hide," I said. And we kissed, inspiring me to tug at the belt loop of her jeans. "Come and sit on Santa's lap." She did, and I wrapped an arm around her waist. "Let's go out."

"Out?"

"Out." I rubbed her calf ever-so-affectionately. "Into Manhattan. Take a carriage ride through Central Park. Shop. Have a drink or two."

Do it all, I wanted to tell her. *Do everything lovers are supposed to do. Get ice cream and go to a movie and get into an argument and make up and make out. All of that. All of the stupid little moments lovers can share together in the course of an evening.* I wanted those moments, and I pressed my lips to her ear and whispered, "Run wild, you know? You and me. Two beautiful, impetuous lovers, out on the town."

"You're not going anywhere," she said. Goddamn, there it was, the voice of reason. "Besides, I have to work tonight."

"You have a job?"

"Of course I have a job."

"Well, of course you have a job. I just don't know why it never occurred to me. So where do you work? Some center for recycling or a literacy council? Battered women's shelter? Animal Welfare League?"

"What? Do I have LOOKING FOR A CAUSE written across my forehead?"

"No, I just, you just seem...I mean, with a heart like yours and your young, idealistic mind...your capacity for tenderness...I thought you'd be out there trying to save the world."

"No, retard." She snuggled against me. "I'm too busy trying to save you."

Chapter 13

Faith left that evening for work, and I couldn't sleep—which for me was nothing out of the ordinary. In this instance, however, my insomnia didn't stem from preoccupying thoughts of death or credit card debt. This time, Faith was the source of my wide-eyed jitters, or rather her impending arrival home from work. She waited tables at Buck and Rita's, a straight club in Manhattan, and got off around 2:30 A.M. After closing, I presumed. After the floors were swept and the band had packed up, if there was a band. After the last of the breeders had paired up for the evening. I put on some music: TLC. Nothing better than T-Boz, the late Lefteye, and Chili to stoke one's already crazy/sexy/cool libido. This was one of those nights when I'd reach far under my bed for the BIG vibrator; only now, I had something—*someone*—better to look forward to. Yes, indeedy. This was a night for *l'amour*.

I switched CDs, boldly opting for the big city sound of Tower of Power. "Clever Girl," a song with loads of fat brass and Al Green-ish vocals. *Yes.* I felt OK, the best I'd felt in quite a while. You could almost say I felt rested. Wasn't I taking my medications like a good little girl? It was just after 1 A.M. Faith would be home in just an hour and a half. Home? Was *mi casa su casa* already? Hmph. I guess it was.

So I decided to do my hair. It was nothing elaborate, mind you—not like I broke out the hot rollers or anything. Just worked some mousse into the natural waviness. Assessed the gray. Added some shine. And, well, once you do the hair, why stop there? Why resist leaping into that big arena of cosmetics at my dressing table?

Please understand. It started out simple, maybe a touch of face powder. But God, all of a sudden my face was a project. Bob Vila's *This Old Whore*. Foundation. Rouge. Eyeliner. Mascara. Eye shadow. Lipstick. Spackle. The works. It felt strange to spend that much time in front of a mirror—I hadn't liked looking that closely at myself in a long time—but I must admit I was pleased with the end result. Sure, in the unforgiving light of day I probably would have looked like some sorry old hooker (Hey, hey, numma one G.I., me love you long time), but—nya-ha-ha!—it was night, and in the soft light from my art deco lamp, I was hot. Lava hot. The lamp itself, a fabulous find from one of my flea market excursions, gave off a calm, greenish glow through its angular shade, muting the otherwise harsh shapes of my apartment. Conical steel mixed with Depression-era cherry wood. Tables with blue glass tops adorned with martini shakers, handmade cigarette boxes, and other stylish trinkets. Wood floors and walls painted deep plum. Once an acquaintance had called my place masculine, but I saw it as rich and sensuous and strong. Frank Lloyd Wright, Philippe Starck, and Early Garage Sale.

I poked around in my closet. Hmm. There *had* to be

something that was sumptuously apropos. At last, my fingers found the silky, silvery gray robe and nighty. Bingo! The tags were still attached even. A virgin outfit! $600?! What violent mood swing had inspired this purchase? It had better be good. And oh, it was, it was. 2:45 A.M. She'd be home any second. I lit some candles and stood in front of the mirror again. Oh, yeah. Dig this. Sinsational. I'd do me in a heartbeat. Come and get it. I stood there and vogued for a few minutes, trying the robe tied, then untied. Then trying just the nightie, straps up. And then, straps down.

The lock on the front door popped. I sprang into bed, sprinkling Chanel as I went. Faith dragged in and headed straight for the bathroom.

Hey! What's the big idea? There I was all painted up and horny and she'd walked right past me. Was the honeymoon over so soon?

I could hear the shower running as I entered the kitchen.

"Are you hungry, darling?" I called out. Boy, I sounded needy. Like rich-old-lady needy. Like Norma Desmond in *Sunset Boulevard* needy. Ick.

"Huh?" She hadn't heard me. Good.

"I said..." I poked my head into the bathroom, swooning at the sight of her wavy silhouette through the shower stall door. "Are you hungry, deaf girl?"

"Death girl?"

"Deaf! Deaf!" A word that seemed ironic to yell. "Like Marlee Matlin!"

"Who? The woman in *Superman* was deaf?"

"You're thinking of Margo Kidder. Marlee Matlin was in *Children of a Lesser God*."

"Oh." A pause. "Sorry."

"Yeah, well, get it right next time." I remained in the doorway, taking in the view. Peeping. How lucky were those beads of water that slipped down and around Faith's curves and crevices. She looked like a piece of fruit just after you rinsed it off to eat. *Let's get down to busin*ess, I thought. *The business of seduction, that is.* Should I just forget all the frosting and go right for the cake? Run on in there and hop into the shower with her? In a movie, it would work. But in a movie, I wouldn't be wearing a cast, not to mention six hundred dollars worth of lingerie that was dry clean only, thanks. Shit.

"So are you hungry or not?"

"Not." She turned off the water.

No? Rats. There went my whole *Pretty Woman*-strawberries-and-champagne reenactment. But then again, what role would I want to play, exactly? Richard Gere? Puhlease. Deliver me from the hamster hall of shame. And Julia Roberts? Well...

"Shall I pour us some champagne then?"

The bottle was already in hand. Verichon et Clerque, 1985.

"Champagne?" She laughed. "It's 3 in the morning. Who are you, Joan Collins?"

"Yes, it's me, Joan Collins. I lost the British accent after *Dynasty*." What was up her ass? I try to be impetuous and all I get is rejection? It never worked this way before. Didn't all women love romance? Weren't we, as a gender, constantly striving to create the perfect mood?

"I'm sorry, Macy." She came out wearing my terry cloth robe, drying her hair with a towel. "Bad night."

I sat down on the end of the bed, motioning her to join me. She did.

"Do tell." Either I cared or it was just an angle to get into her pants—or in this case, her robe.

"Oh, these redneck guys from North Carolina," she sniffled. "They were, without a doubt, the biggest assholes I've ever seen."

"Really? How so?"

"Well, they were loud and obnoxious and they made this huge mess. One of them threw up on the floor and one of them hit the bartender." She continued drying her hair. "I swear, it was like an episode of *Cops*, only they were wearing shirts." She laughed. "You know how on *Cops* every drunk is wandering around with, like, a million tattoos and no shirt? That type of thing, only these guys kept their shirts on."

"Well, bully for them." I patted her knee. "A shining moment in white trash history."

Faith nodded, blowing her nose on a Kleenex she'd stashed in the pocket of my robe. She covered her eyes and moaned, sniffling again.

"What's wrong?"

"Oh, the smoke," she said. "Most of the time, it doesn't bother me, but sometimes it *kills* my sinuses. I have the worst headache."

"Stuffy head?" I asked, not that I needed to ask. She sounded like Edith Ann, for crying out loud.

"Um-hmm," she replied, leaning over onto my shoulder.

I put my arm around her but didn't pull her close like I wanted to. I wasn't used to giving half a shit about any lover, I guess. Was it my fault she chose to work in a smoky bar? Probably just trying to work me, right? Probably wanted me to say, "Oh, you poor little princess! Let me sweep you away from all this and you'll never have to wait tables again." Well, wrongo, missy. I've got your number.

"Why don't you quit?" *We'll see how she answers this one*, I thought. *We'll just see.*

"Most of the time, it doesn't bother me," she smiled, "And I like the people there. And I make good tips, so..."

So she was planning on sticking it out. Maybe she wasn't so ready to reach into my purse, after all. Maybe she just had sensitive sinuses and I should quit overanalyzing everything and just be nice. Like Faith.

But it's hard, you know? Hard to escape the game. Hard to show love in practical ways. I mean, it's much easier to bring a girl flowers than it is to, say, rub her feet or bring her an Alka Seltzer. It's much easier to exhibit contrived behavior in a relationship, to do the dance, than it is to really, you know, care. Caring is risky stuff. And I was truly getting into a risky area with Faith.

"Lie back," I stated, low and strong, like a gentle dictator, "and remove the robe."

"What?"

"You heard me." I made my way into the kitchen.

First-class airline tickets offer a great deal of privileges, one of which being the classic refreshing hot towel. After a long flight back from Switzerland a few years back, my seriously overcoked sinuses were comforted by such a treatment. I trusted that Faith too would benefit from this luxury. And upon finding the softest towel in my cabinet, I soaked it in water so hot I could see the steam rise over my reddened hands as I wrung it out.

"Close your eyes," I said as I reentered the bedroom. She was naked and her skin shone like silk in the moonlight that spilled in through the window. Faith moaned with pleasure as I carefully placed the towel over her eyes and sat beside her, holding my breath as I dared to run my fingers up her thigh, combing through the thick island of curls and eventually coming to rest with a caress at the soft fleshiness of her stomach. She was blind to me now, quite literally, and I felt heated and compelled to take a few liberties. No cheap grabs or fondles, but quiet, measured kisses planted at her hip, her shoulder, her temple—reassurances, I suppose, of our shared intimacy. Her nipples were erect. I slid my hands up to cup her breasts. Cold.

"I'll be right back," I said as I left her again, this time to search for a microwavable lubricant in the confines of my kitchen. Nothing but a bottle of Wesson oil, which was sure to provoke a rash of zits or visions of Florence Henderson, I concluded, neither being the desired result. I clomped into the bathroom and—aha!—took a bottle of baby oil from its spot on the shelf.

The bowl was hot but not untouchable when I removed it from the microwave. Perfect.

Faith had rolled onto her stomach. I tested the baby oil's temperature, then poured some onto the small of her back. She said nothing but moaned and whimpered lazily as I slid my hands up, thumbs tracing her spine until they reached the base of her skull. I repeated this several times, the warm oil allowing my palms to glide across her muscles like her back was a Ouija board and I was spelling out some lengthy message from beyond.

O-h-M-a-c-y-g-i-r-l-y-o-u-a-r-e-i-n-b-i-g-t-i-m-e-t-r-o-u-b-l-e-G-o-o-d-b-y-e...

"Macy." She spoke my name and invoked every song inside me. "Macy." She rolled to face me and invited my hands to touch.

Trembling, I released the last of the oil onto her chest

and stomach and stared into her eyes. Would what I had to offer her be enough? Could I ever be what she deserved?

"I love you, Macy." She whispered it. And from the way her eyes glowed, I sensed it might be the first time she'd ever said it to anyone. She was so young and unbruised, so sure of her profound discovery, so confident. Little did she know my heart had been scotch-taped over and over again until it was a suspicious-looking package no one dared open. Not even me.

You're only 23, I wanted to say, but I couldn't because I wanted to believe her even more than I wanted to be correct. So instead of saying what was right, instead of making a reason to the rhyme, I whispered "I love you" in return.

Chapter 14

I should have waited, you know? I should have found my own perfect timing, my own perfect moment to utter the inevitable three little words. Instead, I frowned and fretted, worried that she might not feel the weight of my reply, that it had seemed more of a natural response to her declaration than an expression of my own true feelings. And what if it *was* only a response? What if it *was* all a fraud? What if I'd talked myself into loving her to avoid being alone? Surely she would see through my ruse, and I'd be unmasked as the consummate liar and colossal fuck-up that I was. Everyone else would see it too, would witness whole the soap opera and *tsk-tsk-tsk* their way through lunch hours and smoke breaks and conversations on the telephone about how I'd blown my big chance, how I'd missed it by a nose, how I could never escape the shallow restraint of my own vanity or insecurity or some emotion as yet unnamed by those best-selling shrinks.

I'd grow old—well, older—and lose my looks, and wander the city: a self-proclaimed superdyke whose only endearing power was her ability to accessorize in the blink

Michelle Sawyer

of an eye. Muttering to myself. Muttering something about maracas that looked like oranges.

The phone rang and I didn't know which territory to brave: the unyielding gaze of a girl I was bound to disappoint or the sickening sink in my stomach I was bound to experience with any late-night phone call.

"Macy..." Faith reached for me with one hand, then two. "Come to bed."

"But the phone..."

"Let it ring," she said, still reaching.

I turned, shuffled over to the sofa, and found the cordless.

"Mace?"

Trish. Crying. Which made me relax a tad, since it meant that she was still alive, that this call wasn't "the call."

"Yeah, hon, it's me." I leaned back into the cushions, observing Faith's silhouette through the crack I'd left in the bedroom doorway. She was giving up, lying back down, and settling herself beneath the covers. Good girl.

"I know it's late...or early...or..." Her voice quaked. "I'm sorry."

"It's all right." I took a cigarette from the lead crystal box on the end table and struck a wooden match against my thumbnail with a pop. "So what's up, Chuck?"

"Is it OK to talk?" She hesitated. "I know you have company."

Since when did she ask permission to talk? "If you mean Faith, she's asleep." I spied the liquor cabinet and considered a martini. God, maybe I *was* Joan Collins.

Trish wasn't sick this time. That wasn't what it was about at all. Not that I had ever minded heading over in the middle of the night to hold her head out of the toilet because she felt guilty and ashamed to have her husband or kids help her puke at all hours.

No, I never minded. Sometimes it even felt sort of good to be so needed. But this call had been prompted by *Bewitched*. Yes, *Bewitched*. Darrin and Samantha. Tabitha. Endora (portrayed by Agnes Moorehead, who I always figured was a lesbian in real life—how could she be straight with a name like Moorehead?). *Bewitched*, the TV show. One episode would have been fine, maybe even two, but after 12 hours of viewing the *Bewitched* marathon on that goddamned *Nick at Nite*, Trish had whipped herself into a frenzy.

"Oh, God, she's dead, Macy!"

"I know, Trish." We'd been through this routine before. Michael Landon. Linda McCartney. And now it was...

"Elizabeth Montgomery! Samantha! Samantha died of cancer!"

"I know," I said, which was not a creative method of consolation, I realize, but I'd learned that it was best to just let her get it out. "And Wonder Woman's an alcoholic and Mr. Brady had AIDS. It's an ugly world, sweetheart. Nothing's sacred."

She sobbed for a few minutes, grieving over the death of television's most beloved witch, then...

"I love you, Macy."

I sighed. That one was always hard to hear—not because she said it, but because of how frantically she said it. Like this may be her last chance to tell me. Maybe it was.

"I know."

"I'm sorry it's so late."

"It's OK."

"But I'm just"—she laughed—"scared, you know?"

"I know."

"Oh, Christ, my life has turned into that fucking *Beaches* movie! And I hate that movie!"

I laughed. "I know."

The conversation stopped for a moment. Trish blew her nose. "I, uh..." She cleared her throat. "I'm glad you've got someone."

"You mean Faith?"

"No, I mean Eric Estrada. Of course I mean Faith!"

"Oh, well...thanks."

"I mean, it's good to finally see you settling down a little. You can't just be a whore-hopping globe-trotter for the rest of your life."

"Hey, hey, now..."

"No, I'm serious." And she was. "It's nice to know you've got someone to look after you."

Look after me? Shit, am I her retarded sister or something? Do I need to be bathed and changed and...

"I'm just glad you'll have someone"—she took a breath—"after I'm gone."

"What?"

"Well, let's face it, Macy, things have let up considerably for now, but it won't last. The fact is, I need a new liver."

"What, are you giving up hope? Jim Nabors got a new liver."

"Yes, and if I knew where he lived, I'd probably hold him at gunpoint and demand that he hand it over to me immediately, but..."

"Mickey Mantle got a new liver."

"And Mickey Mantle died anyway." She was in that mode now.

I felt the tears forming, the heat in my face and behind my eyes.

"I don't need to be looked after." I took a drag from my cigarette. "I'm doing rather well for myself now, with my travel agency, in case you hadn't noticed."

"Well, sure, you've got everything under control at your business, but..."

"But what?"

"Well, you've walked around like a goddamned ghost for the last six months. You're thin as a rake. And sickly. And neurotic. And an alcoholic, if you ask me."

"Yeah? Well, I'm not asking you."

"I'm just saying." She was on track, and Trish was hard to beat when she was on track. "It's nice to see you eating better and going to the doctor. That girl's good for you. See, you're that type of person."

"Oh, pray tell." I had raised my voice, and it was deep and husky. "Tell us, oh, enlightened one. What type of person am I?"

Anyone else would have heard the hostility in my tone and backed off. But not Trish. Trish knew she had me. She always had me. She could push me and I'd take it. Lead me around. Tell me what to do. And it didn't matter how tall I was or how much money I had or how good I looked naked, I'd always back down—mouth off a little, then back down. She knew this, so she was going for it, going for my pulsating jugular, and I was setting her up to do it right. Hit me in the ego, right in the old breadbasket.

"Maybe this is not for me to say," she began.

"Go ahead," I said. "Tell me I'm helpless, that I'll

always be helpless without you or Faith or somebody to tell me when and how to wipe my ass because, let's face it, without my looks I'd be nobody, nobody, nobody, just a two-bit Republican stuck manning the phones at some tool and dye shop in my hometown, making minimum wage, married with two kids, shopping for ill-fitting polyester blazers with matching slacks at the local Kmart, and wishing I had the guts to slice open my wrists because I couldn't help sneaking peeks at the old man's *Playboy*s and wondering how I could get me some of that!"

"OK, well, I can see you're not in the mood for this..."

"No, please, go on with this oh, so well-meaning attack on my character. You, who omitted me from your wedding because I wasn't 'family,' when I knew goddamn well it was because I was gay and your mother thought it was inappropriate, forcing me to watch your homely cousin Edna act as your maid of honor as I towered over every short, hairy Jew boy who dared muster a half-assed hustle at your reception, making me extremely aware of how isolated I was, how threatening I was to the delicate balance of morality established by your family. I was the only one there who could have made that tangerine nightmare of a bridesmaid's dress look less than laughable! But noooooooo..."

"Please." I clenched my teeth. "Please continue. Please subject me to your keen insights and infinite wisdom."

"OK, fine." Trish said. "You're weak."

And suddenly I remembered my mother's kitchen in Piqua—the heart of her house. I was 9 or 10 and had at last found the nerve to spout back. As her eyes sparked hate and despair, I felt proud of my uncharacteristic and open defiance, standing with clenched fists and teeth for about 20 seconds until I crawled under the sink and cringed behind the closed cabinet door as she shrieked, "I'll kill you, you little bitch!" Flinching from the pings and plocks of spoons, knives, and other utensils against the door, I pinched the tips of my fingers trying to hold it shut, to keep me safe in the dank, bleachy smell. Me and my big mouth. All blow and no show. Weak. Even then, I had a decent block but no right hook to follow it with.

"Macy?" She was regretful now. I could hear it, feel it, but gave no response. I'd lost my wind. I was tired. My side throbbed and my eyes itched and it was time to retire for the evening or morning or whatever it was.

"Good night, Trish."

"Macy, I didn't mean it..."

"I know. OK." I sighed. "Neither did I, I'm just... We just both need to go to bed."

Faith was asleep. There was no sense in waking her. I knew what was coming. My chest was already seizing. I slipped down from the sofa and made my way through the darkness and into the bathroom. Once inside, I closed the door behind me and turned on the hot water in the shower full-blast. Asthma is one of those diseases that makes you learn all the tricks, jump through the hoops like a wheezing trained poodle. I'd learned this one at about age 10 when Vi had scooped me into the bathroom during an attack. It worked now as it had then, the steam billowing out through the open glass door and hitting my airways with almost instant relief. I sat down on the floor and rested my head against the cold tile wall. I was a big girl, after all. I could take care of myself. If only Trish could see me now.

I waited there for a few minutes, choking intermittently and taking a deep draw from the inhaler before returning to a comfortable slouch on the sofa. It was early morning, almost 5. The cough was still unpredictable and occasionally explosive, so I opted to sleep right where I was and let Faith get her rest. But first, I opened my planner. Where had I stashed the last of that dandy nose candy from my last venture to South Beach? I'd sure as hell be needing a little pick-me-up to make it through the day at work.

I was expected in at the office at noon, just to go over some things with Lavinia. And then at 2, well, whoa, that was the biggie. Not since early spring had the name Betty Butler graced my planner's lined pages. Pretentious and oversprayed, Betty Butler was no beauty, but to me she looked like a million bucks. 13.6 million bucks, to be exact. Tomorrow at 2 P.M. Tomorrow, tomorrow...

I lounged languidly in the cushiness of my leather sofa, eyes closing to thoughts of Piqua's picket fences, legs pumping the pedals of my pink Schwinn bicycle. My long hair was caught and lifted by the summer wind as I raced down the hill. Those precious seconds of freedom were followed by an hour of secretly picking gravel out of my leg after failing to successfully navigate a "no-hands" turn into our driveway. I was crouched behind the kitchen door, tending to my stinging shin, when...

"What the hell do you mean, you won't deal with him?" It was the raised voice of my father.

I peered around the corner and into his den. Vi stood at the window. From the way she held her cigarette up, arm bent at the elbow *a la* Bette Davis, I knew she was pissed; but she bit her tongue, as was her style when she was angry. Very together, you know. Very collected and smooth. Never intimidated by what Bill Delongchamp had to say. Oh, no. Vi had fried bigger fish than he'd ever be and she knew it. So did he.

That's why it seemed so peculiar that he was blowing his stack to her. He usually knew better. This had to be something big.

She continued to look out the window, exhaling a cloud of smoke with a defiant, red-lipsticked frown.

"I mean exactly what I said," she said tersely. "How else can I say it so you'll understand? In Spanish, perhaps? Russian? Sign language?"

She looked at my father, then looked away, back to whatever it was that had her attention outside. "I won't deal with him, Bill."

I sat down in the hall and eavesdropped. Shame, shame, I know, but shit, I was a kid. It was my job.

"The man brings thousands of dollars to our company."

"Oh, suddenly it's 'our' company." She laughed, looking at him, looking through him, her blue eyes flashing with contempt.

"You bet it's our company!" Dad bellowed. "And we both have to pull our own weight or we'll be in the poorhouse."

"We'll not land in the poorhouse with the loss of Toby Blake's appliance contract, Bill." She shrugged. "I got the contract, and now I'm dropping it. It's that simple, darling. I'll make up for the money with someone else. I've got two new deals coming in next week."

"And both of them together are worth maybe half of what Toby's is." Dad rounded his desk and reached out to touch her arm. She moved away. "C'mon, Vi. Be a sport. The guy grabs your ass one time and you give up?"

"It's not his ass to grab." She continued to concentrate on something outside, something else. "You of all people should feel that way."

"And I do!" Enter Dad, champion cajoler. "But business is business, Vi. You know that. And as your husband,

I completely understand. But as your boss?" He arched his eyebrows. "Well..."

Vi turned sharply; her eyes narrowed. "You know goddamn well that I have nearly doubled our gross revenue in the year I've been married to you."

"Well, now, let's be fair." He said it in such a tone that I knew whatever he was about to say next would be total bullshit. "I'm sure you've done your share, but our company's success is not due to you alone, Vi."

"Oh, really?" She stepped so close that she was pressing against him. "And who do you think should share the credit for this? Ken, your little flunky who wouldn't have the ambition to piss if his pants were on fire?"

"Now, Vi..." Condescending.

Vi grabbed a file folder and blew out in such a rage that I remained unnoticed as I spied openly in the hall. BAM! The door slammed and gravel flew up, hitting the front windows as Vi's Eldorado sped out of the drive, returning hours later at the same wicked pace. The points of her stiletto heels pounded the ground with each step. Dad was still at his desk. Vi hardly slowed her march to throw the manila folder in front of him, unbuttoning her blouse as she headed upstairs. Her meeting with the infamous Toby Blake had been a success, obviously, as Dad whooped with joy upon opening the file and called "That's my girl!" up the stairs.

The shower came on, and as I heard it, I wondered why Vi would be taking a shower so late in the day. But later on I figured it out. When she married an appliance storeowner from the Midwest, Vi probably concluded that her days of having to shake her moneymaker were gone. But business was business, and the term "sexual harassment" had not yet been coined. So much for the good old days. Apparently, penetrating that "good old boy network" sometimes meant letting the good old boys do a little penetrating of their own.

Vi was sitting at her dressing table applying cold cream to her face when I finally had the courage to check on her. I say courage not because I feared her, but because I didn't really know what to say. So I crept in with a drink as an offering, a drink made just the way she liked it. Not like it was complicated—straight Southern Comfort on the rocks—but even as a kid I paid attention to the details, like dropping only two ice cubes, no more than two, into the glass and filling it two inches from the bottom with the remotely peachy-smelling, caramel-colored liquor she loved so well. It had to be just right. An art. A science. I'd watched her do it countless times at the end of the workday.

Since Vi's arrival on Planet Piqua, I'd watched her every move, and had gotten into the habit of taking mental notes of all her behaviors and rituals. I took comfort in the knowledge that every morning she would sit up and stretch, pad sleepily down to the kitchen to turn on the percolator, take a shower and fix her hair and makeup while the coffee was brewing, lay out her clothes for the day, and return to the kitchen in her robe to sit and sip coffee, nibble toast, and smoke her first cigarette. If there was fresh orange juice, she might pour herself a tiny glass, but only half full because it was rough on her stomach (something about the acid in citrus fruit). If I timed it just right, I could sprint out to the front porch before she came back downstairs and have her paper folded nice and neat next to her coffee cup. And sometimes, if I had time, I'd make her toast and have it waiting for her on a plate, all buttered and nicely cut, with a little dish of strawberry jam on the side like the restaurants did it. Some might think it odd for a kid to be so devoted to a stepparent. But growing up in a war zone made me appreciate the stability of her actions, the continuity of her routine. With Vi in charge, there were regular bedtimes, dinner times, and trips to the doctor and dentist. There was never a day when her shoes and handbag didn't match, when her colors didn't coordinate, when her hair didn't look just right. While Dad and I stumbled through the house like crashing cymbals and shattering glass, Vi moved with the cool, sensual rhythm of a stand-up bass. A sultry swing number. Jazz in high heels.

"Vi?" I stood frozen in the doorway, holding the glass with two cocktail napkins, careful not to contaminate it with my messy kid fingerprints or melt the ice with the warmth from my hands.

She turned and smiled, a sad clown in her white painted face.

"Come on in." I handed her the drink and she nodded in approval. "Oh, and I see you've brought my medicine. How thoughtful!"

Vi took a gulp from the glass, and I was thrilled. Soon, she would develop that slight, rosy glow, her voice becoming rich and deep, as if she had a cold. It was a strong voice, like a man's, only smoother, kinder. The thundering resonance of Vi's whiskey-in-the-evening voice always made me feel safe. After all, who would cross her?

"Thank you, my sweet."

"You're going to bed early." I followed her as she gingerly climbed under the covers.

"Oh, I'm just resting for a few minutes." She leaned back and winced. "I think I've strained my back." She must've seen the alarm in my eyes. "Nothing serious, love, just overexerted myself is all."

"What happened? Did you pick up something you weren't supposed to?" I was thinking maybe a stove or refrigerator or something. But looking back, Toby Blake must've weighed in at around three bills. He probably crunched her bones like a big, sweaty steamroller.

"You could say that," she sighed.

"I can get the hot water bottle for you..."

"I threw it away." She shook her head. "Your father was using it last week for *his* back and we woke up in a warm puddle. I thought he'd wet the bed. Say..." She sat up and winced again. "Would you be willing to help me out tomorrow? I'm entertaining the Nickie Loves."

Say no more. The Nickie Loves. Vi said it that way, in plural form, because there were three of them. Three people named Nickie Love, in the same immediate family.

Sunny weekends belonged to our kidney-shaped pool, a must for the average status-seeker in Piqua. Vi and Dad entertained a variety of guests; the most interesting and just plain loudest were the Nickie Loves. Nickie, Sr. was the husband and father of the Love clan. He wore a pinkie ring and gold chains like Johnny Stompanato. A plush crop of chest hair piled out of his white silk shirts. He had olive skin that tanned nicely, wavy hair, a big nose, sensuous lips, bushy brows, and sad, exotic eyes. Nickie Love, Sr. (who had changed his name from Nicholas Taglia upon becoming a U.S. citizen) was the ultimate hot Italian male, a real estate dealer with reputed mob ties whose bar, the Club Love, had mysteriously burnt to the ground a few years back. He was a portrait of masculinity as he postured extensively in our swank pool area, boisterously charming, sweeping Vi off her feet whenever the mood struck him to cut a rug or playfully toss her into the pool.

"Goddamn it, Nickie, you'll drown her!" his wife would yell, jealous but tolerant of the mutual admiration between her husband and Vi. Vi was a good friend to her, her only friend, really, since the rest of the ladies of Piqua snubbed her on a grand scale for being an ex-stripper. Big-breasted and pretty in a burlesque, costume-jewelry kind of way, Nickie looked up to Vi and trusted her. So what if there was an attraction there, right? Who cared?

And then there was their son, little Nickie, whose coal-black eyelashes and muscular frame drove the girls in my school absolutely out of their skirts. Tina Wilson, who rode my bus and was rumored to have gone "all the way" on more than one occasion with several different boys, told Trish and me that you could tell the size of a guy's wang by the way he walked. Like if he walked all stiff and proper, forget it, she said. Cocktail-frank city. But if he walked kind of bow-legged, kind of slow and funny, then you could count on him carrying quite a load behind that zipper. And from the way little Nickie swaggered confidently down the sidewalks of our town, he was definitely of the latter variety.

None of us in our clique ever had the chance to test Tina's theory, however. By the time we were of teen sex-pot age, little Nickie had bought the farm, killed by a drunk driver as he rode his motorcycle home from night class at the community college. His was, as I recall, my first funeral.

"Macy?"

Someone was shaking me, tugging at the sleeves of my silvery robe. Slipping the nightgown up over my head.

Leading me by the hand as I clomped naked through the dark. I was knee-deep in little Nickie Love's Catholic funeral by the time I realized I was back in bed with Faith.

"Oh, God, what time is it?" I was still mostly asleep. "Is it time for work? Am I late?"

"No, Macy."

"Because I really shouldn't go into the office like this."

"Go back to sleep." Faith giggled.

"OK," I yawned. "Good night, Dolores."

"Good night, Ma..." She jerked. "Dolores? Who's Dolores?"

"My sexy little political activist girlfriend." I stretched and popped my shoulder. "From Germany."

"Oh." Faith snuggled against me. "What kind of political activist?"

"She stages protests...against mimes."

"Mines? Like land mines?"

"No, *mimes*," I insisted. "Like Marcelle Marceau. Damned mimes are everywhere."

Chapter 15

Why is it that as men get older, they get more distinguished? Wrinkles seem to suit them, like something they've earned, some classic, necessary accessory. A gold watch. A key to the fucking executive washroom. But women, hell, women just droop and sag and schlep around as monuments to gravity's cruel nature. Like we're punished, you know? Punished.

"It's the Catholic Church again."

This from someone to my left.

"Witch burnings originated as a plot to gain land for the Catholic Church," a man said, eating his cracked crab. "Most wealthy landowners were older women. So when some wretched old crone was deemed a witch, her land and possessions went to the church upon her execution. Thus, the witch burnings and drownings and tortures ensued." He lit a cigar, puffing it lightly. A big cigar.

"Drownings?" the blonde sitting across from him asked—like she couldn't believe it or something. Duh.

So, what was this? Agent and ingenue? Director and

audition? Professor and student setting up a little extra credit at the Russian Tea Room?

"Ridiculous." He continued to puff away.

Ridiculous. Did he know how ridiculous he looked? How blatantly phallic the enormous Cuban appeared as he lovingly sucked at its tip, the smoke filtering through his discolored teeth and mustache? How strange it was to see him cling to its trunk with his lily-white fingers and buffed nails. A primate at best, discussing the desecration and eternal rip-off of womankind. *Men are strange,* I thought. *Quite strange, indeed.* The girl had to be 20 years younger than he was.

And within seconds he caught my glance from behind his Foster Grants and I was on my way, there long enough only to pass judgment as I passed through the crowd.

"I suppose this marks the end of an era," Betty said as we were about to take our seats. Her collagen lips curved with pleasure at her secret joke.

Kiss, kiss, hug, hug. She was in desperate need of a touch-up on those dark roots. That Ivanna-wanna-be fake-and-bake tan look sure was working for her, in a *nouveau-riche* kind of way. Like trash with cash.

"Please clarify." I settled into my chair across from her. "Elaborate."

"Very well, then." She folded her arms over D-sized implants, eyed me through a jungle of false eyelashes, and patted one half of her piled-up hair. "I hear you've been hooked."

"Hooked?" My voice cracked like a boy entering puberty.

"Hooked." She leaned in, watching me squirm. "Landed. Reeled in like the big-mouth bass that you are."

Betty sighed dramatically. "Oh, darling, I never, *ever* thought it would happen to *you*."

Like I had cancer, or something. Like commitment was some incurable, inoperable disease. Like a partner had to be surgically removed but always left you with remaining growths and hideous scars. I couldn't have agreed with her more.

"Hold on, now, my little sliver of angel food cake," I purred, fighting the urge to cough, curbing the manic speech pattern that only cocaine can inspire. "If you believe I am hooked, you are sadly mistaken."

It would be very bad for business if I was known to be hitched—especially with Betty and her entourage of middle-aged lovelies. Yes, indeedy, it never failed. Five minutes after boarding the cruise ship and they were all over me like I was edible underwear. It was my duty to maintain the image of "the single gal." A business thing. I lifted a napkin to my mouth to stifle the volume of my cough. It worked. Sort of. That is to say, the actual noise was muted, but the sheer ferocity of the spell was uncontrollable. Christ. Tears came to my eyes. How embarrassing.

"My word, old girl!" Betty's eyes bulged, herself a bit embarrassed by the length of my spell. "Are you going to be all right?"

I smiled and nodded, trying to be as suave as possible as I sat, choking, in a public place, in front of a major client—in the fucking Russian Tea Room, no less. Our waiter arrived at the table with a pitcher, and I gulped down some water.

"Are you all right, madame?"

Oh, joy. Now he was in on the fun. I made an *OK* signal and he was off to tend to someone more important. Tight-assed little snoot. I mean, who did he think he was with that silly little mustache? David Niven? John Waters, maybe?

"Macy, darling." Betty touched my arm.

"So sorry about the interruption."

"I'd get that checked out if I were you, sweetheart. Sounds like bronchitis and I should know. I've had it three times."

Thank you, Dr. Quinn, Medicine Woman.

"Oh, no." I slid my tongue across my teeth and smiled at the sight of the jewels on her fingers. "I'm fine."

"Whatever you say, lover, but it sure does sound like bronchitis to me." She slurped down the rest of her drink. "And you know, bronchitis nearly *killed* Elizabeth Taylor."

"Not to mention the dinosaurs. Or was it the Ice Age that brought them to extinction?" She giggled at this drivel, if you can believe it. "So," I went on. "Where have you been hanging your garter belts these days?"

"Just got in from Hollywood"—she lit a cigarette, one of those skinny little lollipop-stick deals—"where I was attending a Chakra Khan seminar."

"Didn't she used to sing with Rufus?"

Betty stared at me quizzically. "It's a he that I am speaking of. Abu Chakra Khan." She said it so seriously, obviously having been had to the hilt by this newest of New Age guru dudes. Ah, the idle rich.

Traffic control to cockpit. Traffic control to cockpit. Initiate killer smile. Prepare to kiss ass.

"Well, I hear he's absolutely amazing."

"Oh, he is..."

Blah, blah, blah. So started the ramble onward through the various spiritual journeys that Chaka Khan or Chakra Khan or whatever swami trickster had taken her on.

A young woman walked by in form-fitting slacks, a welcome distraction, needless to say, and I mentally traced the outline of her hips.

MMMMMMmmmmm...

Hmmmmmmmmm... A very fashion mag editor type let her eyes do the same at a table across the room and our gazes met. We smiled "shame on you, sister" smiles at each other and went about our separate business.

"So did you hit any clubs in L.A.?" I asked, as if any self-respecting doorman would let her sorry old ass in.

Never wanting to feel the icy breeze of rejection as a club door slammed in my face, I had long since given up my position in Manhattan's after-hours glam sector. Studio 54 was dead, anyway, its hanging coke spoon moon auctioned off with the rest of the kitsch. But then again, I guess the doors of most any hip, happening nightspot might swing wide when a fifty greased its palm. Miss Butler would always be able to slither in somehow.

"Lunch at the Polo Lounge..."

"Of course."

"And a brief stop at, oh, Johnny Depp's place. What is it?" She snapped her fingers. "The Viper Room."

"Where that young actor died. Oh..." I frowned. "Keanu Reeves or whoever it was." *Boooorrrrring.*

"I believe you're thinking of River Phoenix." She laughed. "Keanu Reeves is very much alive."

"Are you sure?" I snarked. "That might explain his acting range."

She laughed again. A haughty, fake laugh, or at least I hoped it was fake. Dear God. How much longer would I have to stay with this wretched beast? She'd even put on weight, I observed, not that a woman had to be some scrawny little pipsqueak to be attractive. But I didn't *want* to see the good in Betty. I wanted to see the flaws. And there were plenty.

Jesus H. Christ. I couldn't look at my watch, as Betty Butler was the type to be offended by something like that. There simply was no clock when you were with Betty, which meant I would be enslaved by her whims for at least two more hours, not counting any side trips to Bloomingdale's or Bendel or, heaven forbid, Gucci. Ah, yes, yet another drawback of being a lesbian of the lipstick variety and choosing to hobnob with such. A manly sort of lesbo could spend two bucks on a can of Skoal and two hours at a tractor pull and it was all over. But me? No, I had consistently shied from trucker's wallets with their dangling chains and boot-cut Levi's and Harleys. I was the complicated career broad draped in platinum and silk who liked jazz and sushi and the occasional auction at Sotheby's. Shallow. Pretentious. I was asking for it—and I was definitely her type.

We skipped the shopping excursion. Initially, I was grateful for that. But Betty was lonely, and she liked the leverage of her wealth, and thus she had the privilege of shifting up from first gear all the way to fifth.

I don't recall the name of her hotel. It had a marble lobby, which is not a definitive characteristic for a hotel in New York. Every building recycled for the umpteenth time and listed in the historical registry, each brick handcrafted God knows how many years ago. The frigging homeless shelter probably has a marble lobby.

By the time we arrived, I was in this horrid haze, having indulged in a cornucopia of substances. Cocaine. Stoli. Ungodly amounts of cholesterol. Betty was oblivious to my altered condition, however, and as she dragged me by the arm down the hall like a child dragging her mother through FAO Schwarz, I knew and she knew that she had me exactly where she wanted me. I wasn't stupid. I knew what was up. Betty represented 250 customers. Good, cash-in-hand party girls who forked over two grand for a cruise ticket like it was lunch money. And, yeah, ordinarily I wouldn't have thought twice about giving her a little bang for her buck. Fair is fair, after all, and letting Betty Butler go spelunking in my cervix for an hour or so would be the easiest half a mil I'd ever booked. But wait just one cotton-picking minute. Wasn't I attached? Faith was probably doing something cute and domestic right now, buying groceries or making my bed. Our bed.

Betty and I were alone in the elevator, so I lit a cigarette and thought of the commercial where the guy asks, "What do you want on your tombstone?" And the other guy, all dressed for his execution, says, "Pepperoni and sausage." I cracked up laughing. She gripped my arm and marched me off at her floor, giggling. I didn't want to look at her. I knew she'd be smiling that broad smile of conquest, and why not? I'd smiled it too, many times. I ran my free hand through my hair. Nervous. But why? A few days with Faith and suddenly I'd developed a case of the scruples? Shit. No way. Not when business was concerned. Not when it involved money. By conceding to Betty's advances, I'd be doing everybody a favor, Faith included. I was just bringing home the bacon, damn it! What were we to do, scrape by on a waitress's salary? I think not.

The room was nice enough. A suite, of course, with all the unnecessary accoutrement, like a desk and a bar and a refrigerator filled with $5 candy bars. We emptied several itty-bitty bottles of Chivas, and by 3 P.M. I was positively afloat. Meanwhile Betty had been working up her nerve. Small advances. A touch on the wrist, the hip, the collarbone.

"Prince has converted to being a Jehovah's Witness," I blurted out, a last-ditch effort at small talk. "I mean, the Artist Formerly Known as Prince. Whatever."

"Oh?" She didn't care. She was drunk and horny and only humoring me before the kill.

"Yeah, can you believe it?" I was babbling. "Too bad. I guess that's bound to hamper the production of the *A Very Prince Christmas* CD. Such a shame. I was so looking forward to hearing 'Rudolph, the Sexy Motherfucking Reindeer.'"

No response. Just a dopey grin and bedroom eyes.

"They, uh..." I fiddled with my bracelet. "...don't celebrate Christmas."

I was seated in a chair at the desk. Betty knelt before me and began stroking my ankle, then my calf, then...

"While I was waiting for you at lunch, and on the plane..." She slid her hand up my thigh and unfastened my stocking from its garter. "I was thinking of you." She rolled down my stocking. "And it made me wet." And then she smiled sheepishly, yanking at my trousers. "Do you think that's silly?"

"Silly? No, no."

"And I'm still wet for you, Macy."

"Well...uh..." I clutched the arms of the chair. "I can get you a towel if you like."

She stood and took my glass.

"Let's freshen our drinks."

Betty moved toward the bar and I could hear the fabric in her skirt shifting as she walked, hear the clattering of ice into our glasses, hear music? Satie. Yes. It was sad Eric at the keys, or at least a reasonable facsimile. A suicidal interlude sprinkled darkly into the room from hidden speakers.

I wondered if Mr. Satie had ever been happy.

"Are you trying to ply me with liquor?" I clapped my hands together and ran my fingers through my hair. "Because I'm already plied. Plied and plowed."

"I don't know why I'm telling you this, you scamp." She returned with the drinks and was back on her knees. "But I've always had a bit of a crush on you."

"Moi?" What a shock. "And you never said a thing."

"You know what the girls on the ship call you?" She parted my bare knees with her small, cold hands, jagged rings scratching into my skin. "The goddess."

"What?" I laughed, slapping my thighs back together and pinching her fingers between my knees. "That's the most hilarious thing I've ever heard. I..."

Once again, she pried my legs open.

"They say you taste like honey."

"Betty, please."

"And I said to myself, 'I've got to have a taste.'"

I couldn't believe she was saying this shit. Lines from a bad porno comic book were spilling out all over the place. This was *life*, damn it.

"Betty! Hey, listen. Wait." I threw up my hands, praying for some semblance of control. "I forgot to tell you something." I took a breath, calmed myself, and resumed. "I'm straight."

"You're straight." She huffed in disbelief. "You, who wore my gay pride flag as a sarong on the beach in Maui? I beg to differ."

"I think maybe I should go."

Suddenly, I was thinking clearly. You know how it happens, how it comes to you all at once. *Boom*. Faith. This was the first time I'd felt real love, the first time that real love had been reciprocated, the first time I'd have dinner waiting for me when I got home from work. Yeesh. And oh, was it ever work.

Betty pulled at my hands and I resisted.

"Maybe you don't understand," she said.

Oh, I understood. Despite my liquored-up status, I keenly understood the politics of the situation. And then, as if matters weren't gruesome enough already, she uttered those seven little words to me.

"I have a dildo in my suitcase."

I threw my hand to my forehead and giggled, exasperated. "OK, fine." I closed my eyes. "Fire it up."

"I was hoping *you* would..."

I opened my eyes and sat, mouth agape, disgusted by the horror before me. It was a dildo all right, an extra large bumpy fella with a bunch of straps attached. Like a harness. Dear God, not a strap-on! Had I stumbled into a scene from *Blue Velvet* or what? This was not me anymore. I wanted Yankee pot roast with baby carrots and a bottle of merlot and Faith in my king-size bed watching *Laverne & Shirley* reruns. I did not want this.

"Uh, no." I folded my arms. "Just put old long dong back in his travel case."

"Don't tell me you've never seen one?"

"I've seen plenty," I said plainly. "And a few years back, I may have taken on the task, but I'm just not up to it, Bets. Sorry."

The way I saw it, I didn't have a choice. Pounding her into the headboards with this tremendous appliance was sure to send me into cardiac arrest. Strap-ons can be quite a workout, as I recalled from my earlier days in the city, and it was better to know my limitations than to poop out mid-mount and lie wheezing at her side as she struggled to finish without me.

Some goddess.

Betty looked humiliated, then offended, then angry. All this and more with a big rubber dick hanging lifelessly in her hands. A bad visual indeed. Definitely not one for the Christmas card.

"So, what do you suggest we do here?" It was an edgy tone, a tone that told me I'd better do something quick or the deal was down the toilet.

I unbuttoned my blouse and set aside the sick feeling in my stomach. I'd deal with that feeling and all other feelings later, at a more convenient time. Business was business. I slid down in the chair and felt my soul descend into the realm of loveless sex once again.

Betty worked my body like it was a toy, a CB radio whose knobs she twisted without remorse, whose microphone she screamed into and commanded a response. I had rejected the big, fake penis and now I would have to pay for angering the big, fake penis god. So the more I held back from the nudges and pokes of her tongue and nose and lips, the more determined her attack on my clitoris became. Before I could stop myself, she had won.

"I'll see you on the ship," she said, watching me dress.

Chapter 16

Horns blared. Steam hissed out of vents. People brushed against my shoulders and arms as I made my way down the sidewalk in front of Betty's hotel. My body felt bruised, my motion and mind out of sync with the world around me. New York had always seemed so full of light and song and desire, and I had always managed to feed off that tremendous energy. But now I was totally spent. New York's rhythm and throb was working against me on this occasion, and it caught me off guard.

It wasn't that Betty Butler had stolen my spirit. No, no—much worse. I'd simply given in under the *guise* of collecting my check. A big check, granted. But no matter how big it was, there were clearly deeper motives.

Just then, however, I wasn't focused on those motives. I was focused on my guilt, which was a fresh, horrible way for me to feel about the way I'd always done business. Suddenly I had a conscience. Great. I'd always laughed at movies where the hooker has a heart of gold, because as much as all of us might want it to happen, people never really seemed to change. In my world, everyone fell off the wagon sooner or later. Everybody was looking to score. And if you sold out once, it only got easier. Believe me. If it worked the first time, why wouldn't it work again?

But if all this was true, why did I feel so lousy?

I mean, God, it's not like I'm a criminal, I told myself. *Some third-rate gang-banger or something*. It's not like I was being malicious. I was only trying to provide, right? I was only doing what I knew, what I had to do to get what I wanted. I mean *needed*. I mean, you *want* to watch television or read a magazine. You *need* to make money to pay the bills to survive, right? And it's all give and take, all about sacrifices, and that's what I tried to convince myself I had made by fucking around with Betty Butler: a sacrifice. Sealing the deal. Making it happen. Yeah, I'd done what was right. And doing what was right didn't always feel right, did it? Sometimes, it felt...

Sleazy?

I ducked into a cab. The spicy stench of several-days-old B.O. stung my nostrils and I gagged. Why wasn't there a hygiene requirement for cab drivers? My eyes met the cabbie's in his rearview mirror.

"Christopher," I said, flicking my Bic.

"No, no, no!" He tapped frantically at a NO SMOKING sign tucked into the passenger-side visor.

I poked a 20 through the Plexiglas door that separated us. "Come on," I said. "It's been a long day. I'll crack the window."

So he took the 20 and shut up about it. I was a little disappointed, half-hoping he would swear at me in some foreign tongue and hold his ground. Have some principles, for crying out loud. No dice. I removed the mobile phone from my planner and dialed Trish. She was home from the hospital now, maybe strong enough to talk. And I couldn't go home just yet.

She answered on the second ring. Pretty quick, I'd say, for a terminal cancer patient.

"Hello?"

I cleared my throat, lowering my voice, which sounded raspier than normal anyway. "Good day, ma'am. If I could have just a moment of your time..."

"Well..."

"I'd like to tell you about a special offer..."

"Now, wait..." She was getting annoyed. *Yes!*

"...on our collectible 'Serial Killers of the Twentieth Century' commemorative plates."

"Macy..." She laughed.

"Order now and receive a genuine reproduction of the vital organs found in Jeff Dahmer's refrigerator!"

"Hey, kid, I tried to call you at work, but they said you'd left for an appointment. Where are you?"

"I'm in a cab on 44th. I was thinking I might stop over, if you're up for a visit."

Senior year: Trish sits on the bathroom floor under the tampon machine. Her Levi's are so tight she's just had to employ my help zipping them up after she peed.

"Trish, I'm gay."

"So?" She takes a hit off a roach and passes it to me.

"I'm gay, Trish." Maybe she hasn't heard me.

"Yeah? So? And I love you." She reached out and gave me a push. "Not enough to fuck you, of course, but..."

"Of course."

164

"Now, are you going to hit that before it goes out, or what?"

"The prodigal friend returneth!" Trish threw her arms around me and squeezed. She was energetic and had good color but seemed to be...smaller. I hugged her cautiously in return and caught a sudden taste of the day's multiple martinis and fusion lunch disaster boiling up into my throat and mouth. Then suddenly the vivid memory of the stink of myself still lingering on Betty Butler's breath as she leaned in with a satisfied smile. *Don't I get a kiss?*

"Be right back," I said, moving past her, lunging for the bathroom. And not a moment too soon, I might add—the minute the door closed behind me, I was on my knees, retching into the toilet.

"I'll be out in a second!" I called, standing and reaching for a...Dixie cup? Of course. An item such as a Dixie cup holder might seems out of place in my house, but not *chez Trish*. Trish was, after all, a mom, and moms had things around the house like Dixie cups and bobby pins and gallon jugs of milk. Her home was just that: a home. Restored solid oak doors and trim led you from one non-threatening room to the next. Lots of mauve and taupe and other serene colors. Floral prints. And the smell of that stuff you boil—potpourri, I guess it's called, a smell you'd never find in the contemporary confines of my sleek abode. Sleek and clean and, well...cold.

I left the bathroom and found Trish sitting on the sofa, pouring tea. Instinctively, I moved to sit beside her, but stopped myself and aimed instead for the dainty, uninviting Hepplewhite chair in the corner. In the years since her marriage to Hal, I'd trained myself to leave the space at her side open for him, not wanting to put any implied imposition on their relationship. It was not to be a contest between him and me for her affections. I knew that. He was a good guy who loved her and deserved to be at her side. And since her illness, I'd wanted my distance anyway.

I folded my hands on my lap and took another look at my friend. The wig was a tasteful one and very flattering, I'm sure, compared to the wispy tendrils that lay under it. Golden and thick, her hair had come out in clumps and handfuls when the treatments began—a goddamn shame. Other than that, she still looked about the same as she had before: lovely, with chiseled cheekbones and eyes like the girl in *The Last Picture Show*. Trish had been a runner-up the year I was crowned Piqua Peach Queen, and rightfully so. I had banked on her winning, not me. But she'd cheered harder than anyone when my name was announced and even helped me find my tiara later that night after I lost it making out with Melanie Pennbrooke under the bleachers at the fairground.

I smiled and reflected. Melanie Pennbrooke. My first kiss. Real kiss, anyway. An unassuming beauty with brains, she'd sat in the desk in front of me in history class and...

"What?" Trish shot me a look and snapped her fingers. "Hello? Did you stop by to stare at my walls? What are you looking at?"

"Nothing." I blushed. Still Trish, after all this. Only a bit smaller. And I wondered if this is how I would see her go—shrinking away until she simply faded into the conservative tones of her brownstone's interior, gone bit by bit rather than all at once.

I slumped forward and held my head in my hands.

"Macy." She set the teapot down hard onto its tray.

"Surprise me and don't cry today, huh? C'mon. Give me a break."

"OK." I ran my hands through my hair and smiled in compliance.

"Oh, and don't even mention the wig," she warned.

"What?" I sat up. "How am I supposed to respond to that?"

"Just don't tell me it looks natural." She glared at me. "I know it doesn't, you know. Don't patronize me."

"Oh, so I should tell you it looks like shit?" I laughed. "Well, it doesn't. In all honesty, it doesn't. It doesn't look...unnatural."

"Mace, really." She threw up her hand. "Just stop while you're ahead."

"No, seriously." I scrambled for the right thing to say. "It's not a bit overdone."

"Thanks." Trish looked down and let out a self-conscious laugh. "Feels like a coonskin cap."

"Well, it doesn't look like one," I said. "Though that's not a bad idea."

"Yeah?" She grinned and looked up. "You think?"

"Yeah, like a coonskin cap with the raccoon tail hanging rakishly to the side." I motioned dramatically. "A nice buckskin jacket, a musket, some moccasins..."

"Might be a smart look for me, huh?"

We laughed together.

"You take lemon in your tea, don't you?"

Trish had known me for 30 years and I'd never liked lemon in my tea.

"No, none for me, thanks."

"You don't like lemon in your tea?" She squeezed a slice into both cups anyway.

"Not particularly, no."

"Well, too bad." She offered me a cup and I took it reluctantly. "Today it won't kill you to take it with honey and lemon. Good for your throat."

"I'm fine," I said, my hands rattling the teacup in its saucer as I lifted it from the tray. Trish touched my wrist to steady my grasp. Her fragile hand was as pale and cold as the porcelain cup I was holding. I looked away.

"Yeah, you're in great shape." She took her place back on the sofa, perhaps sensing my discomfort. "So what gives? Why so nervous?"

"Oh, just the new inhaler I've been using." I traced the lid of my cup with my fingertip. "Gives me the shakes if I use it too often."

Trish sipped her tea, peering at me over the rim of the cup. "Is that all?"

"Pretty much." I sighed. "Not to mention the personal disaster I'm teetering on the cusp of."

"Uh-oh. Trouble in paradise already?"

"More like paradise lost, I'm afraid. Faith and I are soon to be...um..." I didn't want to say it.

"Kaput?" she asked.

I nodded solemnly.

"Well, what is it this time?" Trish tapped her chin and gave a knowing smile. "No, let me guess. She didn't go with the drapes?"

"It's because... " God, I could feel a stutter coming on. "I...um..." I cleared my throat. "I l-l-love her." Nothing like the "l" word to send this successful urbanite spiraling back into fifth-grade insecurity.

Silence.

"WHAT did you just say?"

168

"It's...it's n-n-not..."

"Slow down!"

Not the thing to say to someone who occasionally stutters. It has nothing to do with talking too fast or being intellectually inferior. Talking down to someone who already feels like Porky Pig can really piss them off.

"I s-s-said..." I clenched my teeth, frustrated. *Spit it out!* "It's not funny!"

"Hey, whoa, settle down there." Trish put up her hands. "Just relax. There's no reason to get all pissy."

I pulled a cigarette from the pack in my coat pocket. "M-may I?"

"Go ahead." She brought an ashtray to the table beside me. "Christ, I haven't seen you stutter like this since we had to recite the state capitals."

I struggled to ignite my lighter with trembling hands. Trish took it and lit my cigarette. "Here." She went back to her seat on the couch, muttering as she went. And as she walked, I noticed that she was a bit stooped, like an old crone. *Which incidentally, she will never have a chance to be.*

"Thanks." I took a drag and blew it out.

"Better?"

"Yes, thanks. I just get..."

"I know." Her voice was smooth, her tone lilting, comforting. "So tell me..."

"What?"

"You're in love with this girl?"

This was not just a girl. This was... "Faith."

"Faith. Right." She picked up her teacup. "And this is why you're dumping her?" She chuckled.

"It's not funny!" I could feel my face turning color, the

heat from the flash of sudden anger itching my ears.

"OK, OK." She cradled her cup calmly. "So what did force you into this decision?"

"I made a mistake."

"A mistake?" Trish tilted her mouth into a harmless smirk. "How big of a mistake are we talking here? Like, an 'I forgot to pick up the milk' type of mistake? Because, shit, Macy, we all make those."

"No." I smirked back, not so harmlessly. "It's more like an 'I let Betty Butler have her way with me' type of mistake."

"Oh, I see." How could she be so cool about this? "Betty Butler? The one who blows all the money on your cruise every year?"

"Yes."

"So this was a business thing, then?"

I hung my head. "Yes."

"Well, I must say, this is a bit of a surprise." I could feel her eyes upon me. "One could say you're moving up in the world. Old big bucks is certainly a step up from some bar-maid half your age."

I straightened in my chair and raised my head to face her. "One could say that, I suppose." I crooked my arm and lifted my cigarette. "If, perchance, one wanted to be a bitch."

Trish laughed, a big throaty laugh that echoed against those mauve walls. "So, anyway." She raised her eyebrows in inquiry. "You're breaking up because...?"

"Because I love her." I sipped my tea and puckered momentarily. "Because I'm going to tell her about my sexual escapade with Betty Butler and I doubt she'll be able to look at me after that."

Trish paused. Closed her eyes. She was getting tired. Weak. Most of our deep discussions ended prematurely those days. Nothing we could do about it, really, except pick up the pace and abridge the conversation to only the important issues. Cancer allows no small talk.

She smiled and opened eyes that were dimmed by fatigue. A sad smile, knowing that I was aware of her sudden weakness and hating it. "How's the tea?"

"Well..." I grimaced.

"That bad, huh?"

"Not if you enjoy drinking warm lemon Pledge."

"Only on special occasions." She laughed again. "So you're planning to tell her of your interlude with Betty Butler?"

"Yes." I set my jaw nobly. "It's the decent thing to do."

She took another drink of tea. "Baloney."

"Baloney?" I folded my arms. "Why?"

"You're telling her because you can't face the consequences of your mistake, Macy. You can't handle the guilt."

"Oh?" My God, since I was born I've been the queen of guilt recipients. Guilt ate up all of my other emotions and left me crumbs on which to survive. Guilt ruled my whole goddamn life.

"I know you, Macy." Trish smiled, eyes still closed, and wagged her finger. "You're not used to being in a committed relationship. So you screwed up once. Big deal. You know it was wrong. You won't do it again." She looked directly into my eyes. "Trust me on this one, sugar. Let it go."

I thought about it for a moment. "You're right." I slapped my knee. "I'll just go home and not say a word about it."

"Of course I'm right."

Of course she was right.

It took nearly an hour for me to get home. In no great haste to reach my apartment, I opted to walk and collect my thoughts and hopefully lose some of my drug and alcohol fuzziness along the way. Yellow taxis swarmed along the littered streets. The obligatory sirens whined. And steam rose from the fresh rolls in the bakery window as I touched the glass with the tip of my nose, wishing I was hungry. Halfway home, I was winded and cold and took a seat at an empty bus stop shelter. My ankle was throbbing. Someone had scratched the word FUCK onto the Plexiglas barrier which was already clouded far beyond transparency with grease and grit and ads for plays and other events. And in the collage, a strange surprise: Partly marred by knife or peeling fingers was a picture of me with my arms open, beckoning. The ever-popular "Come Cruise With Us" campaign. At least five years old, the photo, a friend had once teased, provided choice masturbation material for lesbians all across the land. This was no accident. A few deft motions of the airbrush and computer enhancement had erased my wrinkles and blessed me with bigger boobies, not that I'd looked all that bad to begin with. No. I'd been happy then. Strong and full of lust and greed. Healthy. Bigger than life. I laughed. Funny.

And in one swift motion, I gripped the corner and peeled the rest of me away.

I rested in the shelter for maybe 15 minutes. Its interior was cramped and smelled vaguely of piss, but I didn't mind at the time. I was grateful to find a haven from the wind and a place to sit and attempt to get my breath. Obnoxious city sounds were muffled here, nonintrusive. I was alone. On the sidewalk a cluster of fat pigeons gathered to attack the remains of a sandwich. As I watched them, my ears began ringing. What would I tell Faith? I shut my eyes and thought of her scent: a sweet, sensual smell that had already crept into my clothes and apartment. She was becoming a part of me. I imagined an old farmhouse with a bright red barn and a tire swing hanging in the front yard. I'm carrying groceries and nearly tripping over a lazy dog as I ascend the porch steps. Faith greets me at the door with a kiss. Then we're slicing vegetables in the kitchen. Sharing a good laugh. Indulging in cheap wine. Falling asleep in each other's arms under a quilt before a roaring fire in a stone fireplace.

What would I tell Faith?

Nothing.

"You're home early!" Faith peered through the peephole, and all of my misgivings vanished at the sight of her when she opened the door. "Macy, they're beautiful!"

"Straight from the cemetery to you!" My voice quivered, giddy with guilt. I thrust the bouquet forward with one arm, wrapping the other around her. We kissed, and I collapsed against her in exhaustion and relief, leaning down to rest my head on her shoulder. I expected her to buckle beneath my frame, but instead she was like a rock. She held me firmly, closely.

"Oh, God." I clutched at her shoulders and hair and smiled at the coolness of her skin as I nuzzled my cheek to hers. "God, I missed you so much today."

She kissed me again on the mouth, the cheek, the ear. "Roses! Home early and you brought me roses!" She giggled, biting at my earlobe. "You're spoiling me."

It hit me then. You know how things hit you, revealed like when a book falls open to a critical page? Right then, watching the light from a candle she'd lit dance across her smooth, butterscotch skin, I just knew. Faith was the best thing that had ever happened to me. A fucking godsend. And I'd be the dumbest woman alive not to know that and value it and hang onto it with everything I had.

Faith sent a sigh of her hot breath upon my neck. Yes! I moaned and moved her face to mine, jamming my tongue between her parted lips. She jerked in surprise, then relaxed and returned the gesture, fingers lacing through my hair, feet scuffling against the hardwood floor as they steered us to the recliner, which we toppled onto.

Grappling for each other and for balance, grabbing at hair and flesh and clothing. A mass of groping hands and gasps and grunts. Lights out, radio playing. At last, Faith came to rest on my lap, and I ran my hand up her thigh, marveling at the firm curve of her buttocks and the strong line of her spine as I clutched her to me, feeling her heart, her breath.

"I missed you so much, I missed you so much..." I couldn't stop saying it, couldn't stop myself from dipping her down to lie on my coat, which had fallen to the floor. "Macy!" She seemed all at once alarmed and aroused and she reached for me frantically as I knelt over her, fiddling with the buttons on my suit jacket. "Macy!" She cried out again, louder this time, inciting me to grit my teeth and rip off my jacket, sending several buttons scattering across the floor. Were they lost under the couch? Who cares! Fuck those buttons! Faith pulled off her sweater, and after more tearing and maneuvering I fell against her. Chest to chest, our warm bodies wriggled and melded together in sweat and madness and gold flickering light from the candle on the coffee table.

I raised my head for a moment, slipping my hand down, down...

"Yes?" I looked to her face for approval.

"Please!" Her head was thrown back, eyes barely open to meet mine.

Carefully, I let my fingers do the walking, stroking a steady rhythm until her body arched and twitched and then became still. Faith lay flushed and smiling. I sat up and coughed.

Sitting up beside me, Faith planted a kiss between my shoulder blades. I shook my head and frowned, unable to stop coughing long enough to enjoy the sensation. Sick, still sick, and wondering why.

"My poor baby," she cooed, cradling me against her, stroking my hair.

Her baby. I loved that. I'd never been anyone's baby before.

We sat there, rocking until the cough let up, which was a while.

"Well..." I clapped my hands.

"Well..." She gave my shoulder a squeeze and laughed. "Welcome home. Rough day at the office, dear?"

Chapter 17

We had a quiet, elegant dinner. Peaceful. Champagne and candlelight. Linen napkins. The whole deal. Vegetarian chili with an air of formality. And though we didn't leave my apartment, I did find it necessary to dress for the occasion. Black cashmere sweater and Vi's pearls. Nothing too uptight, but respectful. Serious. After all, this was an important night for us—a turning point. And in the average relationship, this would be the night when I might ask her to... Well, you know.

"This..." I began, then took a sip of water to wash down the huge wad of food I had in my mouth, having already tried to stash it in my jaw so that I might speak. Bad move, as what I was about to say was too nice to be said by someone who looked like a major league baseball manager ready to spit.

"Yes?" Faith leaned in.

I held up my index finger—*just a minute*—and swallowed. "As I was trying to say..." I smiled, gesturing to the fabulous feast before us. "This is exquisite."

She nodded humbly. "Thank you."

"No." I took her hand and kissed it. "Thank you."

"My, aren't we the charming one this evening?"

"My charm pales in comparison to your beauty." I kissed her hand again, and meant it.

"Wow!" She laughed. "Is this how you worked on that Betty Butler woman today, sweet talker?"

Ugh!

"No," I said, wanting to disappear.

"Come on, Miss Flirt, Miss Smooth Operator," she teased. "You never did tell me how the meeting went today."

From heaven to hell in 10 seconds. Just like that.

"Fine," I said. "It went fine. I'm sure we can expect to have a sell-out on the next cruise thanks to Ms. Butler and her friends."

"That's great!" She grabbed my arm. "No wonder you came home in the mood to celebrate." She stood up and threw her arms around me. "Good job!"

Faith moved off into the kitchen.

"I'm going to get some water. Need anything while I'm up?"

I heard the refrigerator door swing open.

"Just a sharp knife to impale myself with."

"What?" she called out.

"No, hon. Nothing!" I took a gulp of champagne. "Faith?"

"Yes?"

"I, uh..." I cleared my throat. "I've been thinking..."

"About what?"

"About..." I paused as Faith returned to the table, a glass of ice water in her hand. "About us."

"And...?"

"W-would you consider moving?" There, just blurt it

out. Not a bad question to ask. Shouldn't be that tough.

"Moving?" She looked confused. "You mean in here? With you?"

"No, no, no." I shook my head. Why was this so difficult? "I mean moving away. Out of state."

"You want me to move out of state?"

"Maybe." I pushed my chair back from the table to look her squarely in the eye. "We could get a nice little farm house. A place with some land."

"Well, God, I mean, your whole life's here, Macy." She seemed surprised. "Your business..."

"I'm thinking of selling it," I said, sounding like I'd really given this some thought, which I had not.

"Selling the business?" She was still reeling. "But you're a workaholic! You're great at what you do."

I refilled my flute and took another sip. "I'm beginning to think it's not for me anymore."

"So do something else. Start another business or something." She shrugged. "This is New York, Macy. You're smart. You can do anything you want to here."

"I know." I lifted an eyebrow and frowned. "This *is* New York. And I don't like you being here." I folded my arms and leaned back into a position of what I hoped was authority. "I hate the thought of you getting mugged again, or God knows what else."

"Macy, that could happen to anybody and you know it. I'm not going to move away from New York just because you want to keep me safe. Look, I'm glad you care about me. Really. And if you have other factors in this issue, I will be happy to follow you anywhere. It's just that..." She placed her hand on my knee. "I don't want you to move because of my safety and end up resenting me for it down the road."

178

"I know." I uncrossed my arms and took her hand. "And I'm not saying that this has to happen right away. It's just a thought. But it might be good for us both."

"Well, I'm sure it would be a lot easier for you to breathe fresh air than it is to breathe this filth."

"Absolutely," I agreed. "You could go to school. Work part time—if you chose to."

"We could get a little dog," she said. "Fence in the front yard so he could run loose and the neighbor kids could come around and play with him."

"Better yet," I said, "we could get a big dog so he could keep the neighbor kids away."

"Yeah, a big dog!"

"Put up a porch swing so we could sit together under the stars..."

"And what would you do?" she asked. "If I went to school, would you start another business? Maybe go back to school yourself?"

"Maybe." I lit a cigarette. "Or maybe I'd just sit around and eat your cooking and read Martha Stewart books and watch talk shows and soap operas."

Faith snatched the cigarette from my lips and extinguished it with a hiss in the remainder of her chili. "And maybe you wouldn't be so stressed out and self-destructive all the time, huh?"

"Maybe."

And maybe, I thought, *in a farmhouse in the Midwest with our white picket fence I wouldn't be so apt to sabotage our relationship. Maybe I'd have no more dirty little secrets to hide.*

Chapter 18

"Mom's worried about you," said Kate, my Hepburnish nickname for the slimmest and blondest of Trish's dynamic duo of daughters. At 17, she was blossoming into a repeat of her mother's good looks and her father's easy disposition. Shapely and cute, she was clad in modern hip-huggers and a top that read IT WASN'T ME in glitter. And in typical teen fashion, she was prone to switching subjects in mid-thought. "Do you think I need a nose job?"

I laughed initially. Such beauty, such insecurity. Ah, youth. "No!" I said, with a frowning resonance that inferred a parental relationship. She was, after all, my god-daughter.

"You don't think so?" She shrugged. "I don't think so either."

The long line at MOMA had hardly moved. Tickets for the Van Gogh exhibit were sold out, but I'd managed to score a pair. Thus, this afternoon found us arm in arm in an interior entranceway. Kate had been my companion for most big exhibits since she was 8. Now that she was approaching college age, I felt sad in the knowledge that—like her mother—she'd soon be leaving me too.

"Tell your mother not to worry," I said, mopping my brow with a delicate red hanky from the Elsa Perretti collection. "I'm on the mend."

Kate fiddled with her bangs. "Good to know."

The two of us stared straight ahead at the distant doorway like the rest of the mob. "God, I hate crowds," said Kate. "Don't you?"

The line began to move steadily, and from being on my feet—or from whatever else was going on with me—I began to feel a bit faint. "I'm not crazy about them. I never used to mind, but now..." I smiled. "Things change as you get older, I guess."

"You've got a great nose." Kate cocked her head and inspected my profile, lifting my chin with her free hand. "How old are you, anyway?"

"Ladies never tell." I grinned, smacking her hand away. "I prefer to remain an enigma."

"Not like I don't know. You and Mom graduated high school together."

"Well, your mother was slow. They kept her back a few years."

"Yeah, right."

Tickets torn, we were finally allowed into the exhibit hall. The show was drastically oversold, so we could only shuffle shoulder to shoulder amongst the crowd. Faint recorded voices filtered through visitor's headphones maintained a consistent buzz. Audio tours had always disturbed me. Amid the occasional hushed whispers, I began to cough, slapping the hanky over my mouth in an effort to muffle it.

"Jesus, don't croak!" Kate sounded like her mother.

I laughed and blushed and continued to cough.

"Here." She produced a hard candy from her purse, hustling to unwrap it and popping it into my mouth before I could protest. Remarkably, it did the trick.

"Sunflowers." I nodded at the canvas before us.

"It smells like ass in here." Kate crinkled her nose. "Doesn't anyone ever shower in New York?"

"Only on Tuesdays." I winked. "And today's Friday, so they're pretty ripe, sugar. Get used to it."

Kate clutched my arm the way she'd come to do sometimes since her mother's diagnosis. Together we eyed the street scenes, the yellow house, the portraits.

"Those eyes," she said, falling in love the way I'd fallen in love the first time I'd seen these same paintings—over 20 years ago, in Amsterdam. "Those are the bluest eyes, like, *ever*."

Indeed, they were. I put my arm around her shoulders, proud.

"Aunt Macy?"

Kate looked up at me with eyes almost as blue as Van Gogh's. I felt the tears coming. A moment.

"Yes, Kate?"

And there we were: Kate, me, Vincent.

"I'm gay."

Gasp! And then suddenly, the candy was stuck. In my throat.

Oh, shit.

I stamped my feet. I flailed. One swift whack on the back from Kate's Nintendo-muscled hand and I launched the starlight mint she'd given me directly at Van Gogh's second self-portrait. It stuck and landed like a red-and-white spiraled pirate patch on his left baby blue.

Thus, the alarm.

Thus, our subsequent escort into MOMA's courtyard.

"You haven't told your parents, I take it," I said, out of breath as always, positioning myself delicately on a bench and motioning for Kate to join me.

"Not yet." She shook her head. "Can you keep it a secret for now?"

"Sure."

Then she hugged the stuffing out of me. Sweet baby Kate, the one I'd always wondered about. I felt afraid for her, felt all the first little fears coming back. It would not be an easy road.

"I'm 46." I felt the tears on my cheeks. "I thought that since you told me your secret..."

"I know." She laughed. "Like I said, you graduated with Mom, so it wasn't a secret."

"Shut up and humor me," I said, hugging her harder, still under the angry gaze of museum security, still feeling my bruised esophagus.

Light shone in through the window from the moon— well, actually, from the billboard on the roof of the building next door to my apartment. I caught Faith's and my reflections in the mirror and wondered to myself if a Boy Scout could tell how old I was by counting the wrinkles on my neck. I thought about having a cigarette and opted not to. The air was so dry it already hurt to breathe, and besides, Faith would get her fair share of secondhand smoke when she went to work later. Perhaps I should only smoke on the balcony. Perhaps I'd get a humidifier or something. Then again, that might be a purchase better made after the move.

The move? The move? It had been a fleeting thought, a chance. Now it seemed so real, so much a part of my vocabulary, my train of thought, and my plans. What exactly was I supposed to do with myself once we moved to this perfect little town? And what would we say about our relationship? Nothing? Let them form their own conclusions? Couldn't exactly attend church bake sales holding hands, could we? Faith would be the social one anyway, the one everybody liked, the one the neighbors would bring fresh sweet corn and homemade jelly to and talk over the fence to and ask about...things. What would she tell them? What would they think? That I was her spinster aunt?

Things might be better if we had a baby, I thought. *One of those you can feed for $15 a month, according to those early-morning commercials. Maybe I can send some kind of lump sum payment, have the kid UPS'd to our door. Yeah.*

We dined in Chelsea, east of Eighth. I arrived first, taking a seat at the bar until she arrived; taking a seat, that is, after popping down the front steps a tad too vigorously and whacking my head on the doorjamb as I entered—rattling the glass just enough to gain the attention of the patrons inside. It was supposed to unfold as a regular dinner date after work, where we would sit together and hold hands across the table and laugh together about, you know, silly things. But even early on in the evening, even before my slapstick entrance, I could feel things beginning to unravel. I left my umbrella in the cab, for starters, my fucking favorite umbrella with the Picasso figures on it. And things only got worse from there.

Faith rushed in, only a few minutes late—but it did annoy me.

"I'm so sorry," she said.

"It's all right." I did not look up from my drink. My eyes itched and it felt like my makeup was running off my face in tiny rivulets of sweat. When I patted my brow and cheeks with a napkin, I saw the foundation. Clammy. Chills. And it ate at me. God, it just ruled me. I was a coward. A whore. A cowardly whore. A whorish coward. A *liar*.

How could I even look at her?

The waiter seated us at a table upstairs. Gay waiter with black, black hair. Like shoe polish. Wet paint! I looked away as he caught my glance, then boldly looked back.

Goddamn, buddy, if you're going to dye your hair that black, that ridiculously salamander-shiny-black, you must want me to stare!

Faith sat across from me, babbling something about spring classes and...

God, just look at her: 23 years younger than I am.

"Uh-huh." I nodded, sore all over. Suffering from a general...what was it? Malaise? Some relentless ague? Suffering from a hard dose of reality was more like it. Christ, what was I thinking? I mean, this was the right kind of thing for a fling, but a relationship? She was a kid! She probably understood rap music and video games and would be prone to waxing nostalgic about the Reagan years after a few Zimas.

Christ...

"Would you like to order, Madame?" Blackie reappeared at our table with his pad and pen, all smiles in his black stretchy T-shirt and black slacks and black patent leather shoes. Black! What was it with everyone in New York wearing black? Like we were all mourning for our lost innocence from living here, or something. And he was sooooo gay. Gay to the 10th power. Flame on, little brother! Was everyone gay? Did everyone have to wear black? Why, yes, on both accounts—unless you ventured up to the Hamptons, which was now P. Diddy territory. He'd been swinging his croquet mallet there lately, according to the tabloids. Perhaps if I moved there, I could be his neighbor. Me, gardening in last season's capri pants. WHITE LESBO BITCH painted on my mailbox in modest letters. Or maybe just HO.

"Sparklings," I said—no, blurted—to the waiter. The very gay waiter with black, black hair. "Do you have any sparklings?"

He gave me a confused smile. "Sparkling water?" Obviously, the dye had hindered his IQ.

"Champagne." I smiled back, so desperately in need of T'aittinger—its effervescence, its flavor—so in dire need of a happy, bubbly fix that I would gladly give Blackie my best smile, showing all of my not-so-pearly whites.

"I'll see what I can find," he said without much hope in his voice.

For the time being, we sipped at our water. Faith's eyes locked on to me and I dodged them as best I could.

"What's wrong?" She was concerned, or was it agitated?

Is she sick of my moods already? My unpredictability? Hell, I can't blame her. I'm sick of my moods too. Sick of it all. Slightly drunk. Slightly disoriented. Did we order our food yet? And where is my goddamn champagne?

"Nothing." I blinked and the room shifted a bit.

Whoa.

"I would like..." That waiter again. Faith was ordering her meal, something vegetable-based and relatively insubstantial.

Fine. Be that way, but I will not be sucked into this Ally McBeal way of life. I will rebel. I will be remarkably Midwestern and order...

"Pork chops," I said.

Two of them. Biggest you've got. Mashed potatoes. Bread. A brick of cheese. Cigarettes. Scotch. Bring it to me. Bring it all! I want to die the overindulgent, American way, and crash a sport utility vehicle into the gates of hell!

"Macy?" Faith slid her foot to meet mind underneath the table. "What is it? What's wrong?"

"Toothache," I whispered.

My God, is this what a toothache feels like? Maybe I need a root canal or some kind of oral surgery jaw realignment procedure. Maybe I do have cancer, a thyroid tumor or gum cancer, something resulting from my experimental use of Skoal as a teenager.

"Hurts, huh, baby?" She touched my face lightly with those tapered fingers.

Oh, God, did it hurt. It had all day—from my jaw down my neck and right down to my fingers. And the more I thought about the Betty Butler thing, the more it seemed to throb and radiate and make me sweat.

I took another sip of water. *Pills! That's what I need. Some of those big ones they gave me for my ankle. Pills as pink as Jayne Mansfield's sweater or slippers or panties or whatever. Hot pink! And I have a stash. Oh, yeah. Right there in the old medicine cabinet, just waiting to be tossed down in a wad, gulped down in one big, last handful by Judy or Marilyn or me—the last of the Geminis.*

"Macy, you're shaking. Here." She came behind me and slipped my coat up over my shoulders.

"What?" I was startled. "Are we leaving? So soon?" My voice grew louder. "Why? We haven't even eaten. We haven't even ordered, I don't think. Have we? Are you sure you want to leave?"

"Just...just settle down. Just relax." She sat back down across the table from me. "It's OK."

"It's not." I laughed, shaking my head violently. "It's not OK."

"Macy..." Faith squeezed my hand. "You've obviously had a rough day, but it's over now. Everything's all right."

"Whoa!" I giggled, trying to appear reassured. "Yes!" I exhaled and lowered my voice. "Yes, it is. I just c-c-can't..." I cleared my throat. "I can't seem to shake this virus."

Or whatever it is.

"Have you called Germaine for another appointment?"

"I don't want to go back to Germaine."

The waiter returned, at last—with T'aittinger! *Oui!*

"I want a new doctor. I don't trust her judgment." I realized what I'd just said and laughed. "Ha! I don't trust *her* judgment? I don't even trust *my own* judgment!" And I gestured with my hand, knocking over my champagne, standing suddenly as it spilled onto the table and floor. Others in the restaurant looked our way, and I greeted their curiosity with a bow. "And for my next trick..."

Faith and Blackie cleaned up the mess, replacing the soaked tablecloth with a fresh one as I stood there, helpless.

"Let's just leave, shall we?" I said, reaching for my credit card.

"No, no, it's OK." Faith sat down and refilled my flute with champagne. "See? Come on and have a seat."

"Please, let's just go." I squinted. "People are staring."

"People are staring because a tall, klutzy but beautiful woman continues to stand in the middle of the restaurant." Faith motioned to my chair. "Sit down."

"No. We...um..." I eyed the door. "We should leave."

"We've ordered. Our dinner should be out any minute."

"I don't care." I folded my arms. "They're staring, and I don't like it. They're staring because they think you're too young for me."

"What?" Faith laughed in disbelief. "They do not!"

"Oh, yes." I nodded frantically, eyes darting about the room. "They do. They think I'm far too old for you."

"That's crazy!"

"Where's our check?"

"Macy!" Faith stood and grabbed me by the shoulders. "Do you want me to ask if they think you're too old for me? Do you want me to just yell it out and ask if our age difference is creating a distraction from their dining pleasure? Because I will. I will do that if you want me to."

Silly. I was being silly. Paranoid. So what if they did think that. I didn't care what they thought. Who were these people anyway? Who cared?

"No," I said, dropping my gaze.

"OK, then." Faith still gripped my shoulders, looking into my eyes. "Now, please, can we just sit down now and have a nice dinner together?"

"Oh, my eyes. I'm sorry." I rubbed them as they teared slightly. "I really do need to get contacts. When they get tired, everything's fuzzy." I felt around in my blouse pocket for my glasses and put them on, shrugging, and looked at her again as everything became clear. "Sorry."

Faith took my face into her hands and pulled me in for a kiss, right there in front of the world. Right there. I sat down, weak, still tasting her and thrilling in the warm slipslide of her mouth against mine. Lipstick on lipstick. Heaven! And at a moment when I should have been reveling in our closeness, something snapped, and I stood up from the table suddenly and just said it, loud and not so proud: "I slept with Betty Butler."

Someone dropped a fork at a table somewhere behind us.

Faith said nothing. Her mouth fell open and not a thing came out. Not one thing. And the moment was long before she was able to speak.

"Yesterday?"

I looked around and felt all the eyes. They really were staring now. And I sat back down, never looking away from her face.

"Yes."

She dropped her head. "Oh."

"Faith?" I reached across the table to touch her, and she withdrew her arms, clutching herself. "Faith, you don't understand. I didn't do this to hurt you. I had to tell you..."

"Why did you do it?" She looked up. Not crying, as I'd expected, but confused. Baffled. Totally lost. "Why?"

I reached to touch her face and she ducked away.

"It was business. Money. A lot of money. For us! It meant nothing, I swear. Faith..."

She swallowed hard. "Macy, I love you..."

"I love you too..."

"No, no, just shut up and listen to me for a minute." She took a slow, deep breath and let it out. "I love you and I think you love me..."

"Oh, baby, I do..."

"Stop it! Just..." She composed herself. "Just stop it, OK? Let me finish."

I nodded eagerly. *Anything!*

"I know it's very early in our relationship and we're going to make mistakes and this...this is a problem. But I've never felt this way about anyone before, and I don't think I could ever love anyone else this much, and I don't want to lose you because of a stupid mistake."

"I don't want to lose you." I felt the lump rise in my throat. "I can't."

"I just need you to tell me that it won't happen again." Silence.

"Tell me, Macy, and I'll believe you," she said earnestly. "And I won't question you or ever throw it in your face. I won't." She looked into my eyes with no malice or anger. She wanted to forgive me. She actually wanted to let this go. "Tell me you'll never do it again."

I knew what would be the smart thing to say. I knew what strings to pull. I'd charmed my way out of worse situations than this in relationships that hadn't meant half what this one did. But when I looked into her eyes, so young and gentle and true, I froze. And before I could stop myself...

"I can't tell you that."

Oh, God. She looks absolutely mortified. What am I doing?

"I can't say it won't happen again."

Faith closed her eyes, held her breath, and when she breathed again and opened her eyes they were distant and dead, and she asked, "So this is the end?"

I frowned. "This is the end."

I slumped. And then I waited. I waited for some sense

of relief, some odd reward for telling the truth that would never come.

And just then the waiter brought our food.

"I'm not hungry now." Faith smiled at him, a pained smile, then turned her glistening gaze back to me. "I'll be by tomorrow to pick up my things—if you could just set them in the hall."

I felt sick to my stomach, felt like a cad. I pulled my checkbook from my bag. "You've done a lot for me. You've been very generous and kind, and I'd like to compensate you for your trouble and expenses, if I may."

She looked hurt. "I don't want your money."

"Oh, come on now." I took out a pen. "It's the least I can do. You're a waitress. Just think of it as a tip."

Faith's cheeks flushed and her eyes shone mad and for a second I thought she would strike me. She was no longer only wounded. She was pissed.

"Go to hell," she hissed and bolted from the table.

"Faith!" I grabbed my cane, shouldered my handbag, and stumbled to my feet. The waiter met me at the door, and I handed him a wad of cash then tripped up the stairs to the street. "Faith!" She was already halfway across, the horns of yellow cabs blaring as she strode boldly in front of them. The same horns blared at me as I hobbled across and watched her disappear into the subway stairwell. "Faith, stop!" I dug for change to drop into the turnstile slot. "Faith! Wait! Honey! Please!" And just as I made my way to the platform, the doors of the car closed and stole her away, speeding off into the darkness.

My scream echoed against the concrete. "Faith!"

I dropped my cane, slid down against a pillar, and sobbed and choked and shivered in the silvery halogen light. A hundred pairs of feet, maybe more, shuffled past. And then...

"It's all right, honey." An Italian woman knelt down and patted my shoulder. "I know it's hard, but there comes a time when you gotta let go. I understand. I got two daughters of my own."

Chapter 19

It's not like I'd never felt love before. Or loss. *Au contraire, mon frère.* But the ups of love are so drastic and all-encompassing, and the downs of it so equally so, you just don't see it coming. You can't.

What was my problem, anyway? Ha—make a list. How could I even consider that this relationship might work? Right from the start I'd been a sickly narcissistic show-off. And a liar. Hell, I'd even lied to Faith about my family. Only my mother had rejected me for being gay. I'd just failed to stay in contact with my dad, and I didn't even know why.

If it hadn't been the Betty Butler thing, it would have been something else. That I know for sure.

I bought a beautiful silk shirt at Barneys. French cuffs, perfect seams...I mean, this thing was gorgeous. Men's, sure, but who cares? When you're a lanky, strapping lass like myself, you can pull it off. Besides, I've always thought there was something sexy about wearing a man's shirt, all white and dressy, that one breast pocket hanging low as it drapes over your belt because you've tucked that roomy sucker in to your knees.

The only thing I've ever swiped from anyone, the only thing I ever openly stole, was a set of cuff links off my dad's dresser. They were shaped like little gold bottle caps. Pepsi. He and Vi had bought a shitload of Pepsi stock and won them at some party. He never wore them. Only offered them at a glance to numerous dinner guests in their little brown box and bragged about how Joan Crawford had presented them to him personally and they had real diamonds in them, blah, blah, blah. After the thrill from their celebrity presentation had worn off, years later, they sat next to the change dish, collecting dust. So one day when he pissed me off about something I just snatched them. He never noticed—or if he did, he never said so.

When you have money, hair stylists make house calls. The right ones do anyway. Never one to demand an hour of fawning and preening from a squad of macrobiotic salon fops with their practiced pouts and space-odditied demeanors, I subscribed instead to the private services of Helena. In 20 minutes of no-nonsense snipping, we were through. Not a buzz cut, but rather short indeed, with the standard crop of loose, natural curls left on top. We'd left the gray for now—it seemed more prevalent with the new do. And as I stood before the full length mirror in my pleated slacks, new silk shirt, and filched Pepsi cuff links, all hollow-eyed and freshly trimmed, wearing only a smattering of makeup...

"I'll send the bill, sweetie." Helena smiled and let herself out, I assume, as I was entranced with the image of my father staring back at me from the mirror on my closet door.

Chapter 20

I am thoroughly convinced that there is nothing more depressing than attending an opera alone. And not just any opera—*La Boheme*. The Met. Wonderful seats. All decked out and shimmering with jewels from Harry Winston. All this and an empty chair beside me.

I sat through the first act, wishing for some miraculous end to the evening but knowing that even if my life were a movie, the best ending I'd get would be to be swept off my feet by someone prominently handsome and decidedly male. Hence, the teary-eyed trudge through Act 2 and numerous flutes of mediocre champagne during intermission. Idiotically, I'd looked for her in the crowd, expecting her to be there for no other reason than the evening's emotional charge. No other reason than that I'd want no other alongside me at the opera.

My continuous pining was futile, however. Faith was nowhere to be found. Women without faces passed me in the hall, urgently steering their husbands and boyfriends in the opposite direction upon catching my glance. I greeted their apprehension with a chuckle. Bad little girls, they were. So eager—desperate, even—to avoid an intersection of their double lives, so quick to recoil in light from the hand they so fervently kissed in the dark. I couldn't help but be amused by their maneuvers to avoid me. The price to pay, I suppose, for being the Harriet Tubman of the gay world. And then it struck me that it wasn't so funny after all; that my life up to then had been a sham; that a great deal of my clients and occasional lovers would never see fit to speak to me in the crisp light of the grocery store or almost any other reality-based environment. And I walked by an enormous mirror. And I knew I was getting old.

"Macy!"

Oh, my. Who else but Germaine and Kristy came drifting out of the corridor, arm in arm. Gutsy. How very *Ellen* of them to be seen together at the opera.

"Well, for goodness's sake! Germaine, darling!" (Something about wearing diamonds always made me prone to calling people "darling." I call it the "Gabor reflex.") "So nice to see you!" I smarmed, campily placing a gloved finger to my chin in mock thought. "And who might this be?"

I knew who it was, knew damn well that it was Kristy, topless treasure of the high seas, unintentional entertainment for those attending my last cruise. Her hair was passable, but the dress, a sad remnant of an '80s prom, had to go. Not to mention it was so tight I cringed in fear of a silicon explosion at any moment. And yes, there was the tattoo. You can take the girl out of the trailer park...

"Oh, Macy, this is Kristy!" Germaine was absolutely beside herself with pride over her perky princess.

I nodded in acknowledgment, not wanting to risk breaking off any of those precious Lee Press-On Nails by shaking her hand.

"A pleasure, indeed," I said, and performed a queenly bow that was made all the more queenly by my scepter, the bull penis. Whatever.

Kristy gave a lip-licking smile and I was reminded of Betty's words—*"They say you taste like honey"*—and I couldn't help but wince. Ha. She remembered me all right.

"I wondered what happened to you." Germaine touched my arm. "I thought you were coming back for a follow-up."

"I'm sorry." I slapped my forehead with my palm, illustrating my forgetfulness. "I've been so busy."

"Well, why don't you stop in next week and we'll go over those test results, huh?" She winked at me. *Winked!* Great. What exactly had she found? Maybe there was some graphic, horrible reason that I felt like total shit. "Say, where's that little gem of yours? Powdering her nose?"

Faith. Now came the awkward and hopefully brief explanation.

"We're...uh..." *Don't stutter!* "We're not together anymore." The words came out heavily, like I was admitting defeat, and essentially I was. I mean, there she was, all happy and kissy with her poorly dressed main squeeze. And there I was, looking fabulous albeit alone at *La Boheme*. A tragedy within a tragedy, you could say.

"I'm sorry to hear that."

"Hey, things happen," I said. "Well..."

"You're not leaving?"

"I'm tired." I nodded. And I was. It wasn't only

emotional—you know, the stress. I felt wrung out physically too. And there was that strange, now not-so-new pain that ran from my jaw down the length of my entire arm. I hadn't gotten a break from it since our break-up dinner in Chelsea. Psychosomatic or otherwise, it was only getting worse.

I did my kiss goodbyes and found the ladies' room. There, I sat on a bench, dropped my head in my hands, and watched as the tiny swirls in the carpet threads danced and ran together.

Craving a quick, cold water facial, I was making my way to the sink when an icy paw greeted my left shoulder. "Hello, lover." It was Betty and Company: Karen "Cokehead" Krane, Barb "Titsy" Baker-Smith, and Moira "Meth-queen" Gruen. The entire foursome was stoned. "We've got plenty to spare. Intrigued?"

Intrigued, I was not, but I had nothing to lose. And so, cramped in a ladies' room stall at the Met, Betty doled out a fat line on her compact mirror and handed me a rolled hundred.

"My Macy." She swooned, rubbing her teeth with her manicured finger to enjoy the freeze. "Still the same, after all. Friends?"

"Friends." I winked, the coke stinging my sinuses. "And may I say welcome aboard for the next cruise, in advance?"

"Oh, honey, of course. The gang and I have been doing your cruise for how many years now? They've spoken of nothing else for months. I couldn't beg out of it if I'd wanted to."

"What?" I shut my eyes hard. "You mean you..."

"Silly! No, you didn't have to sleep with me to make

a deal. We go back, you and I, don't we?" She batted her eyes. "I just wanted to see how much you'd sweeten the pot before we signed on. You know, for your favorite client?"

The room spun, and I clutched the toilet paper holder for support. Betty's laughter rang in my ears as she swung open the stall door.

"And to think the other travel agents only offer frequent-flier bonuses..."

Defeat.

I paused at the toilet, anticipating a nosebleed.

After hemorrhaging briefly, I took my tripping self to stand over the sink basin, as originally planned.

"You OK?"

Ugh. That voice. Well, if it wasn't she of the purple prom dress and fake baby doll voice: Kristy.

"Oh, I'm swell."

She cupped the back of my neck with her hand.

"You're burning up."

"I'm fine." I stooped, splashing my face with cold water. The attendant handed me a towel and I thanked her and handed her a five-spot.

"So..." Kristy clasped her hands demurely at her waist. "How've you been?"

"Exceptional." I smirked. "I'd ask how you've been, but it's obvious."

"What do you mean by that?"

"I mean it's every girl's dream to land a doctor, now, isn't it?"

"I suppose." She began reapplying her lipstick in the mirror. "But the funny part of it is, I love her."

"Ha!" I snorted. "You don't know what love is."

"Maybe I didn't before, but I do now. She's nice to me, Macy. She doesn't treat me like an airhead or a slut." She turned to me. "And I love her."

"Well, goody for you." I carefully patted my face with powder from my compact. "I'm sure that you and Germaine's bank account will be very happy together."

"You don't get it, do you?" Her eyes flashed. "Just because that's all I wanted from you doesn't mean that's all I want from her."

I threw my hand to my chest as if I'd been shot.

"And before you turn your nose up at me, just know that the only reason you were able to use *me* is because I was using *you*."

I paused. Dizzy. Then I put my compact back in my bag and tried to steady myself.

"Kristy, you're right." I couldn't believe I was saying it, but I said it anyway.

"What?"

"I said, you're right." I fanned my face with a program. "Love is, well, an amazing thing. And if you two have found each other, you're very lucky and you should treasure your time together."

Kristy stared at me; then she rose up on her toes to kiss my cheek. "Don't worry, you'll find someone someday."

"Of course. Who wouldn't want all this?" I smiled, hobbling for the door, making myself stand as straight and tall as was possible at the time.

"Wait," said Kristy, moving swiftly up beside me. "Your shoe!"

"Oh!" I smiled, a portrait of taste. "It's Gucci."

"Um, no. I mean, you've got something stuck."

I followed her sympathetic gaze downward to my size 11

pump. The "something stuck," as she'd phrased it, was a trail of toilet paper.

"It's the new thing this season, doll." Blushing and annihilated, I bent to scoop the offending ribbon of white from my heel. "All the rage, darling."

Chapter 21

Sunny September. Her hand pressed to the track, ears trained downwind for the rattle of any oncoming freight—Trish. Always the careful one. Me—forever unconcerned, skipping my big feet and long legs over the railroad bridge's planks, which lay just far enough apart for a skinny teenage girl to fall through and into the muddy current below. The railroad bridge was huge and hideous. There was no romantic, train-oriented vibe attached to it, no stories of tragic lovers leaping from its planks—only a few scattered, gory deaths of derelicts and the like, all buried without headstones and without much said about them in the local newspaper.

The bridge was constructed of steel girders and beams and was nearly 90 feet tall. In its prime it had probably been a marvel, a real showpiece, stretching out across the river to link the thriving cement mill to its parenting town. But the mill had shut down in the late 1950s and the bridge's bright red skeleton had faded to pink, peppered at every joint and rivet with rust and rot, used only sporadically by the dwindling rail freight industry. Like a giant abandoned carnival ride, it still rose above the river, still got plenty of looks from cars passing through on I-40, and still was a constant source of pedestrian traffic—however illegal it may have been to use it in that capacity.

I had no personal attachment to the bridge, but I liked how it felt as I made my way across. I was more afraid of getting a splinter in my bare heel than of plummeting to my death. The cement mill railroad bridge gave me a peculiar power over my peers. For whatever reason, I was not at all frightened. Ever.

But I was frightened now.

Post opera, I opted to limp into a "family" place in Midtown. Deanne's was a "sophisticated lady" type of place, with lots of posing and posturing. That night there were more young ones on the move than I'd expected, countless working gals all decked out in their best *Breakfast at Tiffany's* garb—you know, elbow-length gloves and the essential little black dress. The whole deal.

I'd already had my fair share here and there from the flask in my handbag, but the promise of posturing elegantly with a martini in hand was irresistible. And so, martini in hand and das boot on my foot, I was there maybe 20 minutes at the most when this slick little number comes slinking over in all her china-doll glory. Blood-red nails. Powdered white face. Can she buy me a drink? Why, yes, she can indeed. So I had, you know, another martini, complete with an olive as big and green and saturated as my liver surely was.

"Tell me, doll, what do you do?" I asked, as if I cared about anything but the depth of her cleavage.

She was a window dresser, she vacantly explained, for

Donna Karan. Or was it Anne Klein? Hell, I don't remember. Not important.

Cherise was her name, and she drank one of those big ultra-feminine frozen drinks that overflowed with fruit and miniature flags of obscure countries.

Throughout our short stint at Deanne's, I managed to maintain a marked nonchalance about the amount of perspiration cascading down my back.

I attempted to light a cigarette and trembled noticeably.

"Look what you do to me," I purred and flashed her a smile.

She flashed one right back, the sucker.

I kept my coat with me, kept it pulled over my shoulders in an attempt to curb my shivers. Still, I felt clammy and disconnected and, well, just not well at all.

"You remind me of someone." She spied at me over the rim of her glass, taking a sip.

"Don't tell me." I took her hand. "Your evil third grade teacher?"

"No." She tittered. "It's...oh, what's her name? From that movie..."

"Imogene Coca?"

"*Ripley!*" She snapped her fingers, proud, like she'd just won the Nobel prize. "The one in *Alien. Aliens.* You know, all of those."

"Sigourney Weaver?" said the spider to the fly.

"Yes!"

And so, the trap had been set. I couldn't let it stop there. Not when things were humming along like they were. And, yeah, on any other night I could have surrendered the urge and gone home to bed, sweating out whatever this was under the covers, sipping herbal tea and searching for

Dynasty reruns. Resplendent in my repose, so to speak. But this had been no ordinary day, and it would be no ordinary night. My quest to catch up with true love may have been guillotined by the subway's metal doors, but true lust would be much easier to come by.

After numerous mutual thigh caresses under the table, we cabbed down Fifth. She directed the driver to turn right at the arch. Cherise was rooming at the Washington Square Hotel until she found a place, she said, as she'd just transferred from Chicago. Clean but unimpressive and operated by the standard "speak no English" New Yorker, the Washington Square offered few amenities but a very real sense of privacy.

As for the actual encounter, it was relatively lackluster and brief. The bed was as hard as a goddamn rock, so hard that I felt my spine shift as she tipped me back to remove my wide-legged trousers. I wasn't comfortable flat on my back, couldn't get my breath, but our romp skipped the foreplay and picked up its pace when I attempted to pull myself to an upright position by grabbing Cherise's shoulders and inadvertently slam-dunked her face into my crotch. *Voila!*

Her tour of the Grand Canyon was sadly interrupted, however, as at last she grasped that my gasping was not out of pleasure but urgency. I hobbled half-dressed to the bathroom and braced myself, leaning face first over the john, choking up thick, foul-tasting gunk. And yes, I inspected, like most people tend to inspect when they take an enormous shit. That "My-god-that-just-came-out-of-my-body?" glance into the bowl. Strange. It wasn't vomit. And it wasn't what those of use who have smoked since birth affectionately call "lung cookies." This was different. This stuff was ropy and yellow with rust-colored streaks. Good God. Blood?

"Macy?" Cherise called out and knocked on the door. "Are you OK?"

She sounded afraid. That *Little Girl Lost* voice. I couldn't blame her. I was a stranger to her—a stranger she had sloppily attempted to bring to orgasm, but a stranger nonetheless.

"I'm fine."

I stepped over to the sink to splash my face. Fine? Christ. I looked up into the mirror at my reflection. Flushed. Disheveled. Eyes watercolored with pink. The room spun a bit as I moved for the door, and right then I thought: *God, I could die up here...where are my panties?*

Thankfully, I'd had the forethought to bring my inhaler with me into the bathroom. I hit it once, twice...nothing. No usual shaky wave of relief. Nothing more than a tug, really, at the invisible cord tightening around my throat.

Something clicked, and I turned to see the doorknob turning. Cherise stuck her head inside. Surprise.

"Hi."

She said it timidly, and I noticed then, in the john's unforgiving fluorescence, that she really wasn't all that attractive. Rather nice tits, I suppose, but as for the rest of her...ho-hum. She wore a helluva lot of makeup and had an exaggerated hip-swing when she walked, trying oh-so-hard to be so girly-girlish. The type that needed a real machismo mama, a big broad with a baseball cap jammed down on her head and a chain from a trucker's wallet dangling out of her back pocket. And that was not me.

But I felt bad for her anyway. Cherise stepped in and tried to feel my forehead and extend that maternal comfort they say comes so naturally for women—but to no avail. She wasn't Trish and she wasn't Faith and I wasn't in the mood for empathy from a woman I hardly knew. I didn't want her pity. I didn't want anything from her anymore.

"I...uh..." I cleared my throat. "I need to run."

"Asthma?" Cherise pointed to my inhaler on the sink's counter.

Hmm...let's see, I'm wheezing uncontrollably and I have asthma medication prominently displayed. What gave it away? Oh, well. She didn't have to be a brain surgeon. Looking good in a push-up bra and knowing a handful of state capitals was plenty for her to handle in this life.

"Yeah," I said. No reason to be a complete asshole. It wasn't her fault I felt like garbage.

I took another hit from the inhaler. She handed me my slacks and, of course, my panties.

"I'm sorry," she said with concern in her eyes. "Do you want me to help you get home?"

I shook my head and struggled to dress. She helped me with my coat and kissed me on the cheek as I opened the door.

"I think you should see a doctor," she said. "You're awfully warm."

"Oh, I will." I tried to laugh. "You have a nice evening now. See you on the ship."

Chapter 22

Small towns are often full of bizarre rituals, one of which is the Piqua Live Nativity. Not that live nativities are odd; no, they are not at all uncommon. But my hometown's choosing of the head of the baby Jesus lent an original and somewhat frightening twist to this tradition. What I mean by the "head," well, that takes some explanation.

At an average December temperature of 28 degrees, Piqua's Christmases were too frosty to expose an actual infant to, thus limiting the casting choices for the Christ child. It was suggested by many that a plastic figure of a baby be used, but the city council decided that a *fake* baby amid *live* wise men, Mary, Joseph, and assorted barnyard animals, well, it just wouldn't have been correct. A dwarf would have been acceptable, but as it happened, Piqua's paltry population was entirely dwarfless. Midwestern ingenuity prevailed to solve this predicament, however, and since 1920, Jesus H. Christ himself had been portrayed by a select individual whose head was stuck through a hole in the manger straw with a scantily clad, headless doll body strapped to his chin. And thus, the big-headed Baby Jesus of Piqua was born.

I don't recall, exactly, how my brother fell into the coveted role one year. I'm thinking it was some sort of community service for truancy or small-scale drug possession— or a church payoff by my old man. It being winter, Vi was not at her best. I, being a teenager, could not have cared less. Dad, being himself, had his mind on other things. The prospect of five solid hours in the cold had none of us thrilled, but this being Elliot's debut into the theatrical world, we were all curious. As for Mom, well, she was pleased as punch.

As family, it was our civic duty to stand guard backstage at the manger, periodically pumping my brother the bigheaded Jesus full of hot cider, hot chocolate, etc. After all, the wise men were packing flasks, and Mary and Joseph clutched coffee cups from Schwartz's.

The Nativity began at twilight, outside of First Methodist. A crowd was gathered. Two church choirs, the kids and the adults, dueled in Christmas carols. I was tying the laces of my mucklucks when I felt the tap on my shoulder.

"Heya, glamour puss," Nickie Love said in his undeniably out-of-place Brooklyn accent. "Where's Ma?"

"Vi?" I asked, as if I had to, and he nodded. "She's on the pay phone."

"Go get her for me, will ya?" He slicked back his thinning black hair with a 29-cent unbreakable comb he'd pulled from his coat pocket. "I gotta have a conference."

Bored, I accepted the errand without question and set off toward the church. Nickie and Vi had been having quite a few conferences since little Nickie died in the motorcycle crash. Saturday mornings. Coffee at Schwartz's. Sometimes I'd tag along, eager for the chance to try out my driver's permit. I'd play pinball across the street at the drugstore and watch as they left the diner, heading for the car. He cried in the car, Vi told me when I asked. A man like Nickie wouldn't dream of crying in public, so he cried in the car.

"Goddamn it!"

Vi slammed the phone onto its cradle. I pecked on the door of the booth and she threw up her hands, exasperated.

"You'd think I was talking Chinese to those people! I tell them we're short on stoves and they order refrigerators!" She adjusted her muffler and stepped out into the cold, pulling up my hood. "You cold, sugar? You look cold."

"I'm OK." I jerked my thumb. "Nickie Love's looking for you. At the manger. Church is giving out coffee, if you're interested."

She frowned. "Big Nickie?" Nicki, his wife, had rarely surfaced since their son's demise.

"Big Nickie." I nodded. "Said he needs a conference."

"These men and their conferences." She rolled her eyes. "With women, it's mah-jongg. With men..."

Vi chipped stiffly along the sidewalk, still in her heels from the office. She approached the crowd at the manger and leaned on Dad's arm.

"This goddamned weather..." she said, within earshot of two women who sent her nasty looks. Vi was oblivious and out of breath.

"I told you all about Ohio before you came here, Vi." My father was unsympathetic, eyes staring straight ahead at his son, the savior. "You should have worn a better coat."

"Well, I'm terribly sorry, Bill, that I neglected to dress

appropriately." She slid her hand from his arm, lit a cigarette, and maintained an even tone. "I was too busy trying to fix what those toadies you call employees fucked up at the store."

"Language!" he hissed.

"Oh, I'm sorry. I forgot we're in the presence of Jesus, the pothead."

Dad ignored the comment.

"I'm sorry, Bill." Vi ran her gloved hand across his cheek. "I'm exhausted and I'm taking it out on you."

Ah, yes. Small, yet sweet, victory. Enter the Vi who could extinguish her own bitchiness upon realizing it. I felt relieved. Seeing her resort to snippery made me uneasy; it was the road my mother had always taken, a dirty road that led to constant emotional upheaval. Vi's strength was in coolness, not sarcasm, and she knew it.

"Well, there she is!" Big Nickie Love bounded over to our huddle, the collar of his black overcoat turned up. "Nicki wondered where you were at the bridge tournament Thursday night. She said they was lost without you."

"Vi's not much of a winter gal. She doesn't like to get out much," Dad said, smiling, teeth exposed. "I suppose that's what I get for bringing a Texas one-lunger to the Midwest."

"That's it," she said, her eyes suddenly shiny with tears, rage, embarrassment, etc. "I'm going home, and so will anyone else here if they have any sense."

On saying that, Vi turned abruptly and began crunching her way through the ice toward the parking lot.

"I've got the keys, Vi!" Dad called after her. "Vi!"

He made no move to go after her, nor did she respond to his words. Vi's figure grew smaller and smaller as she moved away from us and into the graying night, arms folded, head down, bobbing slightly as the delayed sound of her deep cold-weather cough reached us.

"Stubborn," Dad said, rubbing his nose. "I don't think she even has her house keys on her."

"If you want, Bill, I'll go pick her up." Big Nickie shrugged. "Take her back to our house until you get home? Just call me an' I'll bring her over when you're back."

"Yeah, I guess you might better, Nick, if you don't mind," Dad huffed. "She'll be in the hospital tomorrow if someone doesn't chase her down."

From November through March, Vi's system fell prey to a multitude of viruses. The bottle of Lavoris-red prescription cough medicine was ever-present on her desktop alongside the IN box, a preface to the gradually worsening symptoms that would have her on her back for sometimes weeks at a time. Over the years, obviously, the romance of having Annabelle Lee for a wife had worn off. My father had lost his patience with her flawed and often inconvenient constitution. I, however, had not. This woman had stuck by me through all my whininess as a sickly kid, and my love for her remained unjaded by her worsening winter health.

"I'm going too," I said, starting off with Big Nickie. Dad caught me by the arm.

"Marcella Antoinette, you are staying with me."

Marcella Antoinette Delongchamp, a name with an aristocratic ring, was borrowed from two women who were anything but. Marcella, after a great aunt I'd never met who'd been banished from her small French village when her practice of trading sexual favors with convicts for pigs from the local prison farm was discovered. Antoinette, from my grandmother, my father's mom, an alcoholic who spoke little English and visited us only once, spending the majority of her stay playing a small, blue accordion between glugs of cheap vino. I was nearly 13 then, and had no intention of following in the footsteps of my colorful namesakes. Ah, how little we know in youth.

"Please don't talk to me that way," I said through clenched teeth. "You've been barking out orders all day. I don't know what the problem is, but I've had enough of it." I jerked free from his grasp, turned away from him, and started walking. "I'll see you at home."

"Marcella, wait!" The softening desperation in his voice stopped me cold.

"What?"

"I...I'm sorry. Come on." He smiled. My dad, the charmer. A man's man whose 5 o'clock shadow occurred way before 5, he moved with a drama that seemed strange for a male. It was at this time in his life, his 40s, that his tall, androgynous good looks were becoming undeniable. Groomed fingernails and cuticles. Soft eyes and smile. The few wrinkles and gray hairs had given a hint of authority to his boyish grin, but it was still irresistible. Even to me.

"Just look at my gorgeous daughter." He opened his arms. "Come on and hang out with the old man for a while, huh?" He took me by the hands. "What, no gloves? Are you crazy?" Dad moved behind me, chin on my shoulder, arms around me securely, slipping my hands up his sleeves. "Just for a while. Don't ditch me in front of the whole town." He pressed his lips to my ear and whispered. "Don't make me suffer through this ridiculous thing alone. *Look* at him up there!"

I laughed, warm and secure against my father, observing the nativity for another hour or so until the mayor came by and started blabbing with Dad and I was able to hit the road. I walked home alongside the river, and through the darkness, I was guided by the lapping sounds of the invisible current to my right, effortlessly navigating the familiar path that lead to the Fox Street Bridge.

New snow sparkled in the moonlight on the bridge rails, and my bootsteps echoed as I clunked my way across. I'd rescued a screaming kitten from under that bridge once. Recalling that happy rush of childhood heroism, I picked up a rock and tossed it over the side, smiling with the splash. This was a lucky bridge to me. A sacred place. At 16, I wondered where my new sacred places would be as I embarked on a life after high school. Perhaps, beyond Piqua, the world would seem more pure and true. Perhaps living somewhere less under a microscope would allow virtue and freedom and the promise of adulthood. Perhaps...

It was at that bridge that I made a decision, the outcome of which would haunt me indefinitely.

The Love household was only a few blocks from the house of Delongchamp. Going back to a dark, empty house held little appeal, so I opted to stop by and mooch a baked ziti dinner. Such was my hunger and naïveté at 16.

Only one window winked light through the blackness of the Loves' front lawn. Shadows bounced rhythmically, like flames, across the features of the frog-shaped cement birdbath in what would be, come spring, Mrs. Love's prized begonia patch. Muffled strains of Frank Sinatra came from inside...

"*When I was seventeeeeeen... It was a very good yearrrrr...*"

...and the awful portrait framed by the Loves' picture window hung before me.

Vi lay on the sofa. Hooded eyes and slight smile. Face flushed. His hands, man hands, cupping her bare shoulders. Square, hairy back covering her almost completely. Big nose buried in the valley between her breasts.

Knees bent and back arched, she raised her body to meet his, their legs lumping beneath a red blanket. Silently, they moved together, illuminated by dying candlelight. Finally, his mouth found hers, and he collapsed on top of her, sliding down to rest his head on her breast, crying. She stroked his hair and cried herself.

I pulled away from the window, sliding against the aluminum siding, reaching the front steps, an unexpected hum of regret in my head. I felt dizzy and so disappointed. And yet I was newly awake, as if maturity had hit me just then like an iron dropped from a 10-story window. Secrets revealed at last. This was how things worked. This was the way of the world. It was a disappointment, but also a relief. If these were the rules, I could definitely play by them. If this was what it was to be an adult, well, I, too, could practice discretion.

Chapter 23

"Faith?"

A girl bumped me on my way out of the hotel. A girl, just a girl of 20 maybe—23, at the most. But she looked at me like I was a ghost, looked right through me. And to tell you the truth, I felt like one.

Pete's wasn't far. Pete's was down the street from my place. Our place. I couldn't go back home, not yet, not like this. So I thought Pete's, you know? Just for a couple of drinks. Just to be around some people. Yeah.

So there I was again at Pete's, too old to know the name of the band, but still young enough to dig the groove and the steady thump of the bass.

Soul.

Someone gave me two tiny pills at the bar and I ate them like Tic Tacs, without a thought. And the magic, it came in waves, steady and violent, crashing into my mind and rolling through my body.

Freak.

Heart beating with the drums, forgetting to breathe

and then remembering in quick gulps. Coming up from the crowd for air. Everything relaxing and contracting and then relaxing again. Awkward dance of involuntary motion. Brief lapses in short-term memory.

How did I get here?

"If you want me, show it...if you need me, prove it..." Lyrics. That song by Brownstone.

Freak.

Whose great idea was it to put gummi sharks in these drinks? They're too sweet, like something out of Willy Wonka. And where are the lights coming from? And where do all these sistas get their great asses? Set a drink on those asses, my friend. Set your watch by the time they keep with those hips. Tick, tock. My God, the looks I'm getting! Can they hear what I'm thinking? Stand still as the sound runs through me like a filter, like a spirit. Bliss and sex and unlimited motion. Fluid. Yes, fluid, for the first time in my life. Unseen and unheard and unmoved by everything around me. A trance? I don't think so. I can't think...

Someone was circling me as if on wheels, as if in flight. Some queen.

I am not a man in drag, asshole. I'm tall, that's all.

Drink me.

The book my mother used to read to me.

Drink me and you'll be small like everyone else.

I had hated Vi for sleeping with Nickie Love, Sr., for falling under his hot Italian spell. Was he that good in bed?

Mother with her perpetual tears. Vi with the power to climb on top. Grabbing the headboard for leverage. Pounding it out of him, angry. The truth, goddamn it! I can hear her saying it without words. The truth!

Touches and whispers. Topless dancing. Girls going

down and then coming up to quench themselves with drinks filled with these stupid gummi sharks. This isn't a gay bar; this is a sovereign nation! No rules in this country, sugar. No holds barred. And I'm alone, man, all alone. A giant redwood ready to fall. Will they hear it when I do? And if they do, will they care?

The finality of it, the stink of sweat and smoke and overzealous perfume application, hit me more than ever during the obligatory third-set "Hits of the '80s" slow dance at Pete's.

A flurry, it all was. A furious flurry.

Martinis and clove cigarettes. Finger foods and human sushi swimming about on trays and high heels. *Purple Rain* had never seemed such a dirge.

Judy and Gina, the Anderson twins, held me up in front and back, wrapping themselves around me like sticky licorice ropes, tough and sweet, when I let my mouth fall onto their necks and shoulders. It was long after midnight and I had let the fever get me. I was past the point of drugging it or dancing it away. Nothing was doing the trick, and nothing would, short of a visit to the hospital followed by extensive, expensive R&R in the tropics. Opportunity was knocking twice, in the shape of the shapely Anderson duo, but while my thoughts were in the gutter, my clitoris was far beyond a jump-start. I was sick and rather drunk, and such sensual, sisterly moments are not to be wasted when one is so...well, wasted.

Convinced that fresh air and a cab ride to the emergency room were in order, I said my goodbyes and mashed my way clumsily through the mosh of bodies toward the exit, smiling over my shoulder at the twins, seeing them surrounded by a misty white light, their faces full and fresh as the 10 year old farm girls they may have once been. I blinked and saw them again, nearing 30 and full of collagen, waving sadly and clutching long-neck bottles.

It was past 2 A.M. Pain licked down my jawline and at the cords of my neck, pulsing within the bones of my shoulder and arm, taking my breath. I had made my way out onto the sidewalk somehow, made my way across the street to embrace a broken street lamp. The sting of cold metal against my cheek snapped open my eyes but did little or nothing to abate the stiffness and the heaviness that had fallen over me.

"Oh, Christ..."

I threw an arm around the lamppost in traditional drunken style and smiled, reassured by its unyielding support. And as the air became thick, as the rows of windows reached up toward the moon before me, I began to recite a poem I'd read in 10th-grade English class.

"From childhood's hour I have not been..."

Footsteps shuffled against pavement behind me.

"...as others were; I have not seen..."

"Ma'am?" A voice.

"...as others saw; I could not bring..."

"Uh, ma'am? Excuse me..."

"...My passions from a common spring."

Three short coughs, wholly unproductive and painful, brought a stream of vomit from my lips and splashed it onto the pavement. Still hugging the lamppost, I turned my head to see his shoes. Worn, soaked Fila hightops. I closed my eyes, steadied myself, and continued:

"From the same source I have not taken my sorrow; I could not awaken my heart to joy at the same tone. And all I loved, I loved..."

I raised up to face him.

"...alone."

He was young, so young—with a face spotted with acne and sporadic beard growth. A smile as ready as any young man's, really, but the eyes remained unwrinkled, unmoved by the smile he offered. Dilated and black. A shark's eyes.

"Ma'am?"

This was it. How many years in New York and I'd never seen this firsthand, though I'd heard about it daily. And now I would experience it for myself. Would he ask me for the time?

"Could you tell me what street this is?"

Directions! He was asking for directions. Not uncommon for hygienically challenged street youths wearing layers of filthy T-shirts to ask for directions at 2 in the morning. Before raping you, that is.

"It's Christopher." I looked him square in the face.

He was shorter than I was, about 5-foot-10. Caucasian. Thin. If I was lucky, this would be about drugs. It was so hard to tell with the young ones. If he cleaned up, he could be a pro, with that baby face. Plenty of chicken hawks would have jumped at him, seeing that last bit of innocence, eager to extinguish it with a session of rough anal in the back of their sedans. But no, this was no pro. He was dirty, probably a junkie. And I would hand him the cash and be on my way.

I hoped.

"Thank you." His voice lost its buoyancy, as did his smile.

We stared at each other for a moment, and I thought he might be losing his nerve.

"You're welcome." I nodded, turning my back to him and taking an unsteady step away.

"Wait!"

Click.

It's said that toughs never use switchblades like you see in the movies, as switchblades are more stylish than practical. They use what's commonly called an "O.J. knife" on the street, a sort of hunting knife with a thick, serrated blade. When I spun around, I saw that the rumors were true. The blade was exposed and locked into place.

"The bag!" He was shaking. Perhaps I was his first. Oh, what a tangled web. "Gimme the bag!"

"All it has is cosmetics and...my organizer," I said, which was true. I opened my handbag and removed it. "See? Phone numbers. If you need cash..."

"Fucking give it to me!"

"What are you going to do?" I smiled. "Call my clients?"

"Now!"

"If you need cash, I..."

"Look..." He jabbed the air with the knife and glanced around. "I'll cut you, bitch. Just..." A car door slammed down the block. He motioned with the knife toward an alleyway. "Get over there." He shoved me, pushed me with a flat hand against my chest. For the first time, really, I was hit with the fear. "Move, cunt!" The fear of being raped, being stabbed, being left dead like others who were found by garbage men and drunks in dark places throughout New York. A secret of the city. A casualty of casual living. A stiffening statistic.

"Fucking move!" He shoved me again and I stumbled, grasping my cane to steady myself, and then...

"Cunt!"

He made his move with the knife, blade illuminated by moonlight. I made my move simultaneously...

CRACK!

...bringing the glans of the bull's penis up swiftly to connect solidly with his chin.

He tumbled back, his knife flying from his grasp and skittering across the concrete. I looked at him as he sat in the alleyway. He was holding his jaw and spitting out blood, some teeth maybe. A noise, a gurgling growl, rose out of him as he struggled to stand.

"No!" I gripped my cane like a baseball bat and stepped into the swing.

CRACK!

"Uhhhh!" He held his head just above the ear, blood and hair sliding between his fingers, and looked up at me. His look was so innocent, as if our shift in power had erased his anger.

"Run." I breathed, raising the cane to my shoulder again. "Run!" And on my second scream, he did just that.

He ran.

Had this victorious moment come at a more opportune time, I would probably have hummed the theme from *Rocky* or wept with joy for my good fortune. As it was, however, I was in no shape for a victory dance. I was quite busy, you see.

I was dying.

A short trek through Washington Square Park and I would've been home free, essentially. A short trek is too much, however, when your heart is literally broken.

Halfway across, I collapsed into the soft snow. The pain had changed from dull to crushing, concentrated jolts. My lungs seized. I clutched my chest, opened my mouth, and watched the stars disappear.

Chapter 24

I awakened to torture, slave to what felt like the prodding hands of every med student on the East Coast. Every joint ached. Every breath they forced into me felt like a thousand needles jabbing into my chest. Shapes merged into a nauseating, kaleidoscopic blur, shapes I assumed were human; but I had no sense of connection to others anymore. In the emergency room, there may be 20 people flashing lights into your eyes and yelling, but the real battle you fight by yourself.

Cyanotic, my hair hanging in frozen clumps against my head, I'd been delivered to the Emergency Room in haste. A well-dressed DOA.

Being in the intensive care unit is like going to Bill Knapp's for dinner: scads of old people and not much service for the price. God's waiting room. Take a number.

The curtain surrounding my bed was mint-green, a deceptively calm color scheme for the severity of the situation. I didn't know much, not even the date or the time, but I knew I was in deep trouble. Waking up to hazy thoughts and tubes jammed into what seemed like every available orifice—including a few that had not been there previously—was my first clue that things didn't look good. Germaine's professional explanation, which she gave while holding my hand ever so gently, confirmed my fate. Hypothermia, just for starters. Pneumonia, of course. And...drum roll, please...bacterial endocarditis. It seems the shortness of breath had not been just an asthma thing. The infection in my lungs had spread to my heart. My heart, only the most important organ in my whole body, and somehow I'd fucked it up. Quite a rabbit out of the hat, I'd say. I knew I was self-destructive, but I had no idea I was this good at it.

Germaine's tone of concern was tinged with "I told you so." She'd been trying to reach me, repeatedly leaving messages at my home and office that the blood work from my last office visit had been inconclusive and she'd wanted more tests, yadda yadda yadda... Was she afraid I was going to sue her?

Then Germaine told me that a friend of mine would be spending some time in the hospital with me. One Patricia Fink.

Patricia was busy in ICU bed number seven—adapting to her shiny new liver.

They'd found a donor match the same night I was brought in and had performed the transplant immediately. Her husband, Hal, had asked if we could share a room once we were both out of intensive care.

I looked up at the ceiling, perplexed. Just like that, Trish was getting her life back? After months of grieving, it had never occurred to me that she might recover.

An actress knows her days are numbered when she is awarded a lifetime achievement award on broadcast television.

Pedestrian folk such as myself know it's curtains when they call in the family, especially when the family actually shows up. So when I fluttered open my tired eyelids to see Phyllis Delongchamp standing at my bedside, she may as well have been holding a sickle.

"Marcella?"

She was more or less a blurred figure—thanks to the primo dope I was getting. But when this blurred figure moved to touch my face, the blips from my heart monitor raced. Was it dread? Hopeful anticipation? I couldn't help it. I wanted her to touch me, to comfort me. Perch on the precipice of death, and believe me, you'll want your mommy, too. But just as her fingers were about to caress my face, she pulled away.

"Jesus, it's hard for me to see you like this, Marcella. You can't understand the kind of pain I feel to see my only daughter lying here in such a mess."

I listened to her pacing alongside my bed.

"I don't know how in the hell you got yourself into this mess, but I've got my ideas. I can only hope that if God has the mercy to let you live through this, you'll change your ways. A person *can* change, Marcella. You may not think you can, but you can. I know it. But a person has to *want* to change. A person has to *want* to survive. You think I didn't want to throw up my hands and give up when I'd been in labor with you for three days? I did. I did, Marcella, but I held on because I wanted my little girl to come into the world and have a chance.

"Of course you don't remember me being in labor with you for three days. Three *days* of no sleep or food or peace, wondering if either of us would survive. You almost killed us both, you know that? You were almost three months early. I

226

was out planting gladiola bulbs when my water broke, with not a soul to take me to the hospital. I had to get the neighbor to drive me and watch after your brother. Your father was at the store and we couldn't reach him for hours. Well, that's like your father, isn't it? And now he's off honeymooning with that new wife of his..."

What? Dad got remarried?

But Mom was droning on about my birth. "It was three days of torture before they pulled you out. So small! Four pounds. They didn't even let me hold you, just took you straight to the incubator. We had to wait almost a month before we could bring you home..."

My mother hadn't spoken to me in 20 years, and brother, was she making up for it. Maybe she thought it was her last chance and, considering this, I couldn't blame her for going on. I guess she had a lot to get off her chest. And I was in no position to do anything but listen. A ventilator makes you the ultimate captive audience.

But thanks to my drug-induced torpor I began to drift in and out of consciousness and caught only snatches of my mother's ramblings. Snatches such as:

"You're like your father, you know that? Nothing was ever good enough..."

and

"Even when they gave you a shot at the doctor's, you never cried. Not once. And you know why? Because you were loved, and you knew it..."

and

"You traded your mother for a substitute who put all kinds of big ideas in your head."

and

"I may have had a problem with Valium, but that

doesn't mean I didn't love my kids. The doctors were handing it out like candy then. How was I to know it was addictive?"

It went on for hours.

Let me die, I thought. *Anything to escape this woman.*

But no.

"You think I didn't know there was something different about you all along? I did. From the time you were a 2-year-old, I knew there was something different. You would look at me, and I could see something. I couldn't put my finger on it, but I knew it was causing you to pull away. Maybe you didn't want to hurt me, or maybe you were afraid of me. Of me—the one who spent sleepless nights holding you and rocking you when you had the German measles."

And later:

"Yes, I punished you, but only to make you behave. I never had any help from your father in that department, so I had to make you behave the best way I knew how. I tried to make you a good person..."

Mercifully, I passed out.

When I opened my eyes again, Faith stood at the foot of my bed. Snow still clung to the shoulders of her purple down coat. Seeing her was a touch of heaven in my hell. The dark eyes and hair. That flawless skin. If I was to die, this was what I wanted most to remember.

My mother hadn't left yet, or even stopped talking. She continued to pace and emote and flail.

"I don't understand. I may be a simple woman, but at least I'll admit that I don't understand how you live. I don't know how you find each other or what you expect from each other..."

Obviously, Faith had introduced herself, as this was

directed as much toward her as it was to me. She saw that I was awake and smiled calmly.

"I won't ever approve of how you're living," Mom ranted. "And I'll never understand it either. I don't want to understand and I don't want to know the details. I'm ashamed. I'm sorry but I can't help but be ashamed of the life you've chosen to lead. I know it isn't right. It can't be. I hate your ways and I'll never accept them. I don't know who you are and I don't *want* to know. I was ashamed of you then and I still am."

Faith looked at me with pity. As pissed off as I'd made her, I knew she could never wish deadly illness and a prolonged monologue from my mother on me. Not even I deserved this, and she knew it.

I closed my eyes.

Faith's voice: "Excuse me, Mrs. Delongchamp, but I think it might help you to take a little break."

A pause.

"I mean, I think..."

"You have no right to tell me anything."

I listened to what sounded like my mother's purse jingling then the slipping on of an overcoat. My mother's voice: "I feel sick. I think I need a cup of coffee or something. Anyway, my son's in the cafeteria waiting. We came in this morning and we've got a flight out late this afternoon."

Faith's voice: "Well, goodbye then."

"Yes, well, goodbye. It was very nice meeting you." My mother moved to the door, calling back to me. "Goodbye, Marcella. Rest, OK? Be a good girl for me and rest."

Faith stood at the foot of my bed. I wanted so badly to speak, but what with the hose I was forced to fellate as it pumped air into my burning lungs, I could not. I couldn't even smile back. Too weak to lift my arms, I couldn't reach for her. Somehow, I shifted beneath the sheets. It startled her, and she stepped back, her eyes widening. I saw the fear in her face.

Pay no attention to the man behind the curtain. It's me.

She moved a little closer, sitting on the bed with her hands in her lap and her eyes downcast. Just then I recalled what I'd said, remembered offering her money and coldly telling her it was over, and all the other moronic, horrible things I'd done. She'd run from me and, shit, who could blame her? So here was my chance, perhaps my last chance, and I couldn't even tell her I was sorry.

Faith slid her hand into mine. She kept her gaze directed at the floor.

"I saw the girl from your office. I saw her with her little boy at the park, and she told me you were here." She finally looked up, and when our eyes met she began to cry. "And I didn't know if I should come to see you. I didn't know..."

I did what I could to comfort her, which was nothing, essentially. Maybe I was able to squeeze her fingers a little. A nurse carrying a pan came in, announcing that it was time for my bath.

"I'll do it," Faith said quietly. "You don't even *know* her..." Her voice wavered and rose, then settled. "Is it OK? I'll be careful. Don't worry, I used to be a candy striper."

The nurse patted Faith on the arm. "Honey, maybe you should let me handle this, huh? Maybe step out and"—her voice dropped to a whisper—"collect yourself a little."

Faith shook her head. "I'm fine. Just..." She sniffled, sighed, and managed to smile. "Would you bring us some more towels, please?"

The nurse looked at me, not into my eyes for a response but more *at* me like the sad mess, the vegetable that I was. And I guess she figured what the hell because she left us and pulled the privacy curtain as she went. "I'll get her a new gown too. Be careful of the catheter there, and her IV, and those monitor wires..."

I drifted for a minute and came to as Faith dabbed at my face and neck with a warm washcloth, wiping away the fevered sweat, rinsing and working her way down until I felt her fingers fumble at the snaps of my gown.

"You gotta hang in there, girlfriend," she said. One fairly swift slipping motion and I was nude to the waist. The fresh air felt refreshing against my bare chest. "It's not that bad. You can handle this. You're going to be fine." She paused at the EKG buttons stuck below my collarbone. "Looks like they've got you all wired up here." She tried to laugh, easing the warm cloth over my arms, breasts, armpits, and ribs before reaching for the towel. "You're going to be fine, Macy. Everything's going to be OK."

I nodded off again, and when I awoke she was finished and rolling me over to straighten my gown underneath me with some help. When the nurse noticed that my eyes were open, she piped, "Much better, isn't it?"

Faith sat beside me again, and we were alone and silent for a while, except for the blips and bleeps and hissing of the machines. I fell asleep again, and she was there when I woke up. Fifteen or 20 minutes later, she slipped on her coat, kissed her finger and placed it over my heart.

"You get well, OK?" she said, stepping back from the bed. "I...um...I don't want to...I don't want you to feel..."

She ran back and kissed my cheek and lay her head gently against my chest. "God, please...*please*..."

Faith stood, wiped her eyes, and backed away.

Then she was gone.

And she did not come back.

Chapter 25

"Hey, kid."

Kid? It had to be Trish. She was a whole month older than I was.

I opened my eyes. Yep. Behind curtain number three in the bed beside mine was none other than the new and improved Trish, waving and grinning. Hal was at her side, looking up from his crossword puzzle to smile brightly.

"Hey." I managed a feeble wave.

Hal walked over to my bed, leaned in, and kissed my forehead. "Glad you're still with us, Mace," he said, and I wanted to cry. "Your roommate and I were starting to worry."

"Kate was here." Trish pressed a button and her bed bent up under her knees with a whirring sound. "We had to kick her out this morning."

"She wouldn't leave you all last night," Hal chuckled. "You know it's a compliment when a teenager shows she cares."

He was a short little fellow, Hal. Bespectacled and

balding, with a general chunkiness to his frame—without seeming actually fat. Hal had worn button-down shirts every day since birth, I think, and Land's End loafers. He had fixed me a big spaghetti dinner on my birthday every year since I'd known him, and he sang along badly to opera. He was a doll.

"So, it looks like you girls have got quite the set-up here. Adjustable bed, cable television..."

"Time for a 24-hour *Smokey and the Bandit*...marathon," I said, still rather short of breath and a bit embarrassed by my halted speech pattern.

"Nothing like Jerry Reed in bad slacks. Oh, baby!" Trish laughed. "Macy-girl!" She applauded. "Welcome back. How do you feel?"

"Oh, swell... And yourself?"

"Good. Better than good." She smiled broadly. "Lucky."

"You were long overdue." I tried to sit up a bit and winced, my back nice and stiff. "So do you know anything about...the donor?"

"Well, he was 18. Hit by a bus." She looked guilty. "A freak accident. The driver said he was holding his mouth, like somebody'd punched him, and he ran right out in front of her."

Hal snapped his fingers. "You know, it happened not far from that bar you live at. On the same night they found you."

The heart monitor beeps came quicker. Suddenly, I was an arcade game.

"What did he look like?"

"Honey, you wouldn't have known him," Trish said. "He didn't live around here."

"But did they tell you what he looked like?"

Oh, God. Let him be black or Asian or wearing an eye-patch...something!

"No, they didn't." Trish shrugged. "All I heard is that he ran right out in front of a bus and he was 18. Probably one of those kids who come here trying to be an actor."

"Or a college student." Hal shook his head. "We're just thankful that he was a donor."

Trish nodded. "Probably some bastard mugger was after him and he was trying to escape."

"Probably." I smiled.

"Well, he had a good heart." Hal dabbed his eyes with a hanky. "That's all I know."

"And a wonderful liver," added Trish.

"Best damn liver in the world," Hal said.

I decided to let it go. What's one more secret in the Village anyway? Besides, I'd never be sure if it was the same guy.

Trish poked Hal in the arm and pointed to the corner. He stood and lifted a shopping bag. "Hey, we brought you a get-well gift. See?" From the bag, he pulled an enormous quilt. Lovely, hand-stitched flannel.

"What do you think? I was saving it to give you for your birthday." Trish perked up. "It doesn't exactly go with your home decor, but..."

"I love it," I said, running my hands along its soft texture. "It's beautiful."

"I made it myself. Don't just stand there, Hal, unfold it for her."

Hal did as he was ordered, spreading it out over the bed and pulling it up till it met my chin.

"There. An early birthday present." She had tears in her eyes. God, did everyone think I was going to die?

"You sure you want to share accommodations with an infamous lesbian such as myself?"

"I'll try to restrain my desire."

And so we lay there that day and began our convalescence. Hal straightened blankets and fluffed our pillows and brought us Junior Mints from the vending machine down the hall. Trish lectured me on eating more and not worrying and obeying my parade of doctors. Eventually, she shut up. Talked herself to sleep, right there alongside me in our hard-as-a-fucking-rock hospital beds. I snuggled down into the quilt she'd made for me and fell into an amused sleep myself—beside my friend, the incredible snoring princess.

I was in the hospital for six weeks. Trish had been home two weeks upon my release. My cast had been removed in the ER, and during the period of time it took me to regain my strength and become medically stable, I was also getting physical therapy for my ankle and learning to walk again. My bull penis cane never made it to the hospital. Near the end of my visit, I weighed in at a whopping 128. At six feet tall, I looked freakishly thin. During what came to be my obligatory shuffles down the hall with IV bottle in tow, people stared, and when they did I made faces. But despite my sideshow-worthy appearance, I had survived, due mostly to the above and beyond attentions of Sharene.

Sharene was a full-figured woman whose squishy-soled shoes could be heard squeaking beneath the stress of her considerable heft the minute she burst through the ward's double doors, huffing and puffing her way down the hall. A respiratory therapist, Sharene accepted me as the ultimate challenge. I was weak and uncooperative. Despite daily pep talks from Trish and visits from the gift-bearing Hal and Kate, I remained heartbroken. Because Faith had not returned since the day she met Phyllis. And for a long while, I didn't particularly care to live. I never mirrored Sharene's smiles.

"Girl, you are too skinny to leave this hospital alive," she said one day as she was taking my pulse.

"It makes no difference," I said, staring out at the gray city skies through the tiny window in my room. "I'm dead already."

"Well, you don't eat. You don't shit. You don't hardly speak to nobody." She plumped my pillows and sat beside me on the bed. "I guess it's possible."

After one restless evening of counting tiny squares in the ceiling, I was unnerved, exhausted, and had a very stiff neck. Sharene sat in her usual spot and pretended to stare at the television with me.

"Cajun cooking." She grunted. "You like to cook?"

"Not particularly," I answered.

"You gonna let me do my job today?"

"Goddamn." I turned my head to face her and winced, throwing a hand to my neck.

"What's wrong? That bed workin' on your neck?" She slid closer. "Go on and lean up a little. We'll take care of this. Go on."

Sharene's hands were tiny and soft and heavily decorated with rings. Delicate as they were, however, I was surprised at their strength. And as her fingers carefully worked away the soreness in my neck, I remembered Faith's hands.

"What's wrong, baby?" Sharene stopped, shocked. I covered my face. She put her arms around me and held me as I wept.

"It's OK, baby, don't cry. Shhhhh." She rocked me against her. "Don't cry." She patted my back. "It's OK, baby. I understand."

"No, you don't." I clutched at her soft shoulders and wailed. "You can't!"

"You bet I can." She snorted and raised an eyebrow, lifting my chin to look into my eyes. "What's his name?"

"It's not a man."

"No woman cries like that unless her heart's been stomped on."

I sniffled. "You know how hard it is to find the right man?"

She laughed. "Do I ever!"

"Well, it's even harder to find the right woman. But I found her." I lay my head on her shoulder. "And I lost her."

"Same difference, baby. Same thing." She patted and rocked me. "You and I just shop at different stores. We're both buying the same stuff."

And we were, I suppose. She was far cooler about it than I could've imagined. Sharene helped pass the time, reading aloud steamy, hilarious articles from *Black Romance* magazine that gave us both quite a chuckle. We were friends, really, which seemed so strange in such sterile surroundings. Our conversations were quite candid.

And on the day of my discharge, I left a check for $15,000 under the windshield wiper of Sharene's primer-gray Nova in the hospital parking lot. Not enough to save the world, of course, but enough for a subscription to *Black Romance* and perhaps a better set of wheels.

Chapter 26

Even after six weeks in the hospital I was still pretty much useless. Consequently, I agreed to stay with Hal and Trish for a couple of weeks.

WELCOME HOME, MISSY! read the banner over the front door of their brownstone. Hanging on to Hal's arm, I was greeted by the entire Fink clan, and after many hugs I excused myself to the bathroom to throw up. Nothing personal, mind you. The excitement was just too much to handle.

As I slept for most of the first day or two, darling Kate woke me periodically for medications, meals, and general adulation. I was no longer just her mother's best friend and her godmother; I was a confidante, an adviser, and—now that I'd seen the white light and survived—a lesbian folk hero.

The room Trish had made up for me was spacious and cheerful, swimming with fresh flowers. She, Kate, and Hal had obviously put a great deal of thought and time into making it as warm and inviting as possible. It was decorated in a kind of homey Victorian scheme, with tea rose sheets and French chairs. A picture of a little girl and a Collie dog hung on the wall opposite a delicate dressing table that had been stocked with my cosmetics from home.

Graceful.

Delightful.

And I hated it.

On the fifth day, I stepped out of my slippers, fell back onto one of the French chairs, and felt the seat cushion poof beneath me. Queen Potpourri sat in the other French chair. Trish, the only woman in the world who could make a Mormon housewife seem butch by comparison. I put my hands to my face and moaned.

"Are you praying?" Trish asked.

"No," I said. "I'm plotting my suicide."

"Well, try not to do it here, OK? We just had this carpet installed."

I uncovered my eyes, staring up at the very mauve ceiling. "I was thinking of doing it at Disneyland. You know: 'The Happiest Place on Earth.' I'll show those bastards."

"God, I wish you'd forget about her." Trish punched my upper arm lightly. "Have you been taking your Prozac?"

"It's not Faith," I said. "It's that I've become your Grandma Walton."

"What?"

"Your Grandma Walton. Your useless burden. I don't want anyone applauding if I accomplish something ordinary. I don't want anyone tolerating my curmudgeon-ness. I don't want to shuffle about your house and have my very presence become an annoyance."

She looked hurt, predictably. "You don't like the room."

"It's not that," I protested. Goddamn her, she was on to

me. "It's just that...I'm too young to be this old, you know? I feel impotent. I can't impose upon you and your family this way, Trish. My recovery is not your responsibility."

"But you are family." She said it so sweetly, so honestly.

"No, no, darling." I shook my head. "I'm not. Hal, the girls...they're your family. And in good health, I'm an interesting addition to your family on holidays. But now, at best I'm a house pet. And at worst, I'm a fashionable invalid.

"I've got to go home," I said.

And just then, just as I had made my stand, Hal came to the door of the ultra femme boudoir.

"Macy?" His face was uneasy. "Dr. Allen just called. From Ohio."

Trish and I looked at each other. Intuition? She took my hand.

"I'm sorry," he said, folding his arms. "Your father's passed away."

Chapter 27

A Midwestern funeral goes something like this: Family and friends are notified of person's death. Everyone prepares some kind of casserole or cake and delivers it to the home of the bereaved, where they all hang around and help the immediate family with chores and crap. There's a general sharing of sedatives. A visitation later that night at the funeral home, which most people skip. There's a visitation the next day too, which about half the people skip. If you really gave a shit about the person, you must attend the funeral by the third day. Things will probably be getting ripe at the funeral home by then, but corpses are like art in the Midwest and must be displayed for two or three days. After the funeral, we all hang out somewhere and drink or go back to the relative's home for a wake or whatever.

I had my pills and the little box that separates them by days of the week. I had several packets of decaffeinated tea bags and Kleenex. I had my warm scarf wrapped around my throat and even a tiny, travel-size tank of oxygen packed into my carry-on valise. I was as ready as I could be for the adventure of my father's death.

Tents were up for the Piqua winter carnival, which was kind of the town's way of tying together Christmas and New Year's and postponing that trepidatious trip to the top of the telephone poles to remove the strands of garland and the gaudy but innocent oversize candy canes that lined Main Street.

A great deal had changed since I'd left. A great deal and nothing at all. Chain stores had bought out many of the mom-and-pops, warping my treasured dime store memories like an unfavorable recording artist remaking a favorite song. Still, there were whispers of my childhood. There were certain consistencies, like the flag flying at City Hall, or the little boy wailing as he sat in the barber's chair, or... well, my own insecurities. I still felt just as isolated as I'd felt when I was ten, scuffing my heels down the uneven side-walks and snapping my fingers in time to a non-existent song in my head, just to look like I was at ease to anyone who happened to notice. And these were small-town folk. It was their job to notice. As an adult, I was still snapping my fingers as I walked through town.

My father's house, once a snazzy brick ranch, was still well tended but tragically outdated. He'd remarried recent-ly—as I'd learned in the hospital—and the new wife had made a few changes to the landscaping, but it was all much the same as it had been when I'd left at 18. A number of cars were crammed into the drive, and as I approached the snowy front steps I wondered why in the hell I'd worn my Blahniks instead of boots. Brrrrrr.

"Hello?" I ventured inside, since the door was unlocked. "Hello?" I called out again, and made my way through the foyer and into the dining room. Death is another word for potluck, in the Midwest. The tablecloth was hardly visible under the palette of covered dishes. I picked up a lid and engulfed my sad sinuses with the scent of home cooked sweet potatoes.

"Macy?"

Lid still in hand, I looked up to find that a youngish blonde had wandered in. Fresh sweet potatoes, and now this. Mmmm.

"Yes!" I dropped the lid back onto the pot with a clank. "Yes, I am. Macy. I'm Macy." I extended my hand and took two steps toward her. "And you are?"

"I'm Lorraine." She shook my hand. "I married your dad."

Whoa!

"Oh! W-w-well..." I stammered. "It's so nice to meet you." Kudos to the old man. Obviously, he liked the younger ones too.

She took my face into her hands, quite suddenly.

I blushed.

"There's no mistaking you," she said, inspecting in awe.

"Oh? Well...I..."

"The resemblance between you and your father." Lorraine remained transfixed, as she turned my head from side to side. "It's uncanny."

"Yes. Well..."

"I'm sorry." She smiled and took her hands away, appropriately embarrassed. "Let me take your things. Would you like a drink?"

"I'd love one, but I really shouldn't."

"How about some coffee?"

"Sure." I lunged and grabbed her arm. "No! I mean...I

can't." I was still blushing. "The caffeine. I'm not supposed to have it. I have my own tea bags, actually."

"OK." She smiled a very nice smile. "Well, why don't I take these to your room, and you can help yourself to some hot water in the kitchen. I think your mom's in there."

Of course. The kitchen. Mom's old turf. Dad had bought her a different place after their divorce, but here she was at the original homestead. She was probably at the sink peeling potatoes, something she used to always do to relax.

"The funeral's not till tomorrow, hon. You can get settled in and rest up."

I fiddled with my watch. "I may need to borrow an iron. This suit has to last me two days. The airline lost my bag, and..."

"No bother. I can loan you something to sleep in." She continued down the hallway. "I'll press your suit out for you in the morning." Her level of organization took me by surprise, though she was simply being a good wife. "Go on, now, and get your tea. I'll turn down your bed. I'm sure you must be tired from your trip." She stopped and glanced over her shoulder. "Or I can get your tea for you, if you like."

"No, that's..." I smiled and relaxed a little. "I'll get it. That's fine." Wow. My father had been spoiled. "Thank you, Lorraine."

"No trouble, hon."

The pipe cleaner ornament that I'd made in second grade still graced a branch of my father's Christmas tree in the living area. He'd remembered me, as this and the cards I'd received commemorating birthdays and holidays over the years demonstrated. I had always answered his brief well wishes with a reluctant sense of duty, and now I felt heavy with remorse. The fact that he'd held on to such an artifact of my childhood proved that he still loved me, he'd never stopped. Flashing back to that snow-covered churchyard where Elliot had debuted as the baby Jesus, I remembered my father's long arms wrapped around me from behind. I remembered the scent of Caswell-Massey cologne as he rested his chin on my shoulder. My dad had been handsome, really handsome, with hair that would never behave and a chiseled jawline. He'd been well-meaning but inconsiderate. He'd been selfish sometimes but not malicious. He'd been an entrepreneur, and a softie, and charmingly fatally flawed.

I'd always thought the old "Hindsight is 20/20" thing was a load of crap. I'd never been much for regrets. But I couldn't help but wish, then, that I'd let him hold me a little longer that night at the live nativity. Maybe then he'd have known that I loved him too.

Mom stood at the kitchen sink, slicing lemons, deep in concentration.

I took a breath and removed my gloves. "Hello, Phyllis."

She said nothing in return, just kept on about her business. She hadn't heard me, perhaps. Getting older, after all. I cleared my throat, and just as I was preparing to say it again with a bit more gusto, she glanced up from the pitcher of ice and said, "You look like shit."

"Yes, I suppose I do."

She turned her attention back to the sink, where she puttered about absently, humming. "There's coffee on the stove."

"I...um..." I watched her for any further and more significant reaction. Nada. "I think I'll pass, thanks." Then I closed my eyes and heard Faith's voice: *I think it might help you to take a little break.*

She's right, I decided, and I walked out of the kitchen.

It was evening, and white lights had been strewn through the limbs of the trees lining a short stretch of the riverbanks. A warm snap had melted the ice, but not enough to prevent sweatered families from carving their way down the center of the river on skates. Somewhere, a cassette player strained its speakers to belt out Christmas music. As the tape was gradually slowing from the cold, the result was a highly mournful, murky version of Bing Crosby's "White Christmas."

My feet were freezing, but I trudged on, as frostbite was a preferable fate to spending more quality time with Mom. Those who had parked in my father's driveway had hustled over for a quick skate before the wake. From the false light glittering against the ice, the river scene was surreal, like a film set. I found a relatively snowless patch of ground and stamped my feet.

"Macy?"

That voice. Was it...?

"Andy?" I smiled. It was. "Andy Babcock!"

"Macy! Well, look at you!" This man, pseudo-love of my teenage years, put his arm around my ass and lifted me up over his shoulder, spinning. "Wow!"

"Andy! Shit! Andy!" I laughed and shrieked and just as I was starting to get dizzy, one snowmobile boot locked around the other and he fell—actually, we both fell—crashing into the snow.

"Oh, I'm so sorry." He brushed the snow from my hair and stood, taking my hands and hoisting me to my feet. "You OK?"

I couldn't stop laughing, my hands still in his, and when our eyes met he said, "I'm sorry to hear about your dad."

"Yeah." I caught my breath. "Thanks."

Andy had a 9 year-old daughter, a wife, and his father's dry cleaning business. He seemed happy and still looked like a boy to me, and he was just about to tell me more when...

"Grace!"

I shot Andy a quizzical expression.

"Murray's kid." He rolled his eyes. "She's always wandering off."

"Grace! No!"

And the unmistakable sound of ice breaking was followed by a muffled splash. Grace Murray, wandering child of Piqua, had wandered onto the thinnest ice on the river.

"Oh, fuck." I couldn't move. Fear tore into me. Grace Murray would be a name in the obituaries if...

Here it was. Here was my purpose for returning to Piqua. Local gal makes good in the big city, saves Grace at winter carnival. It all made sense. I had lived for a reason. Kids had such potential, after all. Why, she might even grow up to become president. And me, well, I'd be given a key to the city.

Through the snow I ran. In my slippery Blahnik flats, I ran. Past the men and the women and the teenagers holding one another, I ran. I meant to stop at the river's edge. Instead I slid out onto the ice and into the hole. Eight ball, corner pocket. *Blam! Crash! Splash!* In I went.

I screamed once out of shock and bobbed up to take a breath before submerging completely. For a moment, all I could see were bubbles and dirt—then, a quick flash of red fabric. I reached out for it, clawed at it through the muddy cloud.

It vanished.

My chest ached for air, and I pressed my face against the ice. I found inches of space between the ice and the water's surface, allowing me a few precious gulps of oxygen. And just as I was about to press on in my quest to save Grace's life and lend purpose to my own, something poked through, dislodging the ice beside me. A shovel handle. I grabbed it and was unceremoniously flung to the riverbank by what felt like dozens of hands.

Spitting grit and regaining my land sight, I shook my head to unclog my ears and was met with raucous laughter.

"You all right, there?" A bearded man in an orange hunting jacket thumped my shoulder.

"The girl," I sputtered, hit suddenly with the shivering wet cold reality. "Where's the girl?"

"Oh, we fished her out. Happens to somebody every year." He laughed and pulled a canvas tarp up around my shoulders. "Getting to be a carnival tradition. But you"—he laughed even more heartily—"you threw a whole new kind of twist on things."

Nathan of beard and Day-Glo hunting garb drove me back to my father's house. Heat blasted from the vents in the cab of his Chevy truck, but it did little to penetrate the sog. Our conversation was minimal.

"We need to get you inside so you can take a good hot shower," he said, reaching over the gearshift to open my door—quite the gentleman. "You'll be fine."

The bath had made me sluggish. And Lorraine had shared her Valium stash. She now sat beside me on the bed.

"How are you feeling?" she asked me.

"Much better, thanks to you. What about yourself?"

"I'm good. I'm fine." She continued toweling my hair.

I grabbed her wrist and gave her a sleepy suspicious glance. "Really?"

"Oh, you want the real truth?" She laughed. "I want a fag so badly I could scream. A cigarette. I'm sorry. My parents were from England and they called them fags. That's funny, isn't it?" She folded her arms and stood in front of the mirror. "I quit five years ago, but.... You comfy, hon? Those shoes! Uh! Such beautiful shoes. Bill said you had style. And that suit! A shame they're ruined." Lorraine spun around. "I'm sorry. You must be positively exhausted. Here, I brought you a plate."

The all-American potluck wake awaited downstairs. I would not be joining. Obviously, Lorraine had valued a chance to escape.

"If I keep moving, I don't think about it. He went easily. He went in his sleep. If I keep busy..." She fiddled with the bedspread. "I put out new pillows for you. Nonallergenic. Are you allergic to goose down? So many people are. Bill told me about your asthma. I thought I should play it safe."

Chapter 28

When the time came for getting dressed the next morning, Lorraine awakened me with a knock and entered with fresh waffles and a gift-wrapped box. Gifts for my father, she said. Clothes. He and I had been about the same size. And since I had ruined my only suit, well...

Don't get me wrong. It was nice enough. The shirt, I mean. Red. A beautiful, Christmasy kind of red. And when I parted the tissue paper and lifted it from its box, the soft-as-a-blanket fabric unfolded into what was a very handsome shirt.

"Handsome" being the operative word here.

The jeans, well, they weren't so bad either. Very loose, boxy fit, though. Levis. Very "guy." Button-flied. Wide waisted. But I cinched them up properly with a buttery black leather belt.

Of course I hadn't thought to remove my shoes before taking the plunge, so even my favorite slings had bitten the dust. Thus, I was forced to open yet another box from under the tree addressed to my father, a box containing a pair of casual black loafers (I'd have to stuff the toes a bit). Coordinating hosiery included, of course. Lorraine had missed nothing.

That had to be a major perk of having a young wife with her finger on the pulse of practical, Midwestern trends. These togs were plain, but high-quality. And...masculine. Perfectly nice looking duds, perfectly innocent when I pulled them from their gift boxes, but putting them on...well, they took on a whole different look. Rather bizarre, rather *Johnny Guitar*. And I wasn't quite ready for this sudden case of the gender bends. Wasn't prepared for the startling resemblance that materialized. Nor was Piqua.

Having lost a contact lens (along with my dignity) in the river, I cleaned my glasses, clipped on the shaded lenses, and swiped my father's black wool topcoat from the rack in the hall. It was only minutes later when I strolled shakily through the double doors of Lauer's Funeral Home. Good crowd, it appeared. Smaller than Vi's, I observed, and smirked. She was probably smirking herself somewhere. Probably taking a head count and having a good laugh.

I paused just inside the door to sign the guest book. A veritable "who's who" of Piqua, which filled all of five pages or so. Concentrating on completing my very long signature, I wasn't aware of the stares. Or the sudden silence. But when I looked up and moved into the viewing room, and moved forward to inspect the casket, I felt the eyes and heard the whispers.

He looked good, my father. He looked handsome. I'd expected to see him bloated and bald. He wasn't. Gray spread from his temples through his auburn hair, which was neatly groomed but still long enough on top to show a few unruly waves and curls. He was clean-shaven, and you could see the clear definition of his features: wide mouth, strong jaw, prominent cheekbones. Still a good-looking fellow, though the deep lines and dark circles denoted a life fraught with...pain? Defeat? Insecurity? Overindulgence? Who knows? If I'd had my handbag with me, I would have opened a compact mirror for a better view and answered the question. No, it wasn't me, lying there amid the scent of cheap floral arrangements. It wasn't, but it might have been. *He's lost his chance to change,* I thought. Then I heard Lorraine sobbing in the front row, and I looked over at her and thought maybe I was full of shit.

Goodbye, Wild Bill. I love you. I reached into my pocket for a small wooden box. *Your Pepsi cuff links...*

In New York, it would have been passé. But in a small-town cemetery, the sound of bagpipes playing "Amazing Grace" seemed hypnotic and unique and tremendously chic. No one seemed to question if Dad was Scottish or not, which he wasn't. Then again, there weren't many "French" things to do at a gravesite. Nothing suitably mournful about snubbing Americans or worshipping Jerry Lewis.

A lone trumpet player, the tail of his mullet flowing down to grace the top of his Metallica KILL 'EM ALL back patch, ended the ceremony by playing "Taps." It was a stark, eerie sound that wound around the trees and headstones and made us all pay close attention as they lowered the casket into the ground. And as the pipers and trumpeter marched past, their reflections bounced across the lenses of my sunglasses. I stood beside Lorraine, my

arm around her shoulders as they shook. Across the grave
I had a clear view of my older brother and his family.
Several stints in jail had obviously agreed with Elliot. In
his khakis and tweed suit coat, clean-shaven and with
neatly clipped and combed blond hair, he looked more
like an Army lifer than a career criminal. I tried to catch
his eye, but instead caught the gaze of his wife, Princess,
who I'd met earlier that morning. She bounced a bun-
dle—my nephew!—in her thin arms, smiling slightly to
reveal crooked front teeth. She was pretty, in a sort of
dishwater way, and I was glad he'd found someone to
keep him on the straight and narrow. Still, it was weird to
think of him as family.

Holding my head high as the crowd bowed theirs in
prayer, I peered over shoulders and hats to view the back
corner of the grounds where Vi had been "banished" (my
word, of course) when Phyllis wouldn't relinquish her
right to the plot alongside my father's. I wondered if she
knew I was here and thinking of her. And I wondered if
my father had found her yet, in the great whatever-after.

Guests were to return to the Delongchamp home. I was,
however, not a guest—or so I rationalized. A strange blend of
medications, shock, and stereotypical homecoming blues was
moving me away. Outside in the cold, I was numb. Invisible,
but anything but invisible. So I was grateful for any safety
and darkness in which to hide my sorry self. The first OPEN
sign I saw drew me in. A bar? No, a pool hall. Even better.

Pool was 50 cents. It wasn't worth any more than
that, as the tables were warped and the edges had lost
their bounce. Impossible to strike any English, lay any
spin on any one of the cloudy striped and solid balls lit-
tering the decayed green felt that stretched sadly out

before me. But the coffee was hot and it was quiet and that was all that mattered. Dark, with no public toilet, or so the cardboard sign said. Pickled eggs in an enormous jar on the counter beside the register. James Brown belting out of a stereo on a shelf with one speaker blown.

Nothing would have done me better than a pack of cigarettes tucked into my shirt pocket and a beer bottle in my hand. An adventure in masculinity, a flip side to the natty prom queen image I'd left them with some 20 years before. But, well, I'd quit smoking, and it was no use to even think of any alcohol being served within spitting distance of the church. This was Piqua. Still Piqua. And if I thought I'd find peace at Mokey's pool hall, I was sadly mistaken.

Three old boys watched me from the bar. I hadn't really noticed their vigil, hadn't cared much. One of them was Ned Reilly, I surmised from an occasional glance toward the counter. Ned Reilly, who drove a big orange snowplow for the county. Ned Reilly, who had frequently plowed the snow from our driveway and stood with his hands thrust deeply into the pockets of his bib overalls when Vi would greet him at the back door. He would take no monetary reward for his efforts—no, ma'am—but would gladly accept any offer to sit and sip warm scotch with her in the living area of our home. There, he'd sit up straight, with his boots left at the rug by the door, his hat in his hands, and his hair parted neatly on the side. Their talks sometimes lasted an hour—even in the thickest squalls, when Ned's services were sorely needed on the drift easy farm roads that ran across our town. But though the topics were scattered and the mood lively, he would seldom dare to look at Vi at all, let alone make eye contact. When he did, he did so apprehensively, eyes darting back to his hat in his hands like a shy child at church. Such a big man too. It amused me to see him be so timid with a woman as small as Vi.

Ned still was a big fellow—a bit stooped now, but big nonetheless. And as he moved toward me, he moved with the sloping shuffle of a man long finished with roaming the roads in his big orange plow. But his bibs were clean, his hair parted straight. He looked at me with sharp, suspicious eyes and asked, "Who are you?"

I smiled, tempted to point a quivering finger and hiss, "I am Death, Ned Reilly, and I have come to take you with me." But I didn't. From his gnarled hands and Hemingway white beard, I could see that the real reaper probably wasn't far down the road for old Ned the snowplow driver. He didn't need an impostor speeding things along.

Ned must have seen a hint of something familiar in my smile because he snapped his fingers and pointed before I could introduce myself.

"You're Bill's daughter."

"Macy." I nodded.

Ned Reilly stood and let his eyes roll up and down my body for a good minute or so before he rested a fist on his hip.

"I don't know what's the big idea," he said. "You'd best be careful coming around duded up like that. You nearly caused that man back there to have a stroke."

"That man" was behind the counter. Short, pale, and bald—something about him rang a bell, but not loud enough to bring a name or any real identity to mind. "Sure do look like your daddy," he said, giggling nervously.

Chapter 29

I suppose we could blame it on the wine. Lorraine, that is...all droopy eye-lidded and blue, the cuffs to her burgundy blouse unbuttoned, her well-heeled hands dangling over the arms of my father's leather armchair in front of the fire. She may not have had breeding, but she was used to money. You could see it in the cut of her hair and the cut of her clothes. Expensive. Blondes of the pretty and petite variety never came cheap. God knows I'd learned that myself. Yessirree, Lorraine Delongchamp was accustomed to the good life, all right, as good a life as one could attain in Piqua. A life my father had provided without question or too many demands and now he was gone. For whatever reason, she missed him. And maybe it was this that made her spin "The Great Ladies of Jazz" CD. Track 10 was playing as I entered the living room at dawn, sneaking down the stairs in the twilight with my carry-on bag, still dressed in the drag of my dead father's clothes. Track 10, the digitally remastered live version of Nina Simone singing "I Loves You, Porgy," so low and lonely and so terribly sad. It stopped me, would have stopped anyone, I think, whose heart had ever been broken.

I thought of turning to leave, thinking she'd be embarrassed. As it turned out, however, she was not. She spun around, hearing my footsteps, and caught me. Caught me staring, pulled into the room by the warm fire and music and whirl of memories that was just beginning to materialize. This had been my favorite room in the house growing up, and the layout was pretty much the same. I could feel Vi here, and my dad—and now Lorraine and I, in this fresh, awkward moment of intimacy, were sure to leave our imprint on this room.

She smiled, lifting a half-empty glass. "Wine?"

"No, thanks, I'm on a whole truckload of antibiotics." Not to mention it was 5 in the morning and even I had always hung a CLOSED sign on my liver from dawn until noon.

"Oh." Lorraine rolled her lazy gaze back to the fire. "Looks like we need another log." She began to rise unsteadily from her chair. "It's about to go out."

"I'll get it," I said, making a quick move for the stack of logs that lay in their brass base in the corner. The heat pressed at my face and hands as I knelt and placed the log with its dry, chipping bark onto the dwindling flames. I was relieved to turn my back to her blatant anguish. "That voice..." I shook my head and let out a short burst of a laugh. "Hoo! Makes me shiver. I saw her, once, in San Francisco—saw her legs, that is."

"What?"

"It was packed, you know. Tough to get tickets. A friend and I, we, uh..." I took the broom from its stand, sweeping the ashes back into the hearth. "We got there and our table was so close, and in such an odd position, that all we saw of Nina Simone was her legs. But it didn't really matter..."

"Macy." She lay a hand on my shoulder, right behind me now, drunk and leaning on me. Wavering like the Underdog balloon during the Thanksgiving parade, tethered by lines held by clowns.

Oh, shit, I thought. *What's this? Don't tell me I have to spend the rest of my morning consoling my father's widow. Don't tell me I have to talk and be sensitive and caring. Can't she tell that I'm completely devoid of emotion, of expectations, of Faith?*

"Yes?" I responded, trying my best to sound cheery, and turning to face her. I was in no place to hear her sentimental tales about my father, no place to hear this song, this fucking Nina Simone song that was fast turning me to jelly.

"There, in his clothes, in this light..." She threw her hand to her mouth, in tears. "Oh, God..."

"I'm sorry." I stepped back, bumping the mantle with my arm. "If I had other clothes to wear...I mean, I know this has to be weird for you." Hell, it was weird for me, weird for the guys down at the pool hall, who'd acted like they'd seen a ghost. I wasn't so sure they hadn't. Ever since I'd hit 40, I seemed to see more of my father in me. I felt him in my squinting leer as I admired the legs of the woman next door. I felt him hiding in my heart when Faith had gotten too close.

Lorraine looked old up close. Not old like me—no, she was still a good 10 years my junior—but hardly the fresh-faced appliance store intern I'd taken her for when we first met. I began to really examine her green eyes and the tiny crow's feet around them. It made her prettier, I thought, to have a few wrinkles.

Lorraine leaned against me, and I could smell the wine and the smoke from the fire and her perfume. Elizabeth Arden. Red. You get to where you know these things when you love women and love being a woman. Simple things like fragrances matter.

"God, I love you." She grabbed at my shirt collar, which was not my shirt collar at all.

"Lorraine, I..." I squirmed, trying not to push her away or touch her in any way at all, trying so hard. And that voice ran over me like warm water...

"Don't let him take me. Don't let him handle me...with his...hot hands..."

This is your stepmother, for God's sake!

"I'm not him," I said.

"Shhhh..." She sighed, resting her head against my left breast, her hands reaching up, cupping the tops of my shoulders. So tiny. I felt her hot, boozy breath permeate the shirt I was wearing and warm the skin between my breasts. I felt her nipples stiffen beneath the fabric of her blouse as she pressed all of herself against me. "God, Bill, please..." She had closed her eyes and was clinging to me now. "Please just hold me." Lorraine opened her eyes and looked up at me, imploring me—seeing it was me, knowing—but still...

"Please. One last time."

One last time. One last time. One last time.

It was about that time that I was beginning to cling to her as well, for once not feeling so alone in Piqua, sculpting the similarities between her body and Faith's as it fit snugly against mine in the heat and light from the flames.

And so, for the remainder of the song and shortly

thereafter, we danced. When it was over, Lorraine ran her long fingers through my hair and gazed up at me blankly. She moved in for a kiss, and I didn't resist her, but let my mouth find hers and linger innocently. Without words, I slipped on my father's coat and headed for the door with my belongings.

"He loved you," she said, turning up my collar.

"I'm sure he loved you very much too," I said, extending my hand for her to shake. She did, and laughed.

Chapter 30

Upon my return to New York, my health became relatively stable. For the first few weeks, I suffered only occasional bouts of low-grade fever and cough, symptoms that surely had not been helped by my plunge into Piqua's icy river. What spring had been lost from my step was beginning to return, and I felt quite at ease with the newfound rhythm of my gait and my life. Quite at ease, indeed.

If a bit lonely.

And it was on such a relaxed but lonesome day that I paused to peruse the display window at Spinnaker Books. A hardcover collection of Hurrell portraits caught my fancy. In no hurry, as I was never now in a hurry, I opted to step inside and treat myself.

Swinging open the door, I was hit with the sweet scent of old paper. I took it in with a smile, satisfied with the scent of history and letters, a smell I found most comforting and nostalgic.

"Excuse me," I said, approaching the counter. "I'd like..."

"Be right with you." I was cut off by a woman's voice that came from a figure completely obscured by the counter. She was either very short, or... "I'm down here on the floor. I'll be up in a minute," she said, sounding somewhat annoyed.

As well she should. She's probably struggling to get by on minimum wage.

"No hurry," I said, moving behind the counter. Then, as her face rose from its position over the recycling bin...

"Faith?"

Choose the path least taken in New York and you're liable to end up right where you started.

Yes, it was Faith.

"Macy," she said, and proceeded to throw up.

Even in a most unflattering pose, she was still beautiful. And she was still Faith. Taking her by the elbow, I assisted her to a chair and crouched before her.

"Here, now. It's all right," I said, pulling a handkerchief from my handbag and dabbing at the corner of her mouth.

"I'm sorry." She shaded her eyes.

"Oh, it's fine," I said. "Women react this way to me all the time."

"I called the hospital and they said you'd been released." Her eyes darted away and then back to mine. "I'm glad to see you're OK."

"Yes, I'm free to walk the streets again." I giggled and ran my fingers through my hair. "Free to turn the stomachs of bookstore employees all across Manhattan."

Faith let her arms fall to her sides, hands slapping her legs. "Is there something I can help you with?"

She looked so tired. Pale. And I had this overwhelming

urge to take her in my arms. As things were, however, I could not. I'd been such an ass, and only a couple of months had passed. But defying all logic...

"Yes, I'd very much like it if you'd join me for dinner."

Faith bit her lip and looked away, steadying herself against the counter. "I, um..." She shook her head. "I don't know if that's such a good idea."

"Well, then..." What had I expected? I sighed, still crushed. "I guess I'll be on my way. Thank you for your"— I turned for the door—"civility."

Shot down and thoroughly defeated, I felt all the worse because I knew I deserved it. Head hanging, I swung open the door and stepped outside, dragging my feet down the sidewalk toward home.

"Goddamn it," I said, looking up at the sky. "I used to laugh at the right-wingers with their signs that say 'God hates queers,' but you do, don't you?" I raised a fist. "You do! Well, I'm sick of it. You get all the credit for the good things that happen to people. What about everything else, huh? Look, I know I've fucked up my life. I take full responsibility for my actions. Full ownership. But why can't I have this one thing, huh? Just one thing!"

A man wearing a Yankees cap snapped my picture.

"Thanks," I said, bowing. "Thanks a lot. Take that and show it to the folks back home. 'Angry lesbian on sidewalk.' And while you're at it, here's another pose..."

And I flipped him off and showed my teeth. "Cheese!"

"Macy, wait!"

The door had opened behind me, and as I whirled to face her, Faith nearly knocked me down with an embrace.

"Here," I said, opening my coat to pull her inside, to keep her warm and close. "You'll freeze."

"I'm sorry." She wiped at her eyes. "I just...I didn't know what had happened to you. I'm just glad you're OK."

I buttoned my coat and waved as she backed toward the door. "Thank you," I said, sincerely, without drama.

Faith stopped in front of the bookstore window and folded her arms, shivering. "Seven o'clock OK?"

What?

"Yes!" I smiled.

"Your place?"

"Yes!" I turned a happy pirouette and waved wildly. "I'll see you then!"

Chapter 31

"Macy?"

I raised my head, my hands still clasped in front of me as I sat at the candlelit table. "What?"

Faith raised an eyebrow. "You're praying?"

"I'm saying grace." I bowed my head in concentration.

"But...you're not saying anything."

"Well." I frowned. "I'm preparing."

"You say grace before meals now?"

"Yes, I do."

"Since when?"

"Since—well, since now, is when." I wrinkled my brow. "Now, stop it, you're making me lose my concentration. This isn't easy, you know."

"OK." She clasped her hands and closed her eyes.

Silence.

"What?" I looked up.

She had placed her hands like a steeple in front of her and looked very at peace with the situation. "I'm waiting for you to say grace," she said.

"Oh." I cleared my throat. "OK. Now..." I cleared my throat again and rolled my shoulders to relax. "Dear God..."

"Is that how you're going to start?" She seemed annoyed. "It's fine, but it's kind of stern. What if the Buddhists are right?"

"Dear Buddha..." I began.

"No!" She laughed. "How do we know who's right? It could be any one of the religions, couldn't it? It could be Allah or Jehovah."

"Attention Allah, Jehovah, and friends..."

Faith groaned.

"All right. OK." I took a deep breath. "To Whom It May Concern: We'd like to pause to pay thanks for the wonderful meal you have set before us. For the Omaha steaks, the fresh olive and pasta salad from Balducci's, the hard rolls and butter..."

"You're making me hungry," Faith said, kicking me under the table.

"And thanks for not striking me dead when I cursed you in the street today, although I still don't understand why AIDS is allowed on our planet and some children go to bed hungry every night. But anyway, I'm sorry for being a bitch, and I am truly grateful to you for allowing me the pleasure of dining with this beautiful"—I took Faith's hand—"and precious woman." I opened my eyes and smiled at her. "The end."

"Amen." Faith smiled back at me and dove for the basket of rolls.

We ate and chatted for nearly two hours. In between bites of steak and baked potato and whatever else was immediately before her, Faith told me of changing jobs and moving. The bookstore was a healthier work environment, she said, and her new roommates didn't charge what the last ones had, although she did sleep in a sleeping bag on the floor. Overall, her situation sounded desperate, but her spirits were high. Faith, the optimist. And from the way she was speed-eating her dinner and part of mine, I could tell that she probably wasn't eating that well on a regular basis. Still, she looked as if she'd put on a few pounds, and Faith had never been the junk-food type.

"This is so good," she proclaimed, cheeks jammed with food and another forkful on its way.

"I can't take credit for the salad. It's take-out." I offered her another roll, which she accepted.

"I'm surprised, though." She swallowed and pointed to her plate. "I know you like red wine with your steak."

"Oh, I don't drink anymore." I rose and carried my plate into the kitchen.

"What?"

"I said, I don't drink anymore." I took a glass from above the sink and filled it with water. "With all the medication, I couldn't have it. Just got out of the habit, I guess. Ready for dessert?"

I heard a muted belch and returned to the table.

"I think I'd better let this settle." She leaned back in her chair. "By the way, I like the glasses."

"Oh, these?" I blushed at the compliment and was surprised at myself. "I lost one of my contacts and never had them replaced." I shrugged. "Got out of that habit too, I guess."

For the first time since she'd been in my apartment, Faith looked at me without chewing. She smiled.

"And no smoking?" she asked.

"And no smoking." I sighed wistfully. "That one truly sucks."

"You've made a lot of changes," she said.

"You could say that, yes." I grinned and framed my face with my hands. "The new me."

"I like the new you."

I laughed. "Didn't you like me before?"

"No, Macy." She gazed at me intently. "I loved you before."

So things had changed. That was then, this is now, as they say. And she would gladly partake in my steak, but not in my love life. There it was.

I turned my back to her and moved out of the dining room. "Let's sit in the living area, shall we? Where we can relax and talk."

"Did you go to A.A.?"

"Alcoholics Anonymous? Hell, no. Support groups are so trendy." I rolled my eyes. "I had to stop, so I stopped."

"You needed to stop a long time ago."

"Well, yes, perhaps." I licked my lips. "After Trish got cancer, I had a real problem."

"It started long before Trish got cancer."

I sighed. "Well, yes, I suppose it did."

"I still love you, Macy."

Back still turned to her, I began to shake. "I'm sorry I did what I did," I said, wiping the tears from my cheeks with the back of my hand. "I was wrong and I know it. I never should have done it and I never should have treated you that way."

"Macy?" Faith came up behind me and wrapped her arms around my waist. "Don't cry." She turned me at my shoulders to face her. "Do you love me, Macy?"

"Yes!" Boy, I was really bawling now, snot flowing and mascara running. So much for pride. "I won't do it again. I promise!" I blubbered. "Please come home. Of course I love you!" I buried my face against her shoulder. "I'm sorry! I'm so sorry!" I started to choke, which only added to the spectacle.

"Shhh." Faith guided me toward the sofa, where she stroked my hair and kept an arm around my waist. "My poor baby gets so upset," she said, kissing my cheek.

"It's just that..." I took a Kleenex and blew my nose with a mighty honk. "I m-m-missed you."

Faith remained strangely calm—solemn, even. She appeared so committed to me, so intense, the light of love shining brightly in her eyes as they gazed into mine. And when she knelt before me and took my hands in hers, I had no reason to believe that she would say:

"Macy, I'm pregnant."

"You're WHAT???" I pulled back, pulled my hands from hers in order to gesticulate wildly. "Was this...was it...rape?!"

She shook her head. Stood up. Moved to seat herself on the arm of the recliner.

"What the fuck was it then? Immaculate conception?"

Faith hung her head. "It was Marcus."

"Marcus? Who...?" And it struck me then. Marcus. Farm guy. Marlboro man. The rugged individualist in the Michigan wilderness who smiled at me through his blond mustache and stared at my tits.

At least the kid would be cute.

I sat beside Faith and said nothing. I waited. In an instance such as this, you never know what's going to send you from the status of "reconciled lovers" to "ex-lovers who are now best friends."

I looked at Faith. *Pregnant! With child! Knocked up! Ugh!*

"May I ask...what was...the motivation?" I said, with feigned calm. "I mean, I know *what* happened, obviously. However, I would like to know *how?*"

Faith's explanation was brief. She said she couldn't stand to be with another woman, which stroked my ego. She said it was a mistake, a one-time thing they both regretted. And without understanding or anticipating the logistics of it all, the paternity issues and such, well...

"I'd like for you to stay here." It was surprisingly easy to say.

Faith raised her head. "What about the baby?"

"The baby can stay too," I said, deciding that it would be best to call the movers in the morning. For now, we would collect a few of her essentials ourselves. And for now, I would sit with my arm around her and enjoy the moment and try not to think about things too deeply. The prospect of becoming a stepmother was not particularly appealing, but the prospect of turning the love of my life into a best friend or casual lunch date was out of the question. Was I cutting her slack? Sure. But perhaps this sort of slack was what was required to achieve a real relationship. Perhaps this was family.